THE WIDE ROAD

AN AFRICAN PATH IN A WORLD OF THE WEST

ÒGÚN YẸMÍ

Order this book online at www.trafford.com
or email orders@trafford.com

Most Trafford titles are also available at major online book retailers.

Note for Librarians: A cataloguing record for this book is available from Library
and Archives Canada at www.collectionscanada.ca/amicus/index-e.html

Printed in Victoria, BC, Canada.

ISBN: 978-1-4269-0819-4 (sc)
ISBN: 978-1-4269-0821-7 (e)

*We at Trafford believe that it is the responsibility of us all, as both individuals and corporations,
to make choices that are environmentally and socially sound. You, in turn, are supporting this
responsible conduct each time you purchase a Trafford book, or make use of our publishing services.
To find out how you are helping, please visit www.trafford.com/responsiblepublishing.html*

*Our mission is to efficiently provide the world's finest, most comprehensive book publishing
service, enabling every author to experience success. To find out how to publish your book, your
way, and have it available worldwide, visit us online at www.trafford.com*

Trafford rev. 8/4/2009

 www.trafford.com

North America & international
toll-free: 1 888 232 4444 (USA & Canada)
phone: 250 383 6864 ♦ fax: 250 383 6804 ♦ email: info@trafford.com

The United Kingdom & Europe
phone: +44 (0)1865 487 395 ♦ local rate: 0845 230 9601
facsimile: +44 (0)1865 481 507 ♦ email: info.uk@trafford.com

THE WIDE ROAD

AN AFRICAN PATH IN A WORLD OF THE WEST

I

For my wife, Yinka.
She has always been there for me.
And our Son, Jimi.
A source of inspiration to us both.

Acknowledgements

My discussion with Sèyẹ in 2003 at Ìdó-Èkìtì was purely incidental. It was what set me on the path to this book. A great deal of gratitude to you, Sèyẹ.

There is the lady I simply call Alhaja; my humble, hardworking typist at Ùsì-Èkìtì in the later half of 2004. Your help is greatly treasured.

I acknowledge the professional insight of Jacobus Aucamp and the roles played by Tesleem Ọréwọlé, Ìsínkáyé Ayòdélé, The Dùnmóyès, Ìbítómi, and Dr Olúsọlá Adéwálé Adédípè.

Special mention needs be made of two persons so very dear to this book. Ncube Solomon and K.J. Ayòdélé. Both devoted chunks of their precious time poring through this book so it could come out this delectable.

I acknowledge the immense contributions of hundreds of Books, Magazines, Newspapers, Independent Articles, Documentaries, Interviews (casual and formal), and countless other sources of learning and databases that served for my research tools in writing this book.

Special thanks to the entire staffs of Trafford Publishing for working tirelessly to make this book see the light of day.

Last but not the least, this book acknowledges past and ongoing sufferings of All Victims of Apartheid and Slave Trade Worldwide.

TABLE OF CONTENT.

THE WIDE ROAD

BY

ÒGÚN YẸMÍ

PART I

STEPPING ON QUICKSAND

2 - 102

1

Lagos, Nigeria
January 2006.

The choking lump in Ikeh's throat melted as soon as he got out of the elevator at ground level.

Science called it claustrophobia; Ikeh knew better. If you worked as an International Sales Agent for a company like LAZULINE LIMITED (LZL), you never had peace. You went around with lumps in your throat and knots in your stomach.

Moments later, Ikeh was out on the street. The open space was a relief. He took a deep, deserving breath of fresh air off the nearby Atlantic and felt better still.

Crossing the busy street to the other side he lifted his eyes to the imposing grandeur of the fifty-floor, seafront building that housed LZL. As usual, the sight awed him.

Atop the building was LAZULINE's majestic emblem, the imperial eagle. It was cast, complete with the top ends of an equally regal Ìrókò tree. The eagle was frozen in its last moments of taking flight. Its huge winds seemed forever spreading, the neck a little tucked in, and the powerful legs perpetually leaping off the strong Ìrókò branch. Even from this distance, Ikeh could feel the scrutinizing glare of the imperial eagle. It seemed to watch over LZL in its resplendent spread. Atop a tree known for its ability to tower above and easily dominate thick African forests, LZL's message through the eagle was stern – we know everything!

A huge wave from the roaring Atlantic broke Ikeh's almost hypnotic concentration. He sighed, peeled his gaze off the eagle, and took off his Nike cap. The coolness that assaulted his clean-shaven head was so welcoming. He set out at a trot.

The exercise helped him in dissipating heat and nervousness. It also did his trim body a world of good. A round hairless face completed Ikeh's features, cutting years off his thirty-seven.

While he trotted, Ikeh thought.

Within minutes, he drew sweat, making his ebony complexion glitter in the early afternoon sun.

Under the able leadership of Yòmóyè, LZL administered over thirty-two blue emerald mines scattered in south western Nigeria.

Over the years, Ikeh had realized that Yòmóyè was simply a surrogate, as his two gofers. Somewhere within the United States of America embassy here in Lagos was the real show runner. Ikeh had no clue as to who exactly it was, but he was sure that the person operated from the embassy.

Ikeh knew that Yòmóyè and his two stooges got 10% of the yields from the mines as payment for fronting. Scores of International Sales Agents like Ikeh were in the employment of LZL. They scouted the world's black market to peddle this 10%. Which was why Yòmóyè and his cronies were filthy rich.

The going market rate of Crude Oil was about U.S. $60 per barrel. Simply put; to make U.S. $60 from the almighty crude oil, which everyone cried about in the world today, you needed an entire barrel of it. To make same from blue emerald, you needed a size less than a baby's thumb. In going into emerald trading therefore, Yòmóyè and his gofers had made a sound business choice.

A month earlier, Ikeh had smuggled into the United States a consignment of Blue Emerald and had succeeded in selling it to waiting black market buyers without any incident.

Today, he had supplied the technical and financial details of the transaction to the threesome who ran LZL and had passed their grueling interrogation.

Nevertheless, Ikeh was always unsettled. What if he came for the usual post-trip briefing and they found out that he had skimmed a few thousand dollars from the proceeds of the sales? Which he normally did.

What if they found out that he usually cornered a few of the stones, salted them in a safe place for disposal later? Which he practiced all the time!

What would they do? Kill him like Dìrân? Maybe!

Dìrân had disappeared after such post-trip briefings and turned up floating a few days later on the lagoon nearby. The case was never solved. Dìrân drank like a fish. Everyone knew. The big question that was never answered was; did he fall into the lagoon while drunk? Or was he conveniently pushed? There were stories.

"Hi Ikeh," a passer-by hailed him.

Ikeh snapped around from his personal

reflections, came to a stop, and looked in the direction of the voice. It was Tolú, a colleague from LZL.

Tolú was with Exports Department run by a paranoid and spiteful Délé. Export Departments in LZL was vested with the responsibilities of devising appropriate methods of smuggling the gemstones off Nigeria into countries where Sales Agents had contacts in the black market.

Now, Ikeh grinned and shook hands with Tolú.

"Hi Tolú," said Ikeh. Tolú was a very likeable person, a struggling youth with promising future if he could summon the courage to leave LZL with his talents. "Are you okay?"

"Yes. Just went down the street to get the Newspaper."

"Job adverts?"

"Yes!" whispered Tolú glancing furtively in the direction of the imperial eagle atop LZL. Ikeh could not help noticing that, even out here, amidst hordes of Lagosians, and half a mile from LZL, Tolú still felt naked, watched. "Always watching us!"

"Yeah! Bloody eagle!" said Ikeh sympathetically. Despite the distance the eagle was still intrusive.

"Don't tell anyone that I was trying to get a new job!"

"My mouth is zipped. Good luck."

"Thank you. Are you working out?"

"Sort of. Just done with the big guys up on the top floor."

"Was everything okay?"

"Yes. Thank God!"

"So? Where to?"

"Ìsàlè Èkó."

"See you around."

"Yeah. Bye Tolú."

Ikeh broke into a trot again, snaking his way amidst a sea of bodies. Now, he dripped water and breathed deeply. Good for exorcising the demons of LZL.

Ikeh had put in place some reassuring personal arrangements. These would not prevent LZL murdering him if it came to it but it would see to it that his family was taken care of financially. It was like being on a treadmill; you had to keep running at all times just so you could stay in one place.

His next smuggling trip to the United States was likely going to be booked for the following month.

Now, Ikeh just wanted some cold Palm Wine. He headed for a joint in Ìsàlè Èkó.

2

By noon, Ikeh was home happy.

He slept off the Palm Wine until evening. And the alcohol-induced euphoria went with his dreams.

7pm on the dot, his wife – Florence – was onto him, forcing him into a discussion about his debriefing that morning. Ikeh never liked discussing his report sessions. So demeaning.

Ikeh left the bedroom for the living room and plastered himself in front of the TV, leaving Florence, who was having a change of cloth, to her thoughts.

Few minutes later, Florence emerged. She looked concerned. This showed by the wrinkle, which destroyed her otherwise perfect face. She was ripe-orange, unlike Ikeh's dark features. Thin nose. Sharp face. Her long tarry black hair was braided and bound into a ponytail by a string of brown African beads.

She wore a light brown evening caftan that further set off her color, making her glow in the coolness of the softly lit living room. Ikeh surveyed her as if seeing her for the first time in his entire life, and whistled his admiration.

"Wow! Stunning!"

"How was the briefing this time?" asked

Florence, ignoring Ikeh's amorous advances.

"I would rather like to discuss some other more pressing matters," said Ikeh with a knowing smile. "You glow, my love."

"Ikeh?!"

"Into my lap first," insisted Ikeh as he pulled her on to his laps and delivered a good kiss. "Aaah! There. Now shoot!"

"So?"

"Those guys don't trust me much, Flo," said Ikeh as he played with Florence's long braids. "But I passed their scrutiny anyway."

"Maybe you should leave now. We've got enough stashed away. We could start something!"

"Not yet. I can hold on a little longer. Besides, those files are enough back-up. If anything happens to me all of a sudden, they will have to pay you at least two-fifty thousand U.S. dollars or LZL sinks."

"Oh … those files! The thought of them makes me shiver, Ikeh."

"Well, nothing good comes cheap, my dear. It sounds bad but we've been all over this enough. With LZL, it was necessary! The files are not for me; they are for you and the children. You have a set of files; I also have mine. If they kill me, simply send one of your copies to the first address on the list. Then wait for their response. If after a month they are yet to pay up, send another copy to the second address and wait again. Believe me, they will make the deposit. Two-fifty thousand dollars is nothing to Yòmóyè. He will make the payment; otherwise, he loses everything. You and the children won't lack money for the rest of your lives. Call it our Life Cover, an Insurance Policy."

"I don't want to talk about the files, Ikeh."

Ikeh's telephone next to him on the sofa rang, helping Florence change the subject.

"Hello," said Ikeh, answering the phone, while his left hand played romantically with Florence's supple breasts.

"It's Johnson."

Johnson was Ikeh's best friend – business and social. He worked with the U.S. embassy in Lagos.

"Hi. What's up?" bubbled Ikeh. Johnson was always fun.

"Can't talk about it on the phone!" said Johnson sullenly.

Ikeh's heart flew. His roving hand on Florence's breasts stiffened. So did Florence who was listening.

"Did anything go wrong with the visas?"

"No. The visas went well; they are ready. It's not the visas, Ikeh. Can we meet at 9pm tomorrow?"

"The usual joint?"

"No, not this time."

"Wow! Are you okay?

"Yeah, sort of. Let's meet at NightPranks at Òpébí, Ìkẹjà, tomorrow. 9pm. Okay?"

"Yeah, okay."

Ikeh cut the call. Expectedly, Florence pounced. "Is everything okay?" she said worriedly.

"Nothing to worry about, Flo," said Ikeh, trying as gently as possible to wrestle his wife off the edge of panic. "You know Johnson; he will always have something to grumble about."

"Sure?"

"Positive."

"You feel tense," said Florence massaging Ikeh's stiff shoulders.

"Maybe I need the angel touch from those tender fingers of yours," said Ikeh.

"Mmm!" said Florence delivering a perfect kiss on Ikeh's lips.

Ikeh carried Florence to the bedroom.

Chinedu Johnson was the computer whiz kid who graduated cum laude in Computer Programming from the Federal University of Technology, Akúré a decade or so earlier.

For two years, he walked the streets of Lagos without a job. Hungry and exhausted, he accepted a Security Gateman's post at the America Embassy in Lagos.

Soon, he found himself in the very profitable visa racketeering business. And he made money. Ikeh also made money from Johnson by sourcing him clients in needs of visas.

Being an International Sales Agent for LZL had some perks too. Ikeh got to meet international travelers who were in need of visas and who were too impatient or too dubious to appear at embassies.

Johnson helped. For a fee. Ikeh's commission was satisfying.

3

Ikeh was prompt at 9pm on Saturday.

Johnson was already seated at a private booth for two, drinking Guinness. The atmosphere was hush, mature, and upper-class with soft lighting playing on booths carved out with clear plexiglas.

Ikeh surveyed Johnson carefully. And found that the uneasiness that had latched onto him the previous evening was starting to dig its teeth in his skin. Johnson looked drunk. In itself, that was not unusual. Johnson drank and it was weekend.

But there was something bordering him, which showed on his furrowed forehead as he stared into his glass of foaming furry – Guinness.

Ikeh said, "What's up, Johnson?"

"I hate these Americans, Ikeh."

"That's the feeling about town these days what with the Bush wars and all. But for you who work for them and make so much money from a parallel issuance of their visas, I'll say it's a huge conflict of interest!"

"Conflict of interest? I have a first class degree in IT and they know, still they can only employ me as a Gate Security. That's mean!"

"They did not force you to take the job, Johnson. I would say you were very fortunate to be on the payroll of the Americans. Thousands around here

10

envy you ..."

"Don't lecture me, Ikeh!"

"Sorry. But you worry too much. That's why you are balding at thirty-three."

"Leave my head alone! Besides, no one knows. Except you tell on me! My head is always clean shaven like yours!"

"And the pot belly?"

"None of your business!"

"For a friend who is just five feet seven and weighing seventy two kilos, I make it my business. You are going to have a heart attack if we don't do something about it."

"When you see what I have for you, you're going to be the one having a heart attack, not me. Better take a seat."

"You're kidding!"

"No! I'm not," said Johnson, taking a side-look at Ikeh from under his hooded black eyes. His breath was coming out in wheezes. And his voice had that characteristic nasal twang one found with overweight people.

"You are serious!" said Ikeh taking a seat.

"Damn right!"

"So, what's eating you?"

Johnson gave him a sealed brown envelope and said crisply, "In there!"

"What?"

"The passports are in there. With the visas!" snapped Johnson.

"The two of them?"

"Yeah! Thought I just said that! One is for the Dúró fellow; the other is for his buddy, Emeka. You skinned me for those guys, Ikeh! Anyway, it's done with. My best wishes as they sojourn in the United

States!"

"Yeah! Thanks! So, what's eating you?"

"Also in there, Ikeh. Go home and read it. It's all in a DVD-R. You love stuffs like that. Besides, it also relates to the company you work for. I've always told you LZL is odd, didn't I?"

Ikeh's mouth turned dry.

"I need some beers!"

Johnson dissolved into a convulsion of cough as he tried to laugh. "Now who is having a heart attack?"

"Really, I need a beer."

"Not this night; another night maybe. You need a clear head to understand all the stuffs in that DVD-R. My visa program dragged it out of the embassy computers yesterday. Inadvertently, I may add. So don't you go thinking that I hack into stuffs that are none of my business."

"All right. All right. See you later," answered Ikeh, looking worried.

"See ya, Ikeh," said Johnson as he went into another fit of cough while laughing.

Ikeh headed straight home.

The DVD-R contained 4GB of data. In the privacy of his study, Ikeh went through the content in fine details. He was not done until early dawn of the second day.

In it was enough to prove in any law court that some U.S. officials at the embassy were hiding under diplomatic relations with West African governments to steal the region blind of its vast resources in solid minerals.

It was a carefully run multi-billion dollar gemstones cartel with webs spun not only in

Nigeria but the entire West Africa sub-region. This was the fourteenth century all over again.

Back then, the marauding Spanish conquerors massacred the Muzos – in the now Columbia – for decades just so they could wrap their hands around precious stones. Eventually, Columbia produced the finest emerald the world over.

Ikeh knew that Nigeria was rich in the blue variety of emerald. Though not as craved as green emerald, it fetched good money as well.

Now, his knowledge of LZL and the American owners was complete. As dawn came in Ìkẹjà, Ikeh began making plans.

4

Lagos Island was on the other side of the Lagoon from Ikeh. There, other worries were taking root even as Ikeh sat crafting his plots at his Ìkejà home.

Presently a bedside telephone was ringing stridently. Roland woke up to its insistence with notable reluctance. He thought it odd. It was 6am on Sunday. Curled around him was Lará's remarkably beautiful body, exhausted from hours of sex.

He disentangled himself and picked the phone.

"Roland here," he said.

"Good morning, Sir."

Roland broke out in cold sweat. It was David Terence, his Chief Technical Officer at the embassy. Something bad was up. Terence never called him to say a hello or to find out how sound of health he was. Terence hated him. Now a call at 6am on a Sunday! Except Terence was trying to find out if he was dead in bed!

"Yeah, Terence?"

"I've been trying to reach you all night but couldn't!"

Roland's mouth went agape. His cellphone was missing and he had been too drunk and sex-hungry to realize it. He made a mental note to take care of that problem later.

"Anything?"

Dump question, if there was nothing bad, Terence would never call!

"There has been a security leak," said Terence in the most cryptic manner.

Roland sat up and threw his legs over the edge of the bed. His heart was pounding. He said, "How bad?"

"Very."

"I am on my way," Roland said hanging up. "Get dressed in two minutes, I am off," he flung at Lará and jumped out of bed, racing for his walk-in wardrobe.

"Why the hurry?" Lará whined with disappointment as she woke up to an unexplained hostility.

"The show is over baby. Time to go," he answered, hurriedly dressing.

"Will I see you again?"

"Depends."

"Can I call?"

"No."

"Hey! Don't be snobbish."

"No commitments, remember."

"Oh sure, anyway nice getting to know you."

"Yeah; me too. Are we set?"

"I'll just get my clothes."

"You may look in the living room."

5

Fifty minutes later, Roland was at the embassy; driving towards his private entrance.

He was blonde, tall, and good looking; giving him the coveted Yale look which he felt he lacked because he never had the luxury of attending Yale. This horrible morning however, he couldn't care less how he looked. Which was why his hair was mated to his head by sweat of anxiety and he did not care. The sweat coalesced and dripped down his face, stinging his eyes as he drove. And still, he did not care.

A security man logged him in as he drove his luxurious Porsche into the sprawling, desolate compounds of the embassy. On a typical work day in years past, the place was like a carnival ground – filled with Nigerian youths deserting the country for the United States and seeking appropriate visas. Finally, the consulate could no longer have any of that rowdiness; it was now online application or nothing.

Terence was waiting at the carport.

Roland got out of his car and hurried to Terence who was as broad as Roland but a head shorter. All so well. Roland could look down on Terence. Literally. Satisfying.

They both talked as they walked towards Roland's office on the top floor of the embassy, an area that was off limit to most staffs.

"What's going on?"

"Someone had accessed DRAINPIPE," Terence said.

Roland could feel his world tumbling down.

In DRAINPIPE, he was the Head of Operations; had been from the inception of the program. For that, Terence envied him. Now, Terence was going to do all at his disposal to ensure that the blame for this leak was laid squarely at his feet. Goddamn jealous fool!

"Who accessed it?"

"Chinedu Johnson," Terence answered crisply.

"Jesus!" spat Roland. "That fat Nigerian fellow in security, right!"

"Yes, sir."

"When did this happen?"

"Friday, 4:15pm. Just before he got off duty."

"Where the hell is he now?"

"Just got to his usual church at Ìkejà with his wife and children. I've got Drefeus trailing him everywhere he goes."

"Good. How the hell did he get a line on DRAINPIPE?"

"It was incidental," pronounced Terence. "He is the one involved in the visa racketeering thing. He was trying to break into the program on visas when he incidentally hacked into DRAINPIPE. He hacked from his office."

Roland sat down at his office desk, thinking. Terence took a seat opposite him.

"Are you sure of this analysis, Terence?"

"Hundred percent. I've pulled from the system

all the technical support to prove the intrusion. You'll have a copy within the hour. Johnson is the major leak we have been trying to plug on the visa program for onto a year. DRAINPIPE had just now given him off. He must have made millions with the visas he had been issuing."

"Fuck the visas," cried Roland. "That is the Ambassador's headache! My concern is the safety of DRAINPIPE!"

"Safe, Sir ... if we can get rid of him as soon as possible."

"Beautiful! Then do it, Terence. They are a group of expendables, all of them! Get rid of him!"

"Yes sir."

"Make it look like it's a ritual-killing again! Okay?!"

"Yes sir."

"But his head should be on his neck! And they shouldn't deface him. Maybe ... have them chop off the genitals this time!"

"Yes sir."

"When the newspapers carry his death, I want to be sure it's him! They will blame it on the usual ... ritual-killing! Got that, Terence?"

"Yes sir," Terence said. His distaste for Roland was hardly concealed from his tone.

Bloody imbecile would always whine, Terence thought. The fool made thousands of dollars from each shipment of gemstones from the mines, but he still whined. He sat around, playing God while he, Terence, took care of the dirty details, and he still whined. Incompetent fool!

"One more thing, Terence," continued Roland.

"Yes sir?"

"If the Ambassador wants to know what

happens to Johnson when you are through with him, let him ask the Nigeria Police or the goddamn President up in Aso Rock."

"Yes, Sir."

"Another thing, Terence! Set the boys loose on all the mines and the administrative offices. I want detailed security work-up on all of them, ranging from the STAR mine up north, LAZULINE mine in Ẹpẹ, to LZL here in Lagos."

"Yes sir."

"And if there is so much as a speck of dust looking funning, I wanna know about it."

"Yes sir."

"Keep me posted."

"Will do, Sir," Terence said and left.

6

While Terence stormed off, Roland Edward sat thinking.

He was the CIA Head of Station who supervised all of CIA activities in West Africa.

The embassy, which was the largest and most intricate of all U.S. missions in Africa, provided the CIA with a legitimate cover and enough spread to house its various divisions.

The U.S. Department of Justice had a similar section run by the FBI. Still a third department existed. This was the Drug Enforcement Agency, DEA, concerned with fighting the illicit but flourishing trade in narcotics.

The thinking of policy makers in Washington was that drug trafficking went around with money laundering. And that laundered money was one of the financial lifelines of worldwide terrorism. Therefore, the DEA, the FBI, and the CIA went around like conjoined triplets in all of America missions all over the world.

Yes, the CIA was legitimately in Lagos, lodged at the embassy. What was not so legitimate was DRAINPIPE and Roland's very lucrative role as its Head of Operations.

Roland knew that the facts could not be allowed

to leak. Too dangerous, too destructive. Again, this security breach in DRAINPIPE. Roland's aim was to confine it to his office. No need to inform the big guys in Washington. Terence would take care of Johnson and, if anything escaped Terence, Roland was prepared. He was bringing Thompson, a very useful and trusted friend over in New York City, down to Lagos to keep eyes on things from a discreet distance.

Roland heaved a big sigh and placed a call to Thompson. The line connected at the other end and was answered only after several rings.

"It's Roland. Wake up, Thompson."

A whistle came clearly down the line. "What the hell, Roland! It's the middle of the night here; what's eating you down there, man? Yesterday was Saturday, wasn't it?"

"Yeah! Sorry, Thompson! I may be in big trouble. You better hop on a plane right now."

"What! What the hell is going on?"

"You'll know when you are here."

"No shit?"

"No shit! Eh ... one more thing ..."

"Yeah?"

"You will be going around here a lot ... yunno ... possibly doing your stuff. So come well equipped."

"Jesus Christ! What have you got your ass into?"

"That's what you're gonna find out, Thompson," snapped Roland. "Can we cut the crappy questioning?"

"Awright! I'll be down ASAP."

"That's the spirit, keep in touch."

"Sure will."

What a way to start a new year! At least, there was a consolation; if Terence began getting smart,

Thompson would take care of him.

7

LZL's huge cargo room on the twenty-third floor was awake and running.

Machines hummed and whined as workers labored with the characteristic frenzy of all smuggling outfits.

Overseeing the details was the Head of the unit, Délé. There was a deadline to meet. Ikeh's trip was due. It was the last week of January. Délé had to get five International Sales Agents on the road. Ikeh was the third on the line. Two others had departed in the last three days. Délé was overworked. And noticeably edgy. Which was bad news for Ikeh. Délé and Ikeh were not the best of friends. Currently, however, Délé was briefing Ikeh about his trip.

"We are sending the stones using the Bible this time," said Délé staring down at Ikeh over a broad nose.

"Why the Bible? We could use a thousand other books!"

"Not while I'm sending two thousand copies that had to look and weigh absolutely same! Where would I tell Customs and Immigrations that I'm sending two thousand copies of any book but a religious one? Besides, what's this sudden sentiment about the Bible?"

"I have no qualms using the Bible!"

"Good! So?"

"I need the details," said Ikeh.

"Okay. Fine with me. We use the biggest King James around. We hollow each out and put in the stones ..."

"Immigration will pick them out! Won't work!"

"Why?" challenged Délé. His frame went into a slight hunch as if prepared to box. He disliked Ikeh. Both knew. The feeling was mutual.

"A typical King James does not weigh more than twelve-fifty grams. You hollow it out and ..."

"And we stuff it with just enough for the Bible to weigh about thirteen hundred."

"Oh!"

"Yeah. Leave us to do the thinking as far as export technicalities are concern, Ikeh. Your job is with the black marketers."

"I don't mind that! But I won't go with any consignment whose shipment is not to my satisfaction."

"Have we ever disappointed you guys in Sales?"

"There had been cases! I don't want to be part of any failed data."

Délé's face went rigid. "You'll get what you need on this shipment, Ikeh," hissed Délé. "Satisfaction guaranteed!"

"No offence, Délé," said Ikeh. "Just have to be careful. It's a dangerous word out there."

"Yeah. What else do you need?"

Ikeh did a rough calculation of the weight expected of two thousand King James Bibles and said, "net weight should be twenty-five hundred kilos or thereabout!"

"Yeah. But we made it twenty-six hundred. How

about that?"

The margin is within acceptable limits, thought Ikeh. He said, "That's okay. Then the X-ray machines at the airport. How are we going to beat them?"

"Our sources in Mexico City say they have only conventional X-Ray machines at the airport and not CAT Scanners."

"Are we transporting through Mexico this time?"

"Yes. We've got good contacts in there."

"So?"

"The stones are all wrapped in X-Ray-proof foils of same density as the leaves of the Bibles. On the sort of X-Ray machine available at Mexico International Airport, the package will appear as books ... Bibles. Satisfied?"

"Did you put it through X-Ray tests here?"

"Yeah! In there," said Délé sharply, pointing at a huge corner of the cargo room with the insignia of irradiation. "Want to repeat the test yourself?"

"No need."

"Like I said, I know my job."

"Yeah."

"What else?"

"When is my ticket booked?"

"Day after tomorrow. We want you arriving in Mexico City early Sunday morning. Mostly, the immigration officers are tired. They just want to up and go home. Besides, our contact will be on duty."

"Good!"

"What else do you need?"

"Where are the Bibles going?"

Délé held up a package in a brown envelope. It was at least three feet above Ikeh. Jeez, he is tall, thought Ikeh.

Délé said, "The cargo is addressed to a Christian NGO at a suburb of Mexico City. The address is in here."

"Genuine?"

Dele chuckled derogatorily and said, "Of course not. Thought you should know better. It's an address of our office there. We opened it a month ago. It is registered in Mexico as a Christian NGO. Now, apparently, we are stocking it with Bibles."

"Naturally."

The brown envelope came down, saving Ikeh the embarrassment of having to jump up to retrieve the package.

Délé handed the envelope to Ikeh and said, "The details are in there. You have two hours to memorize it and then I want the papers back."

"Okay."

"From our Mexico office, you are on your own. How you get into the US is your headache. Draw funds as usual and let Accounts Department have the details when you are back. Have a nice ride."

"Thanks."

Délé wheeled around and stalked away.

"Arrogant imbecile!" spat Ikeh as he headed for the Sales Department a floor up.

8

Ikeh, Dúró, and Emeka were chilling at Corner Bar Club in Ọgbà, an Ìkẹjà suburb.

It was a Sunday evening. The club was packed. Strobe lights flashed, setting the floors in flames of different colors.

Music played gently at the background, creating a soothing contrast to the dancehall blare, which seeped through the acoustic padding a floor above.

This was where club goers came to talk, to flirt, to strike business deals, or to simply sit and reflect in relative quite. You wanted a roller coaster ride through the club; you went to the floor above.

"I'm leaving for Mexico City this night," said Ikeh.

"Mexico City?" boomed Emeka in a unique, baritone voice that always drew attention. As usual, heads turned.

This was more so because Emeka was a lanky dark fellow. No mustache. Thin, almost feminine lips. His crew cut and narrow face made him more youthful and even more alien to the baritone.

"Leaving for Mexico City?" said a surprised Dúró. "I thought you said USA last week?"

"Yeah," answered Ikeh. "Got some business to take care of in Mexico. It came up a few days ago.

When I'm done in Mexico, I'm off to California."

"Oh!" said Emeka, eyes wide, making his naturally intense look more penetrating.

"Bon voyage," said Dúró, raising his drink.

Dúró was a head shorter than Emeka. Like Emeka, he carried a crew cut. A hitlerian mustache completed the picture. Even without a beard, he seemed to radiate authority and confidence unlike Emeka who seemed to effortlessly exude Rock-and-Roll demeanor.

Emeka and Ikeh had been friends from a long time. As the year 2005 drew to a close, Dúró and Emeka had decided to flee Africa's decay to the United States of America.

Emeka had approached Ikeh for help. All he and Dúró needed was a roof over their heads until such a time they could get jobs and be able to fend for themselves. Ikeh had agreed.

"Our tickets are booked for the 25th of next month," said Emeka.

"And thanks for connecting us with Johnson for the visas," said Dúró.

"Oh! It's okay. Everyone benefits. Johnson makes his bucks. You guys get your travel papers. And if Johnson were to keep his end of the bargain, he should be making certain deposits in my account for sourcing him clients."

"Commission?"

"Yes," laughed Ikeh. "But in your case, Johnson may give me nothing."

"Why? Because of the discounts?" asked Emeka.

"Yes. I begged him for special rates ... seeing that you guys are hard on cash."

"Thanks, man," said Dúró. "Let's drink to success in the US of A."

"And to Ikeh's happy flight tonight," added Emeka.

They all drank. And kept on drinking. It was a happy day, the beginning of hope and a better life for Dúró and Emeka.

Later that night, Ikeh flew out of Lagos to Mexico City. A week later, he was in the United States sourcing buyers for the consignment of Blue Emeralds from LZL.

With him also was the DVD-R from Johnson.

In the last week of February, Emeka and Dúró flew into LAX from Lagos. Ikeh welcomed them into his home in L.A.

9

Los Angeles
USA.

Ikeh shed his cloth and headed for the bathroom.

It was a tiring day. He needed an invigorating treat in the bathtub. And thereafter a big meal. He had just concluded the sale of the last shipment of Blue Emerald from LZL.

While still in the bath, the telephone rang in the bedroom. After a few rings, the extension in the plush bathroom picked the bedlam.

"Hello."

"Darling," the voice said worriedly. It was his wife, Florence. Ikeh's stomach went into a tight knot.

"Flo? What is it?"

"Darling, it was Johnson ..." she began sobbing.

"Johnson?" An alarm bell went off in Ikeh's brain. "Johnson?" he repeated nonplussed. His mind was whirling, narrowing possibilities, sieving through options.

"Yes, Darling. Diane discovered that he would not wake up this morning. He was dead in bed ..."

"No! Couldn't be! What happened? How could Johnson be dead, Flo?"

"I've been trying to reach you all morning …"

"I'm sorry, Flo. I went out early on business. I just returned. What happened?"

"No one knows yet. Apparently, he was hail and hearty last night when he returned from work. Diane said both of them slept in same room, same bed … as usual. At five this morning when the house was supposed to wake up and have the morning prayers together, Johnson wouldn't wake up. That was when she discovered he was dead."

"God!"

"The corpse had been taken to the morgue."

"How's Diane?"

"Devastated. It's horrible to find your husband dead beside you all of a sudden. I've been there all day. I only now came home to take care of the kids. It's about 10pm here."

"I better speak with Diane!"

"Yes! Call her! She needs our support. Then we wait till the date of burial is set so you'll know when to come and pay him your last respect."

"My God! Johnson is truly dead, Flo?"

"Yes, Darling. Johnson was so young and he was not ill. What happened?"

Ikeh had no answer to the prodding of his confused wife. Rather, he would not want to tell Flo what he thought might have killed Johnson.

This sudden death out of nowhere might have to do with the US embassy. Now, scary questions started popping up in Ikeh's mind. Had the guys at the embassy somehow found out about Johnson's link to DRAINPIPE? Were they his killers? Did they know about the DVD-R from Johnson to him? If yes, was he next on their hit list? Ikeh did not know for sure. He did not want to exclude the possibility.

Now, he needed to be careful. Time was running out. He needed to make his move. And fast.

Even as he sat perplexed in the huge bathtub, his mind was already engaging other worries. Dúró and Emeka were out sightseeing and basking in the glory of having made it out of Africa and into L.A. a fortnight ago. They would soon be back. They would know about Johnson's death. And they would want to know what happened; while a man that sound of health would suddenly turn out dead in bed. Ikeh had to have the right answers ready. Now, his mind was in overdrive.

Over in Lagos this instance, other plans were afoot by the same men who killed Johnson.

10

Surulere was only a quarter of an hour's drive from Ìkẹjà where Ikeh's family lived.

As Florence was hanging the phone up at Ìkẹjà, having talked with Ikeh in California, Thompson was heading for a meeting at Nox Nite Club in Surulere.

He was edgy and furious. His cab was in a traffic snarl at 10pm. In itself, this was not a big deal. He had been in Lagos several times in the past and was used to traffic snarls, which were constant features on the road … at any hour. No big deal. Problem was; he was in one hell of a hurry today.

In the last half an hour, it had been a perfect standstill. Thompson sat in the rickety taxi, his shirt glued to his hairy chest.

Three buttons from the top were open. Still, he sweated. The night was torrid. The asphalt, which had stored tropical heat during the day, now radiated heat from below, creating a continual swirl of hot current.

Outside was worse.

Added to the discomfort was the cacophony created by a unique blend of horns that blared impatiently from hundreds of automobiles. Angry motorists and frustrated commuters snarled and swore at each other as their endurance was pushed to the limit.

The general trend in the last few minutes had been for passengers to push for and get a refund, disembark, and then pad-out the rest of the journey. The negotiations were not very smooth in most instances. Here and there, things were so bad that arguments degenerated into fisticuffs. Still, others would hop on motorbikes called Òkadà to get to their destinations. These motorbikes were used as commercial transport services.

Thompson loved this ambience about Lagos. Always thrilling. Even hilarious in some instances. One thing was for sure in the Lagos environment; you were never bored. Even when penniless. Here in this beautiful, albeit congested city, even the crooks had a comical demeanor below the portrayed hard look. Altogether, you loved the city. You felt alive. You felt loved. You felt cared for. You never felt alone. Your burdens were always automatically shared by the city. It was for these that you were hardly ever psychologically stressed in Lagos even with the absence of the conveniences that you found in typical first worlds.

But today, Thompson was not enjoying himself. He was uptight. He was late for Roland's appointment slated for ten. Which was bad. The luminous hands of his Rolex said three minutes after the hour.

"Shit!" he muttered for the umpteenth time, the clump of hair left on his balding head dripping sweat.

The taxi driver took a curious look at Thompson in the rearview mirror and found his field of view filled with a broad forehead and two hollow sockets. A pair of green eyes below forests of eyebrows bored into his from the dark interior of the taxi.

For a reason he could not entirely understand, the taxi driver found the hairs at the nape of his neck suddenly bristling. In nervous staccato, he stuttered in Lagos pidgin English. *"Sorry Ògá; na ... na dis nonsense ... go slow* (Sorry sir, it's the damn traffic jam)."

Thompson snorted and said impatiently, "As if I cannot see. Goddammit!"

Now, Thompson's aquiline nose looked more intimidating. He brought out his billfold, peeled off the taxi fare of a thousand Naira, and handed it to the cab driver, saying in heavily accented yorùbá mixed with English: "Here, gbà, (Here, have it). I will take my leave now."

Thompson decided he needed an alternate transportation. The cab thing just wasn't working.

Thompson looked over his shoulder through the cab's rear window before attempting to open the cab door. His anticipation was just in order. An Òkadà laden with two passengers lurched precarious by and was away. Pedestrians flew out of the way, as the Òkadà careened through the snaky traffic. Rains of expletives followed. All so good. Thrilling!

In spite of himself and his situation, Thompson grinned. Seeing that it was momentarily safe to emerge, Thompson opened the cab door and jumped out.

The traffic snaked into the distant dark night. He was somewhere between Stadium Bus Stop and Shitta. He knew the environment quite well. The bottleneck must be somewhere around Shitta

Roundabout.

The night was alive. Titillating. Hawkers of all sorts of wares were taking advantage of the traffic standstill to make brisk business. They sold anything from cold drinks, aspirin, to electric iron and cellphones.

Thompson bought a cold can of coke and drank it in a single gulp. He belched gas and felt better. Then he hailed an empty Òkadà.

"Where to?" said the Òkadà rider.

"Nox Nite Club on Olúkólé."

"Five hundred!"

"*Say wetin happen*! (What the hell!)," said Thompson in the popular Lagos pidgin English. "Five hundred Naira! For what? Riding a plane?"

The Òkadà rider started as if stabbed. He looked Thompson over with surprise mixed with admiration, then busted into a guffaw. "So you understand pidgin, sir?"

Thompson ignored his advances and drove for a hard bargain. That was his primary concern, not the advances of an Òkadà rider intent on skinning him because he thought Thompson a novice to pidgin and Òkadà-riding. Thompson said, "One-fifty Naira?"

"*Okay Òġá*! (Okay, sir)."

"That's the spirit. Let's ride!"

———

Thompson made Nox at Olúkólé Street in ten minutes. It would have taken the cab at least two hours to crawl through.

———

Roland was waiting anxiously.

"What took you so long?"

"Go take a peep outside, man. This is Lagos."

"Yeah! Damn traffic jam!"

"I need some beer. Colder than ice."

"You're in the right place," said Roland snapping a finger. A waiter materialized. Thompson ordered Star Larger.

Two-Face laced the air with alluring romance. Which was all Nox wanted.

Roland said, "I got us a quite air-conditioned booth at the back. We can talk over beer in relative peace."

"Good."

Thompson had landed five weeks earlier. Roland had wasted no time taking him through the details of what trouble he had in his hands. Roland was however very careful. He needed to be suspicious of everyone. Better be paranoid than sorry.

He had told Thompson only what Thompson needed to solve the knotty problem at hand and nothing too detailed about DRAINPIPE. Roland had his reasons.

If his success in Nigeria was getting to Terrence, it could also get to Thompson or anybody else. With so much money at stake, there was no telling what anyone could do, including the very dangerous Thompson.

If not for the tangled nature of it all, why would he have any dealings with a psychopath like Thompson in the first place? But then shit had happened and here he was.

Thompson had spent most of the day at the Ìkejà General Hospital morgue, where Johnson's body was kept. Characteristically, Thompson had done some detailed checking of his own.

Now, Thompson said, "Terrence's men poisoned him. There was nothing at all in Johnson's death smelling of ritual killing; not even in the remotest sense."

"Are you sure?"

"Hundred percent! Terence carried out his order, not yours!"

Roland ignored the insinuation and said; "How did they get the poison into him?"

"They laced his lunch with it at the embassy restaurant yesterday at 3:30pm. The poison has a latent period of twelve hours. He must have died at about 3 or 4 this morning."

"And if there was a post mortem ..."

"With the unsophisticated level of postmortem done around here, they will get nothing, Roland. Your guy Terence knows his tuft. My hat is doffed."

"Yeah. Terence is good."

"The poison he used is lethal even in the minutest quantity. I know it very well. It is hardly detectable in victims. The damn thing is an extract from the back of a tiny rare species of toad found only in the Amazon ..."

"Yeah?"

"Yep. Stops your lungs in its track! Chokes you to death."

"Yeah," said Roland getting edgy. He knew Thompson enough to realize that he was building up to something.

Thompson was saying, "If you handled the toad with your bare hands, you felt nothing. No problem you would think. But wait about half a day thereafter and you would suddenly realize you were in deep shit ..."

"Then what!" snapped Roland, his voice sharper than he had intended.

"Then you are fucking dead, Roland!"

"What now Thompson! Are you some kind of a frigging expert on Amazon toads?"

"Yeah! You may say that!"

"What the hell is the point, Thompson?"

"You gotta be careful of that guy, Roland," Thompson said ominously.

"Oh sure! I watch him like a hawk. Why do you think I sent for you?"

"That's not what I mean."

Roland froze, the hand taking his beer to his lips arrested midair. "What exactly do you mean?"

11

"You think you are running the show around here! Yes?" asked Thompson.

"What are you driving at?" shot Roland.

"What if you are not? Have you ever considered that possibility?"

"Explain."

"Should be obvious," said Thompson sarcastically. "Terence directly disobeyed your instructions!"

"Look! He probably thought death in bed while sleeping was better to pull than making it look ritual-like, Thompson," defended Roland. He was beginning to feel the start of a nasty headache.

"Maybe!"

"So!"

"Maybe not!"

"What do you mean?"

"The big deal was ... simply put; brazen insubordination. You gave him instructions; he went along; but changed your orders thereafter without the recourse to consult you. Meanwhile, all the time, you were either a-phone-call away or on hand in an office next to him. Still, he never saw it fit to tell you a thing ... even as we speak. Nothing could be more dangerous. It placed you directly in the line of fire had a detailed postmortem been done and that poison picked up."

"So what do you think?"

"With that guy around, you, my friend, may be living on borrowed life."

"We shall see about that."

For the next few minutes, each just sat silently, drinking beer. Then Thompson broke the silence and said, "Have you made the list?"

"Yes," Roland answered distantly, gulped more beer, and seemed to wake up to the immediate challenge of the list. "Fucking Terence."

The list was actually why Thompson was in Lagos.

It was to be an itemized chronicle of those Roland wanted screened. From this, Thompson was expected to draw out those he would have to take out in addition to Johnson (already taken out by Terence) in safeguarding DRAINPIPE.

"Keep your eyes on Terence and his activities, man," advised Thompson. "You don't wanna wake up struggling to breath like the Johnson fellow."

"Cut it out, Thompson! I told you things are under wraps!"

"Good to hear that. I care, that's all!"

"Yeah! Thanks! You want the list or not!"

"Let's have it."

"Goddamned Terence!"

12

The Igbo tribe to which Johnson belonged quickly interred their own.

A week after he was found dead in bed, Johnson's solemn burial was in full gear at his hometown of Orlu, Imo state.

Thompson was in attendance. Finally, he had his hit list – Two. Ikechuckwu Ikade; Ikeh for short. And Abíódún Òtòlòórìn, aka Bíódún. He had decided that they were the ones who could constitute any threat at all to Roland and the big guns up in Washington.

Bíódún was based in Germany, while Ikeh shuttled between L.A. and Lagos. They were both at the funeral.

Good prediction.

Twenty minutes into the funeral, Thompson cornered Bíódún at the restroom.

"Hi there, it's a pity about Johnson," he started with a long face, opening his fly to relieve himself.

"Yeah really," Bíódún answered. "Quite a pity. Such a young man. Very vibrant, nice, affable, always ready to help his people."

Sure, thought Thompson, by issuing fake U.S. visas.

Aloud, Thompson said, "He was such a nice person to work with."

"The best there was. This town had lost a gem," concluded Bíódún who was tidying up. "What's the name?"

"Mark Foster, SPO to the U.S. Ambassador."

"SPO?"

"Yes, Senior Protocol Officer."

Thompson knew that the SPO thing always got to crooks like Bíódún. They believed you were big.

"You are welcome, Mark. I'm Bíódún."

Bíódún was built like a battering ram. Thick, fleshy head. Full hairless face. Hooded eyes. Thick lips. Short, heavyset neck atop a broad menacing chest. Six feet frame that dwarfed most people around.

"You are welcome," Thompson said.

"Good to know you, Mark. May I call you that?"

"Yes, Bíódún, call me Mark."

"Here is my business card, Mark," Bíódún said handing a beautiful gold-inscribed card to Thompson. "I'm based in Germany. I deal in importing electronics from Germany to Nigeria."

"Glad to know you, sir," Thompson said, shaking an offered hand again. "I will be sure to keep in touch. Unfortunately, I do not have my business card here."

"That's not a problem," Bíódún said. "There is always a next time. You have my contact details."

Both headed for the exit.

As they got to the door, Ikeh was coming in.

"Ikeh," Bíódún cried in the subdued tone characteristic of funerals. "Meet a friend of mine from the U.S. embassy. Mark Foster, Senior Protocol Officer to the Ambassador. Mark, meet a special friend, Ikeh."

Ikeh's hand short forward and Thompson

grabbed it.

"Happy to meet a friend of Bíódún," said Thompson.

"Ikeh was quite close to Johnson," Bíódún added.

"Very close," Ikeh reechoed. "His death was a shock."

"It was also a shock to us all at the embassy, sir," Thompson said with another of his long faces.

"We'll all miss him," said Ikeh.

"We sure will," said Thompson.

"Excuse me," Ikeh said and disappeared into the restroom.

Bíódún shouted after him: "We will just have a drink at the house in case you want to join us."

"No thanks," Ikeh said from the depth of the restroom.

———————

Johnson was buried at a corner of his palatial country home.

Ikeh had lost an important friend and he felt he knew why. He quickly put the offered friendship from Mark Foster out of his mind, SPO or not. He knew it would take a while before he could make friends with anyone in that embassy.

13

It was two days since Johnson's burial at Orlu.

Ikeh was flying out of Lagos to L.A and Bíódún was there at the Murtala Mohammed International Airport to see him off. Having made sure that a distraught Ikeh had boarded his flight, Bíódún headed straight for Rhythm Night Club at Allen Avenue for a good night life. He was unaware that he was being trailed by a killer. Even Thompson did not have to trail Bíódún for long; Ìkẹjà's Allen Avenue was a stone throw from Murtala Mohammed International Airport.

Thompson knew Rhythm well enough to know that it was ideal for his purpose. He would not stand out as a white client, which was paramount to his success. The club had sizeable patronage from the white community in Lagos.

Presently, Thompson sat in a rented old Honda Civic parked across the street from the night club and prepared for the next stage. He checked his gun. Satisfied. He screwed a silencer on its barrel then stowed it away at the inner right pocket of his jacket.

It was time.

He got out, crossed the street, entered the dimly lit barroom, and ordered a beer. He was just in time

to see Bíódún disappear up the stairs with a call girl.
The glow of the key holder with him showed the
room number. Room 13. Thompson decided to
allow a half hour interval before heading for room
13.

Half an hour later and a few beers down,
Thompson was at the door to Room 13.

It was located at the extreme end of the corridor
down from the second floor landing. Coming up the
stairs, he met no one. Just as well. Thompson
listened for a while but heard nothing. He tried the
door; it was locked. Naturally.

He bent to the keyhole. The tip of a key was
visible from the other side of the door. He
straightened up and assessed the situation.

How would he get into the room with the key in
the lock from the other side? There was only one
solution; fire a shot through the lock. A shot
through the lock would however rob him of his
surprise edge over Bíódún. Reasonable risk.

Glancing up the corridor again and satisfied that
he had the whole stretch to himself, he withdrew his
gun. As he thumped off the safety catch, he heard
shuffling of feet behind the locked door. Then the
key turned and the door flew open.

There was no hiding place. Thompson found
himself face to face with the person he had come to
kill.

Bíódún's reaction was instantaneous as he saw
the gun in Thompson's hand.

His right hand disappeared into the inside of his
suit jacket while he ducked backwards into the
room, slamming the door on Thompson at same

time.

Thompson's right foot shot forward and blocked the door. Behind Bíódún, the call girl screamed and grabbed him for protection. Bíódún tripped on her and both sprawled on the carpet, the call girl on top.

Thompson acted fast. He shot the girl first, cutting short her screaming. Bíódún had gotten out a handgun. But that was as far as he managed. Thompson shot him twice. He needed not look; Bíódún laid still. Dead.

Thompson peeped into the corridor. Nothing. Satisfied, he made a quite exit. He headed for Providence Hotel in Lagos Island where he had lodged since coming into Lagos.

Hours later, Thompson was ready to get out of Lagos Island. He called Roland for a rendezvous and then checked out of Providence. Thompson was done in Nigeria. The next target was Ikeh who had just flown out to Los Angeles.

Roland picked him up a few blocks away from the hotel and headed for Lagos mainland. From Lagos Island, they quickly gained access to Third Mainland Bridge. At nearly midnight, the whole stretch was devoid of traffics.

While en route the mainland, Thompson brought Roland up to date on his activities over the Bíódún case. By the time they exited the Third Mainland Bridge, the longest bridge in Africa, to Èbúté Méta in Lagos Mainland, Roland was fully informed.

Satisfied by Thompson's progress so far, he enthused happily: "One down, one to go."

"Yep," answered Thompson. "Ikeh just flew out to LAX. I'm out of here in a day or two."

"Yeah, sure. I'll conclude another payment

tomorrow morning then."

"Not later than 10am, Roland. I'll be running a check on my account at ten."

"No problem. I'll pay the balance when Ikeh is dead."

"That was the agreement, yes."

"Where do I drop you?"

"Stop right here and I'll find my way. Thanks."

"Sure man," Roland said stopping the car. He offered a hand and Thompson shook it firmly.

"Thanks for helping me, Thompson."

"My pleasure, Roland," Thompson said opening the car door and stepping onto the street.

"Hear from you soon," Roland shouted after the departing Thompson.

"Yeah," Thompson threw over his shoulder, disappearing into the Èbúté Méta night. An hour and a half later, he was in a hotel room at Maryland, Ìkẹjà.

14

Los Angeles
USA

Ikeh was generally chilling at the Temple Bar on Wilshire Boulevard in Santa Monica when his cell phone rang at 8pm.

It was Rèmí, Bíódún's business partner. Ikeh's mind was automatically flooded by the terrible memories of the just buried Johnson; the very memories he was trying to drink out of his system.

"Rèmí, hi."

"Ikeh; did you hear of Bíódún's death?"

"What?" Ikeh cried in shock disbelief, feeling the floor swing towards him. He grabbed a pillar for support. He had flown out of Lagos a mere forty-eight hours ago and Bíódún was there at the airport to see him off. Now, he was dead! Dead?

"Hello ... hello. Are you there?"

"Yes, I am, Rèmí. I don't get it!"

"Someone shot him dead at a night club in Ìkẹjà. It happened same night you flew out of Lagos. They think it is one of our business rivals, Ikeh."

Ikeh felt otherwise.

Moments after getting off the phone from Rèmí,

Ikeh's hands were still shaking as he punched a contact's number. And it was not out of fear, but rage.

He needed to get rid of the explosive DVD-R now. It was leaving dead bodies in its wake. Two of his best friends were dead. All of a sudden. Now more than ever, he needed a buyer fast!

15

Washington D.C.
U.S.A.

Roland and Terence had been recalled to the United States by DRAINPIPE's overall boss, Kim Holland.

For Roland, that was a very bad development. His hope at the outset was to keep the leak within the confines of Lagos. That was why he had authorized the death of Johnson and employed the services of Thompson to take care of other loose ends.

But Terence was ahead; he had started a dangerous game. He was using the leak as a platform from which to launch a desperate bid to oust him as DRAINPIPE's Head of Operations.

Terence's first move was to make sure that the leak was not confined to Lagos. Behind Roland, Terence had furnished Kim with details of the leak. And Kim had responded by recalling them both as well as demand a list of all of Johnson's business and social associates.

Kim was the master-minder of the money-spinning mining ventures all over West Africa.

Along with Neil Simon, his Deputy, Kim was drawing up a list of potential risks to DRAINPIPE from that supplied by Terence.

There were six persons in the United States who might have had contacts with DRAINPIPE and therefore needed monitoring. There were also nearly two-dozen others scattered in Africa, Europe, and Asia to be kept under surveillances. One was already dead; shot at a night club in Lagos.

Kim knew that it would cost a bundle to pull this vast network of surveillances. For a delicate program like DRAINPIPE and its financial firepower, Kim felt it was indispensable.

In all the cases reviewed however, Ikeh was in the forefront. For a number of haunting reasons, Ikeh became a special target for surveillance. One; Ikeh worked for LZL, which housed the administrative arms of DRAINPIPE's mines in Nigeria's southwestern states. Two; Ikeh was a notorious criminal of the gemstones underworld. And three, the most damning of all of Ikeh's attributes, he was a police informant.

Kim and Neil went digging. The more they dug, the more they found. What they unearthed about Ikeh was unsettling, given Ikeh's proximity to Chinedu Johnson who accessed DRAINPIPE.

Now Kim, Neil, Roland, and Terence were in a suite in Washington Hilton far removed from prying eyes at the office, discussing some interesting points about Ikeh.

"Helluva guy, Roland," exclaimed Kim, glaring over a horn-rimmed reading glasses at Roland who was shifting uncomfortably in his chair. From the corners of his eyes, Roland could see that this moment was for Terence.

Kim's right hand shot towards his head, running over the wig that concealed his baldness. His tall, bulky frame hunched over, making him more imposing and forbidding. His blue eyes had taken on an icy coldness that seemed to stab into Roland's.

Kim shifted his gaze over to Neil and said, "What do you think Neil?"

"I agree," said Neil. "A guy who squeals on his people to LAPD on a regular basis in the course of earning a living is someone I will not trust at all. He'll do anything for money."

"Yes! With Ikeh, we have to be very watchful," said Kim, directing himself at Roland who was doing his utmost to disappear into his seat. "Johnson used a disc to copy those files from your records. We know he took it home and had the files copied into his computer. Now what we did not know for sure was what happened to the disc thereafter. Was it destroyed or what? You guys had searched his house top to bottom; no dice. Where is the bloody disc? With an LAPD informant as resourceful and as crooked as this Ikeh fellow close to Johnson … we simply cannot be too careful."

"Yes, Sir."

"So we keep eyes on him and his daily dealings!"

"Yes, sir."

"And you two better get off your asses and do your goddamn job. Got it?!"

"Yes sir," chorused Terence and Roland.

Half an hour later, both Terence and Roland left. In his mind, Roland was a relaxed man. With no worries. For a reason. Kim and Neil had come to the same conclusion Thompson did. The most prominent target on Kim's list was the same on Thompson's. Anytime now, Thompson was going to call him to report the death of Ikeh. He would await words from Thompson.

Shame on Terence.

When Thompson was done with Ikeh, the next assignment was Terence. Of that, Roland was certain. Now, unlike in times gone, Roland's mind was made. Terence had to go or Terence would get rid of him first.

———

"What do you think, Neil?" said a worried Kim.

"We don't need this, Kim," answered Neil. "Not now of all times. We've got enough to chew over in Iraq and Afghanistan! And that's not mentioning the tricky business with an unstable Musharaff. Look, Kim … we've got to nip this right in the bud. Cannot risk an explosion of the stuffs we got going. Roland is a fool! A billion-dollar venture is threatened and all he could think was confine the leak in his office! Unbelievable! Anyway, bottom line is; we can't afford a disclosure."

"Especially now! Not with the American public threatening to take apart the bloody federal cabinet every time a suicide bomber blows himself off in Iraq."

"If this gets out," said Neil, drumming his fingers on Kim's table for emphasis, "membership of George Bush's cabinet will be the last of our worries."

"George will personally fry us!" snapped Kim as he stood up and drove his hands into his pants pockets so hard they tore. "And that's irrespective of what we've done for him on FLIGHT."

"It's why, Kim … it's why we're going to make sure this never leaks! Never! No matter what!"

16

On the west coast, a number of things had happened in the last few months.

Emeka and Dúró had found jobs and were earning money. Both had merged with the huge city of L.A and its eccentricities. They looked ahead to a very bright future in the United States.

Ikeh had been to Nigeria and back with another shipment of Emerald. He had run around California the whole of July trying to sell the gemstones to waiting clients.

Dan had helped. Rick as well. Both were Ikeh's business associates with contacts in France where emerald of the varieties Ikeh brought from Nigeria was always in high demands in the jewelry world.

Done disposing the stones, Ikeh got down to the business of getting a buyer for the political missile he got from Johnson.

If you needed to sell hot stuffs on high-profile politicians in Washington and top State Department technocrats, you visited places like Busby's.

Conveniently situated on Santa Monica Boulevard, Busby's was an up-market club whose clientele spread from middleclass Americans to the rich.

Chauffeur-driven limousines with darkened

windows ferreted clients to and from the club. No one was ever interested in anyone's identity. Visits were just to have nice times and be off. Until the next visit. Therefore, you could jump and prance in Busby's incognito.

Occasionally, you saw a face you had seen more than a few times on the political pages of Washington Post or New York Times. Those were in the class of the big shots whose dirty laundries were in Ikeh's DVD-R. But those were not his targets.

His targets were their agents. In Busby's, the agents for these rich clients were in abundance and readily approachable.

Ikeh had visited Busby's twice. One or two guys had shown interest. As it turned out, one of them worked for Dan. Just as well. He knew Dan enough to be able to discuss the sale of the DVD-R with him.

Dan was into everything that fetched money, especially monies he could salt away from the long hands of the IRS.

Dan was good-looking, lithe, fast, with sharp features to complement his fast-track mind. Dan carried himself well and prided himself on the way he dressed, which was not only expensive but confidence inspiring.

In the last few weeks therefore, Dan and Ikeh had regularly met. Dan was sourcing clients for the DVD-R. The preliminary talks had been concluded. Now they were meeting for the final negotiations.

They were in Ikeh's Dodge in a public parking lot in downtown Los Angeles. Nearby, the rumble of an overhead train passing intruded into their discussion.

Dan said, "Look, I understand your need for secrecy but I need a few tidbits on what may be up for grabs, Ikeh. Besides, that will help in setting a price."

"I set the price, Dan. I thought we agreed on that a few days ago."

"No doubt. Still, there is the need for negotiation. I'm under tremendous pressure here! My clients want some juicy bits. Whatever you have on those guys will help in driving the bargain. It's also to your advantage, Ikeh. That's the truth."

"I've got named banks, account numbers, and fund transfers."

"Over how long?"

"Years, Dan. Years."

"I need one or two names."

"No! No!"

"Look, it ..."

"I cannot tell you names, Dan! But I can tell you this; they are as high as they come."

"I need a little something, Ikeh," said Dan desperately.

"State Department. The Congress. High-profile players of the Gulf War. It's a bomb, I guarantee you!"

"My God! No shit!"

"No!"

"Convince me, Ikeh!"

"It's all about Africa's gemstones. These guys operate a web of gemstones cartels with a spread the size of the Amazon. These guys had raked in almost five billion U.S. dollars in just ten years! Tax free! Hidden in carefully created accounts all over the world! Expectedly, a huge chunk of the monies is over there in those secret vaults for which Swiss banks are noted! Safely hidden from IRS!"

"Diamonds?! Right?!"

"And much more, Dan! Emeralds! Sapphires! Topaz! Hundreds of mines, all carefully structured. Can operate in wartimes and peacetimes. Attracts no undue suspicion from local officials."

"What's that mean?"

"They got people, Dan! They got ... locals fronting for them. The locals usually get 10% of the yields from each mine."

Dan was thoughtful for a while, his face crinkled from thought. Then he said, "These guys who supply your stones, Ikeh ... they are part of the ring. It's how you got this bomb! Right?"

"Sort of. So now you know that the stuff I'm selling is core!"

"My God! What's your asking price?"

"Two million dollars, U.S.!"

"Are you kidding me? Who's going to pay that sort of money? We are talking about old politicians here! Most of them are damn poor! Besides, their political futures are damaged anyway! I mean judging by Bush's escapades, these guys running around with him are history!"

"That's the cash, Dan."

"Yeah, yeah, yeah. I know all about that trick! The more damaged these guys in the DVD-R are by current political games in Washington, the higher the stake. Is that it?!"

"Right, Dan! Bush is retiring! These other guys are still waiting for their turn to preside over the most advance economy in the world! Right? Right! If the stuffs in my DVD-R can redeem the political future of any of them, whoever it is will pay anything to acquire it! So, it's one of two choices you have Dan. You can sell to the guys in the disc. They'll pay anything you ask them ... even if only to snap it off the market and keep it away from political foes. On the other hand, you can locate their sworn political foes and sell to them."

"Ikeh!" snapped Dan, "can we leave the bloody lectures for another day?!"

"Yeah. Maybe. See, Dan, my concern is not the sentiments."

"Glad to hear that. Emotions cloud things. Bad for business!"

"Right! I could not care less whose political future is amputated in Bush's cabinet. Over in Africa, Bush and his guys are doing a whole lot more than amputate political careers."

"Yeah! Sort of! Can we get on with the negotiations? You said your concerns are not the sentiments, man. Leave the politics to the politicians!"

"What I care about is who pays the highest price."

"All the more I need a peek into the DVD-R. I need a few names, Ikeh, please!"

"Kim Holland!" Ikeh whispered as if the inside of his car was bugged.

"The CIA Director?"

"Yes."

"I'm listening!"

"Bush's boy, Jerome Hughes!"

"Cat-with-nine-lives Jerome?!"

"You got that right! It's cat-with-nine-lives Jerome."

"My God! You got these guys on record ... on this DVD-R?"

"In minute details!"

"I'm listening!"

"That's all I'm ever going to tell you!"

"One more name please!"

"Look Dan ..."

"Please! I'm on my knees here! Besides, you're asking for millions, Ikeh!"

"Yes! And rightly so! I know the DVD-R's worth!"

"Good! So?"

"Todd Broadmann!"

"Rice's Under Secretary of State on Africa?"

"Yes!"

"My God! What's your bottom line?"

"Still two million. If a cent less, don't bother calling me."

"Jesus Christ, Ikeh! All right, talk to you later," said Dan as he opened the door and scurried to his Jaguar.

17

Two weeks had passed since the discussion with Ikeh.

Dan had been in a frenzy of activities, crisscrossing the country sampling opinions, and rating potential buyers of the bomb with Ikeh. Finally, he had selected the most enticing of all the clients – Jack Nicholas. Now, Dan was in a meeting with Jack in Washington to conclude the sale.

Jack had booked the meeting to take place over lunch at the exclusive Sea Catch Restaurant on 31st Street in Georgetown.

The atmosphere was hushed and auto-cooled. Kenny G's saxophone spiced the air delectably. The tables were far apart and gave an air of strict privacy to diners.

Dan's aims had been to get Ikeh to come down on his two million dollars price tag as much as possible. At the same time, Dan had been racing to push the price up with potential buyers as far as he could. Only in this manner would Dan be able to rake enough from the transactions.

Ikeh had finally agreed to a million and a half. Now, Dan needed to add a little something on top.

Dan was saying, "I've done all I could, Jack! He's simply not ready to drop below a million and six hundred thousand."

"I was counting on a million, tops!"

"Then you may have to talk to him yourself. And fast," said Dan tasting his drink. "You can get him in one of those sleazy bars in Santa Monica."

Jack shot him a poisoned look. His asthma was threatening to shut his breath off. He brought out his inhaler and puffed at it vigorously. A little bit relieved, Jack wheezed, "Can't afford that, Dan. And you know it!" He took a momentary break from the exertion and then continued. "I cannot be seen with that guy! Not now; not ever! So you swing the deals, Dan!"

Puff! Puff!

"Then you need to start listening to my story, Jack. He is not dropping below a million and six hundred thousand bucks. That is a big difference from a million you had in mind! I had a hard time getting him to come down from his initial two million. But a million? Six hundred thousand bucks off? You talk to him yourself! Santa Monica is a flight away. Your boss has a plane!"

Puff! Puff!

"Cut the shit out!" spat Jack, his breath still coming out in wheezes. "There is always the need for negotiation! Everything has a bottom line! And you know it!"

"Yeah! Sure! Still, we have to move fast. Otherwise, someone else may snap up that DVD-R."

That got to Jack whose wheezes increased.

Puff! Puff!

"Look, Dan ..."

"Even Kim himself," said Dan, deliberately cutting into Jack and doing his best to drive the nail deeper under Jack's skin. "Whatever that disk has on Kim is hot! Ikeh knows it! Otherwise he would not be talking in millions instead of a few thousands. This transaction breaks all barriers!"

Puff! Puff!

"You can say that again!" cried Jack. "This is unprecedented! U.S$1.6m!"

"Know what Jack! This guy has a good grasp of the politics around here and what role the information he has can play. He knows he is dealing with crooked multi-millionaire politicians and exactly how to rip them off grand-style. He's got us by the fucking balls, Jack! Wake up!"

"He is a Nigerian, Dan!" said Jack breathless. "Don't set stores by them this much. You're getting sloppy!"

Puff! Puff!

"Jack! Quit this moral high-ground. We most probably made them into what they are today. And if you spoke with a guy like Wells, you might just discover that your great grandpa or something was one of the Slave Traders who fucked up their life and mind or something!"

"Dan! Dan! What are you saying?!"

Puff! Puff!

"Simple! Crooks are everywhere in this messed up world! There are worse crooks in this country than any Nigerian crook out there. Dubious characters out here had tried everything imaginable ... from trying to sell the Brooklyn Bridge ... the Brooklyn fucking Bridge! ... to selling the Eiffel Tower! What the bloody World Bank is doing with logging in the forests of the Congo's pygmies is worse than any scam ever pulled by any combined group of Nigerians!"

"Are you trying to lecture me, Dan?!"

"No! Just letting you know that these Nigerians you call crooks happen to be the ones exposing a multimillion-dollar illegal gemstones cartel formulated by 'good' American guy Kim. And by so doing, Ikeh is saving you and your boss. What I'm saying in effect is for you to leave the fine details and the morals, Jack!"

"What are you implying, Dan?!"

"Simple, Jack! The bottom line is; I know this guy well enough to know how he operates. We are business partners; we know each other well!"

Puff! Puff!

"You guys deal in stolen gemstones, Dan! Stones you smuggle across borders! You guys forge official documents and sell them for money!"

"Look, Jack," retorted Dan. "This guy has the stuffs that can save your boss's ass from guaranteed political extinction. You want it or not?"

"What's the bottom line on your commission?"

"It's usually 5%, Jack! You know!"

"We are running short of cash, Dan. A little favor here can be repaid back in the near future. The NSA is not likely to forget such gesture."

"By sourcing out this hot stuff on Kim in the first place, I have already made more contributions to the NSA's political future than any campaign donations, Jack. Without me and this DVD-R, Reeds is history! Kim has your boss by the balls from the rumors making the rounds! I need some credit here."

"Still, cash is in short supply, I say."

"Oh boy!"

"So ... what will it be, Dan Boy? You owe me!"

"Yeah! I know!"

"Big time! Don't forget!"

"Yeah. Look, I appreciate your role in making that sonofabitch cop drop those charges ..."

"Ten years, Dan," said a very intense Jack. Now his pale cheeks were red. His short hair, patted at the vertex, was in disarray. Otherwise, his features were a perfect Aryan, which he was always proud of. "You would have gotten ten with no option of parole, Dan. Don't forget! Nevertheless, I made it go away. Now you drive one of those fancy cars! What's the name again? Yeah, a Jaguar. A Jaguar, Dan! You are doing well I suppose."

"All right! All right, Jack! My five percent here is eighty grand. Right?"

"Yes."

"I drop ten. Give me seventy."

"Let's split it down the middle, Dan. Forty-forty."

"Come on, Jack! I have a living to make, bills to pay. sixty."

"Fifty. Not a cent more!"

"Awh God!" lamented Dan running his right fingers through his hair. "All right. Deal."

"Thanks," said Jack relaxing back on his seat and grinning knowingly at Dan. "The NSA is never going to forget this."

"Yeah, yeah! How about payment?"

"I'll have it deposited in the usual account as soon as I get the DVD-R. So speed up the exchange and keep in touch."

Dan finished his drink and hurried away happy. He was going to rake in one hundred and fifty thousand dollars in all. Tax free!

Not a bad deal.

18

Jack sat in his car at the parking lot of Sea Catch Restaurant, trying to catch his breath.

He puffed at his asthma inhaler several times to help with his breathing. Excitements like these always brought on his attacks. Soon, the wheezes subsided. The tightness in his chest relaxed. The pounding headache of anticipation receded.

There were other worries of course; but they could take a back seat for just a few moments. For the next few minutes, he simply basked in the glow of his success. Alfred Reeds was going to worship him for eternity.

For a reason.

Finally, Jack had gotten the best weapon with which to clip Kim's wings and rescue the political future of his boss from – how did Dan put it – yes, guaranteed extinction.

But for nearly two million dollars! That was the other worry! Where were they going to source that kind of money?

It took Jack half an hour to calm enough to take the next step. From his car, Jack placed a call to Alfred Reeds' Personal Secretary.

"Nancy?" said Jack into the phone.

"Yes, Jack?" answered Nancy.

"Is the boss busy?"

"Yes, Jack. He is still in the middle of the Saudi meeting ..."

"Interrupt him!" instructed Jack.

Nancy was almost apoplectic. "What?! Jack! It's the group from the Saudi military!"

"Yes, I know, Nancy! I set it up and opened the meeting an hour or so ago before I slipped away, remember?!"

"Right! Yes! It's why I'm shocked!"

"Interrupt him!"

"Sir ..."

"Nancy! Interrupt him!"

Nancy was desperate. "Sir, I might just point out that the Secretary of State was participating via video conference."

"Is she on line right now?"

"No. But she could come back on the screen anytime! The line is open; you instructed me to keep all such lines open at times like this, Jack!"

"Good job, Nancy," said Jack. "All the same, interrupt him! Place the call through a Red Line and have it scrambled, Nancy!"

"All right, sir! Right away, sir."

A few clicks and hums sounded while Jack waited. Then the country's National Security Advisor came on the line.

"Jack!" cried Alfred Reeds. "In the middle of a Saudi military deal! What's got into you? You should be somewhere close-by if I remember your job stipulations right!"

"I slipped away for a quick meeting, sir. And nice that I did. Now, we got Kim Holland cold turkey!"

"Come again!"

"I got a line on Kim! He's got some dirty deals going on in Nigeria! Big, big stuff!"

"My God! How solid?"

"Solid enough for us to put him away for good!"

"Are you kidding me?"

"In the middle of a hundred and seventy-five billion dollars military deal with the arrogant Saudis? With Bush on your tail?! You underestimate me, sir!"

"What do we do?"

"We are going to hunt for funds! We'll need some couple of millions to pull this through."

"Million?!" cried Reeds, feeling dizzy. "What do you mean millions?"

"I'll get down to the details later."

"Oh! All right. I take it this call is scrambled?"

"Yes."

"Good! You're the best, Jack. You know that?"

"Thanks for the compliment, sir. I'll be with you in two hours. There are things I need to set in motion to see this through."

"Thanks Jack."

19

"How the hell are we going to get a million and a half, Jack?" cried Alfred Reeds. "And for a mere DVD-R!"

In his mind, Reeds was thinking in the range of fifty thousand dollars or thereabout. A million and a half?! And counting?!

"That DVD-R, sir, is our only ticket out of the Iraq wilderness. With it, we can wash you clean and watch Kim and Bush go down! Same with half a dozen other high profile politicians here in Washington. The wave will propel you into the forefront of the elections!"

"Oh, Boy! You do have a fertile mind. As for the DVD-R, what makes it so hot? A million and ..."

"I've asked around, sir. It is a political bomb. State Department, the Congress, Kim, and his CIA. It is a coup! Numbered bank accounts; movements of funds in and out of Africa in the last ten years. Names of gemstones buyers in Europe, Asia, and the Americas having contacts with Kim, Jerome, and guys like Todd! Black market deals! Hidden money inaccessible to the tax guys! IRS will have a fit! It is explosive! Kim won't make it."

"Boy! Kim will want that DVD-R badly!"

"And he and his cronies in there have enough

salted away from West Africa's gemstone business to snap it up. A million ... two ... or three means nothing to these guys! The only thing is; they are not aware yet that their dirt is up for sale. Which exactly is why we should move fast."

"How the hell am I going to get a million and a half just to buy a DVD-R, Jack?" Alfred lamented.

"Lewis is a multimillionaire. He is your pal. You are in same political boat. Lewis faces as much political death as you with what Americans perceive as *the Iraq mess*. You are each other's confidante. Talk to him. I think he will jump at the chance to redeem his image in this administration by exposing the dirt buried in that embassy in Lagos. A million or two means nothing to him."

"Well ... you ... you could be right there, Jack!"

"You could make him your Secretary of State or something ... in return ... if ... if we won."

"Yes. I'll talk to him."

"Before or after Camp David?" pressed Jack.

"Afterwards, Jack. Let's make it afterwards."

"You will talk to Lewis, sir, wont you?"

"I will. I will, Jack. I will think everything through during the retreat. The fresh air out there will benefit me greatly. If I need any more clarifications, we'll talk."

"Yes, sir."

20

Since Jack told him about the DVD-R, Alfred Reeds could hardly think of anything else.

For the first time in a year, there was real hope that he could actually clinch the White House.

Reeds was fifty-eight and looked younger than his peers who had aged considerably from the high-tension political games of Washington.

He had been a successful Republican Senator and the Chairman of Arms Services Committee in 2005 when President Bush invited him into the Federal Cabinet as the National Security Advisor.

Walter Elmer had taken over from Condoleezza Rice. Rice had been moved to State Department to take over from Powell whose potential political future had been amputated by the Iraq imbroglio.

In three months flat, Walter had run America foreign policy further aground. Bush felt Reeds' experience was vital in undoing the damages. Reeds' experience cut across international diplomacy, national security, and the military. Taken alongside his experience on the Hill and his role at getting backings from the senate for Bush's invasion of Iraq two years earlier, Reeds looked tailor-made for the job.

Even the public wanted him as the NSA. It was

almost like graceful old Powell whom the Democrats courted even while he actively campaigned for Bush, a Republican, in 2000. Such was Reeds' charisma and political experience.

Now barely a year into office, Reeds was as good as politically buried.

From the dept of the dark tunnel now emerged this ray of possible hope. Ikeh. And the DVD-R. And of course a whopping million and a half dollars.

Reeds was troubled.

Lewis was a good man. Honest. Trustworthy. Generous to a fault. But sourcing a million dollars from him was buying too much into his debt. Most times, he who paid the piper dictated the tune.

Reeds' mind had been awash with plans. Alternate plans. Plots. Counter plots. What else could he do? How? What means were available to him?

Then he realized. The answer was there at his fingertips. Would it work?

Reeds had gone into his private vault at the office and brought out a thin file. It was a copy of the file compiled by the New York Police Department on the murder of his first wife, Claire, fifteen years earlier.

The murder was never solved. Reeds could have helped NYPD solve the murder but had chosen to keep mum. Back then, the murder was better unsolved. Better for his career; better even for Claire.

Now it might serve a useful purpose in avoiding the payment of a million and a half dollars for the only commodity he knew could realign his fractured political future. A stone for two beautiful birds.

As he left with President Bush for the Camp David Retreat northwest of Washington, Reeds took the file with him, locked within the safety of his briefcase.

Amidst the demands of Camp David, Reeds had moments to shape and reshape his plot. Two days later, he was set. Late at night while Camp David lay sleeping for the night, Reeds briefed Jack in the safety of his private quarters.

Jack read the file and listened to the missing part, which Reeds could supply to get a conviction.

"What do you think?" Reeds asked.

"Brilliant! It will work, sir. All we have to do is let him read the file compiled by the police fifteen years ago and the missing part we can supply to get a conviction."

"Think so?"

"Yes, sir. It was a Midas touch for you to have followed him through the years. He will be looking at twenty-five years to a life sentence. He will play."

"I sure hope so."

"He will! Or he will lose all the millions he had amassed. He will make the rational choice! When money is involved, huge piles ... men always prefer to preserve the money. He'll play!"

"I feel so terrible dragging Claire into this!"

"Believe me, sir; she would want that you made this move."

"We have to be careful, Jack."

"We will."

"What if he plays rough?"

"He won't!"

"So we make Lewis a back-up in case this does not work!"

"Yes. But it will. I am so sure."

"How long do we give him?"

"Two weeks or thereabout to work out the details and for us to gauge his reactions."

"All right, Jack. Let's go with it."

21

Both were in Fort Meade in Maryland.

Alfred Reeds always retreated there if he felt insecure as was the case in recent times. It was not until November that Jack gave Reeds the go ahead to meet with Lewis.

Lewis Howitzer was the Special Political Adviser to the U.S. President on Middle East.

Both were desperate men.

The indirect cause was President Bush. The direct cause was the thickly disguised, very ambitious and patriotic program, which the President personally named FLIGHT.

Simplified, FLIGHT's goal, amidst several, involved the invasion and occupation of Afghanistan and Iraq as a part of a larger economic and strategic game Washington had going in the region. Otherwise, the despotic ruling class in both Iraq and Afghanistan would present perpetual obstacles to Washington's ambition in the region.

Installations of puppet democratic governments in Kabul and Baghdad were thus core parts of the multi-pronged program.

"Timing is of essence if you want to go, Reeds," said a very worried Lewis. "Mine is a different ballgame. It is irreversible. I'm leaving!"

"Not if there is an alternative. We may have found some sort of leverage, Lewis."

"What leverage?"

"Jack is working on it."

"That's what you want to talk to me about?"

"Yes."

"Must be sensitive then for you to bring me into your fortress here just to clue me in."

"Yes, Lewis. This thing is very delicate. But it may give us a platform from which to spring out and launch into the White House ... not irrevocably destroyed by Kim's FLIGHT."

"Oh ... FLIGHT," spat Lewis.

"If this thing with Jack works out, we can cheat political death, Lewis."

"Tell me about it."

Reeds did. More importantly, he intimated Lewis with the financial implications. A million and a half dollars. Lewis went along, promising to shell out a million if it came to such eventuality.

"But we wait for Jack."

"Agreed. We wait for Jack."

22

Ikeh had been drinking alone at Temple Bar, his usual joint in Santa Monica.

All around him, Temple Bar hummed delectably. But Ikeh was not in the mood for flirting today. He was sad. And nervous. He had worked his way into a lion's den. A buyer was what he needed for the DVD-R from the U.S. Embassy in Lagos; a buyer was what he got.

Ikeh's asking price had been U.S$2million, hoping for about a million or thereabout. Dan had screamed and complained and Ikeh had settled for a million and a half.

Somehow, Dan had delayed paying the agreed fee and Ikeh had gotten another offer.

Still at a million and a half price offer, the total package was better than Dan's. Ikeh was going to be paid in uncut diamonds. Meaning, the diamonds were stolen and untraceable. It was a whole lot better than cash.

Ikeh was down with it. What he was not down with was the buyer. Pablo.

Pablo was the chief of all crooks in Los Angeles. He was wealthy and dangerous. What a person like that wanted with such DVD-R puzzled Ikeh.

Nevertheless, the fact was that Pablo wanted the

DVD-R and the price was right. A deal was struck. Not that Ikeh could have turned him down. Whatever Pablo wanted Pablo got.

A few days later however, a third offer came. The price offered this time was a whole lot better. Too late. If you struck a deal with Pablo and fucked him up thereafter, you would never live to regret it.

Suddenly now, things had taken on a new look.

The exchange would have been simple really – he handed over the DVD-R and Pablo gave him the uncut diamonds.

This could have been done in a pub or a park. Even on a side road. A few minutes for either side to confirm the authenticity of the merchandise and the deal was done. However, things had changed by the buyer turning out to be Pablo.

Ikeh knew that if he got Pablo's diamonds, he would need to leave the USA. Permanently. Never to return. He did not mind that. It was about time really, LZL or no LZL.

The big question to ponder seriously was what Pablo could do thereafter. Would he want to retrieve back the diamonds? A big yes! Would he want to get rid of him? Another big yes. What if Ikeh skipped the USA and holed up for a while in his village in Nigeria? Would he escape Pablo's clutches? A huge no!

Pablo would take less than a week to locate him! How? Emeka. Even Dúró. They were his two fellow Nigerians. They were his friends with blighted youth driven out of Africa by the sorry socio-economic decay into which Africa had turned. They were in the USA to make a clean start.

Both had been with him for about ten months, living in his house in West Los Angeles. By now,

Ikeh was sure; Pablo knew everything about them all. Why would Pablo choose to pay him in what Ikeh was best at smuggling – gemstones – if Pablo did not know these details about him?

Granted that Dúró knew next to nothing about him. But Emeka did. Pablo would use them both. Ikeh had walked headlong into a rattler's hole. Backing out had to be methodical. Backing down was out!

What Ikeh needed was a foolproof plan to deal with Pablo and still stay alive to spend his one and a half million dollars. Therefore, he needed time; time to formulate alternate plans. He had already started stalling Pablo for time. These days, his mind was in overdrive. He slept poorly and drank more. A simple exchange had turned terribly complex.

One thing had to happen; he had to find a way to get Dúró and Emeka to vacate the U.S. after he sold the DVD-R to Pablo. That possibility could only come to reality if Emeka and Dúró could be so financially successful they would be willing to leave the U.S. for good after the exchange. The corollary was simple; Ikeh had to share his million and a half dollars worth of diamonds.

His first move then was to start hanging out more with Dúró and Emeka. He needed to study them and assess their demeanor as it related to his livelihoods.

He knew Emeka well enough to know that Emeka might not present much of a problem. But Dúró could. He was the sort who had his head in the clouds most of the time.

Ikeh sighed as he kept drinking at Temple Bar. Even as the yuletide loomed in the horizon, Ikeh knew that his life was becoming quite complex.

23

Over in a hotel suite in Washington, Kim and Neil were not having fun!

They were in fact far from happy. The heated discussions between the two were frantic. Both were scared men! Desperate also! So much was at risk!

Finally, after months of dogged surveillances on all DRAINPIPE targets, things were happening. Nothing had surfaced from the surveillances in Europe, Asia, and Africa, but the U.S. axis was a course of concern now. And so suddenly.

Ikeh was the subject.

The DVD-R with him was the development.

Missing via Johnson, it had now crawled back to life with all the damning implications. Simply put, DRAINPIPE was for sale.

Worse still; by the time the news got to Kim and Neil, a buyer had turned up and a deal had been struck.

"Isn't there a way we can change his mind?" prodded Kim.

"There are! But I don't think we should pursue them! It may precipitate a blowout! We have to adopt other tactics to get at the DVD-R. He is scared of that crook, Pablo. I offered him up to two and a half million dollars but he would not bulge."

"We can take out Pablo."

"We can't! You attempt taking out Pablo, there will be a bloodbath for sure. LAPD will sniff around and some smart ass may connect Pablo to Ikeh. Once Ikeh comes into the picture, we cannot keep the FBI out ... since Ikeh is an immigrant. FBI will connect Ikeh to Johnson and to LAZULINE. Both will lead to DRAINPIPE. We will be sitting ducks, Kim. It will be a media circus. Abu Ghraib will be child's play."

Kim shivered at the mention of Abu Ghraib.

"This is a nightmare!"

"We need to be careful, Kim."

"What beats me is why a crook like Pablo wants to buy a set of files like those on DRAINPIPE and so desperately. I don't get it!" Kim stated angrily. "A million and a half of his money? Don't make sense!"

"No, it doesn't! Something is not right here!"

"What do you suggest?"

"For starters, we have to get at the disc. We have to get it off the market! The safest option is to contract the deal out."

"Who do you have in mind?"

"Terry Valentine."

"All right."

"If there is any bloodbath or fall out, he's got no connection that can be traced directly to us. Even if Pablo is buying to resell or working for someone, everything can still be nipped at the stage of the exchange."

"Perfect," Kim said, snapping his fingers. "Yes, contract it out. Use Terry! Pay him whatever he asks but get that damned disc to me! Whatever is peddled in Washington thereafter will remain just hearsay once the DVD-R is safely in our hands."

"Yes. I will get Terry Valentine to handle this. He will deliver."

"Good. But this is spinning out of control. First, a mere security officer screwed up Roland in Lagos! Then it is a police informant in California! Now we have to contend with a crook like Pablo and a psychopathic killer that no one uses except people as crazy and as trapped as us!"

"Things are desperate as they stand, Kim."

"You can say that again. Then recall that your goddamn boy Roland! I want him out of that damn country. I want him off DRAINPIPE! Terence can take over the Head of Operations!"

"Yes Kim."

24

"Okay! Out with it, Alfred!"

Alfred Reeds started as if stung.

"What?"

"You've been staring at that page for five minutes."

"Oh ..."

Reeds and his wife had attended the Christmas party hosted by George and Laura Bush at the White House. They had however lingered on until midmorning before leaving the White House.

"You've not been yourself since we left the party!"

"Aaah," sighed Reeds closing the book he was pretending to read.

"What's going on, Alfred?"

"I'm just all wound up!"

"2008?"

"Yes."

"Kim again?"

"Yes."

"Don't you think I should know about this thing? In a year or two if things work out, I should be your First Lady ..."

"If I don't get buried by Kim ..."

"No, you won't!" shrieked Jennifer. "We work so

hard to get here, Alfred. I need to know whatever is going on!"

"It's top secret, dear."

"Still, I have the right to know if it's affecting you … us this badly …"

"I agree with you, Jennifer … but …"

"I promise to protect your secrets, Alfred. I will never do anything to jeopardize your ambitions … political or not."

"Yes. I know that."

"So what is this all about?"

For a few moments, Reeds was silent, weighing what to tell and what not to. Finally, he began.

"One of President Bush's focuses the very first year he came into office was to begin tackling our energy issue head on – addiction to crude oil and undue dependence on foreign crude. In 2001, the President set up a think-tank comprising members from core Republican loyalists, the National Security Agency, the CIA, State Department, Department of Energy, Military Intelligence, White House Aides, and Energy Specialists from some of the big oil companies around here. It was a bold and courageous policy move. The think tank's mandate revolved around three points: to map out the country's energy needs of the next two decades and how to secure it; reduce our reliance on the Middle East for oil; and wean the country off its addiction to crude oil. Laudable! Kim chaired the team. Six months later, the team produced 1,478 pages of recommendations. Bush called the project 'FLIGHT'. He was still to give his nods to begin the implementation of FLIGHT when Osama Bin laden hit us."

"My God!"

"Bush simply called Kim and gave his nod to swing FLIGHT into operation. I walked into the second stage of FLIGHT's implementation when I accepted to serve under him last year."

"My God! What was the first phase?"

"Should be obvious! Afghanistan! As part of FLIGHT's short term strategy, Afghanistan was the starting point!"

"Makes sense!"

"The underlying principle is simple really. At a stupendous daily need of 20million barrels and a strategic stockpile that cannot last more than forty-five days in the event of an oil meltdown, we needed to, as matter of urgency, locate and secure more stable sources of oil ..."

"A sort of get in; settle in; secure the sources solidly; and begin tapping ..."

"Yes; in summary! But I would not put it so harshly!"

"Come on, Alfred! Quit the sentiment! It's only patriotic! I probably would have done same as a president!"

"Well, for the First Phase, Kim needed Afghanistan. He needed it to be able to tap into the vast oil reserve around the Caspian Sea Basin. In there lying around is about fifteen billion barrels. Afghanistan was strategically vital to peace in the region but the Taliban in Kabul presented a huge obstacle."

"So the Taliban had to go?"

"Yes. Really, Kim was right. Those people were nothing but monsters preying upon their people under the name of Islam. They killed and maimed the citizens while the economy spiraled into the abyss and the country descended into total ruin.

Meanwhile, the country strides oil, natural gas, one of the best grades of emerald the world had ever seen ..."

"And countless other precious stones, arts and the rest!" said Jennifer with dejection in her voice. "The women in that country ..."

"Oh come on, Jennifer! This is not about women rights and Islam! This is about a project I know nothing about blowing up ... taking my career down with it!"

"Now you are really wound up!"

"Shouldn't I?"

"Calm down, Alfred!"

"Aaah! Anyway, Afghanistan worked well. So Kim moved into the Second Phase! Iraq! It was well underway when I took oath of office last year.'

"Of course! Makes sense! Organized chaos!"

"What?! What was that?!"

"What was what?"

"The thing about chaos!"

"What about it?"

"How ... how did you learn about that?!" Jennifer.

"What's the big deal?!"

"I need to know, Jennifer!"

"Why are you alarmed?!" asked Jennifer. Then as a wave of insight hit her, she said, "my God! Alfred! That was Kim's exact words?!"

"Yes, Jennifer. An entire section of the report was devoted to the principles of *Organized Chaos*. Post-Saddam Iraq will be very sectarian; so, Kim was set."

"It makes good common sense!"

"Well; you had me worried for a moment."

"It was just my personal choice of words. It's

what makes sense to me. With over two hundred billion barrels of the best grade of crude lying around while Saddam terrorized his people, Kim could not have wished for a better field from which to tap oil ... under the cover of chaos!"

"Something like that! Yes! With that country and its oil solidly in our hands, we would be in control of a whopping four out of the only five oil fields in the world today capable each of over a million barrels a day production. See? We got the Saudis and their Ghawar, Burgan in Kuwait and Canterell in Mexico. Kim's aim is to conquer and develop Iraq's Kirkuk if all works out. See? Makes sense! Besides, if we don't get a good hold on the Middle East, China eventually will. Even Russia! Don't forget ... the fifth mega-oil field, Da Qing, is China's. See? If China wraps her hands around the Gulf, it can be very bad news for us ... not only politically but economically. China's recent disdain for us and our views and influences is a confirmation ... all stemming from the burgeoning economy and the half a trillion dollars budget deficit it had helped us finance."

"So it is true?!"

"What?"

"The Weapon of Mass Destruction thing? Kim dreamt it up for Bush to wrap his hands on Iraq's oil!"

"Coming from the wife of a serving National Security Advisor in the Administration pursuing the Iraq war ... that was a wrong thing to say! Crude too! Cruel in fact! Knew I shouldn't have told you these things!"

"But everyone in town is saying the same thing, Alfred! Even Larry King! So what's new? Have it on

Oprah?"

"Oh stop it, Jennifer! What's new is the wife of the country's National Security Advisor and one of the proponents of Saddam's deposition joining the fray! What is new is my wife using the phrase *'wrap his hands on Iraq's oil'*. That's what is new!"

"The fact that I said I would protect your secret did not mean I should not have my opinion, Alfred! I happen to have something called a brain within this thick head of mine! Wouldn't you agree?"

"That's not in dispute. Just keep this opinion within the bony confines of the thick head you talked about! That's important to me as well as us!"

"Alfred! You did not just say that!"

"Let's not make a scene. You started this; not me!"

"Still!"

"Oh come on, Jennifer! You just love it, don't you?! Sitting up propped in quilt and Stephen-Sackuring me while I sweat it out!"

"Alfred!"

"Sorry I said that! I retrieve it!"

"Good. So it is true?"

"What?" snapped Reeds.

"What else? What people say about the Weapon of Mass Destruction?"

"You don't give up, do you?"

"Confession time, remember!"

"Oh come on!"

"True or not!"

"It wasn't true!"

Jennifer was shocked. She had expected a big YES; that the WMD was dreamt up so Bush could go into Iraq seemingly legitimately. She gasped, "What do you mean?"

"Military Intelligence did actually believe that Saddam was mass-producing chemical and biological weapons ..."

"Where was the backing?!"

"Intelligence reports for the Iraq invasion were based on projections, not real-time facts, Jennifer! They never found any real-time factories manufacturing Nerve Gas or Anthrax or something! They never had any photos in the first instance. And unlike what the country now believes, the Bush Administration did not lie to Americans about the war."

"What?! Hans Blix said ..."

"Forget what Hans Blix said. Yes, Hans never found Weapons of Mass Destruction; but he also never found incontrovertible evidence that there was definitely none."

"That's some whacked-out reasoning!"

"That was Bush-Kim's game; it beautifully checkmated Hans. That exactly was why a lie was no longer needed at that stage in implementing FLIGHT. Even if a lie was deemed appropriate to sell the war to Americans, the Bush Administration never had enough time to prepare any."

"What's that mean?!

"No President in his right senses was going to call a press conference and tell Americans about FLIGHT."

"That would be political suicide, yes."

"Still, Bush needed the backing of the Congress as well as the American public to get into Afghanistan and Iraq. And the reasons had to be tenable enough to warrant the invasion."

"Yes."

"Bin Laden and the 9/11 incident was enough

reasons for Americans to allow Bush in Afghanistan. Bin Laden helped Bush start FLIGHT ... inadvertently. So Bush hadn't lied; he just never told the whole truth; he never mentioned the other reason – the Caspian Sea Basin deposits. So FLIGHT's phase one went well. But Iraq was a different ballgame. There had to be a reason to go in; but there was not a single one as solid as any one of those with Afghanistan. So Kim and his buddies devised a set of reasons. Emphasis was shifted away from Bin Laden himself."

"Of course, he could not have been in two places at same time."

"Yes! Emphasis was shifted to Bin Laden's al-Qaeda connections. Kim linked al-Qaeda with Saddam. And Americans believed him. Done deal! But then the United Nations came in with Hans Blix and things changed."

"How?!"

"Bush's FLIGHT team knew that it was one thing for Bush to have *no tenable reasons to want to move into Iraq* but another for him to have *tenable reasons not to move in*. And Kim knew beyond any shadow of doubts that, given enough time, the Hans Blix inspection group was going to eventually give Bush and the UN enough tenable reasons not to invade Iraq. That would have decapitated FLIGHT in its track and cornered Bush. That was unacceptable. So the Hans Blix group had to be rushed out, his inspections concluded, and FLIGHT's second phase started. See?!"

"Yes."

"No time for any lies; but enough to stop short of letting the truth come up."

"But the thing about pepping up Hans Blix

report on the Weapon of Mass ..."

"Come on, Jennifer! Sit down and think about it for a moment. You think the combined team of Kim and his intellectuals are dumb enough to make the mistakes everyone on the street talked of the Bush Administration?!"

"But the ..."

"The country's fourteen-trillion-dollar economy did not get to this level of sophistication on the platform of naivety; it took hard work and intelligence on the part of the political leadership ... not mediocrity ..."

"Well ... the whole thing may start to melt down! If that happens, we'll all be paupers!"

"Maybe! But the thing is; such economic meltdown is not going to be as a result of mediocrity but capitalistic greed taken to the extreme by the very bright minds which created our prosperity. That is the point to realize here."

"Still ..."

"The thing is; why would these politicians in the corridors of power suddenly turn up as dumb overnight as for them to make these petty mistakes people sit around street corners and yak about! Most times, things are not what they seem, Jennifer."

"Obviously so, Alfred."

"The fact is that the Bush Administration had taken it upon itself – and at great personal costs, I must add – to protect the country's energy needs at this stage of economic vulnerability."

"So after all ... after all, General Powell did believe in the invasion."

"No, he didn't ... for the simple reason that he was not part of Kim's team. He was not privy to

FLIGHT. He only knew what the ordinary man on the street knew; the same things you could read from any ragtag tabloid – Saddam's evil, Bin Laden, Terrorism, blah, blah, blah. He had no choice, Jennifer. The moment FLIGHT was formulated, fall guys were needed. Powell happened to be one ..."

"Powell was special! Impeccable!"

"No doubt! It was exactly for that reason he was used to sell the war to the U.N. Security Council. He simply was in a wrong position ... but at the right time!"

"Poor General! They promptly gave his job to Rice!"

"Yeah, the next victim!"

"Poor girl!"

"Rice may not have enough record to march Powell's but she is as impeccable. They tell you only what they want you to know! I am the National Security Advisor ... and what the hell do I know? In principle, FLIGHT was laudable but, by its nature, I cannot identify with it. Not now!"

"That much is obvious! I heard they've signed something about a trans-Afghanistan pipelines project, haven't they?"

"Yes. That's what Bush needs to get at the Caspian Sea Basin deposit. We've got Georgia and Azerbaijan as close allies. So, in that front, we are sitting pretty. Really, FLIGHT had been as successful as it was intended. Eventually, FLIGHT is going to be able to tap Iraq's oil in much the same way we have Kuwait's."

"Then?"

"It moves to the Gulf of Guinea."

"Will be cheaper to source oil in there these days ..."

"Yes. There is Sao Tome and Principe. And there is Nigeria's Niger Delta. Both are chucked full of oil and gas. Between us, Britain and France, we've got a good grip on these areas. FLIGHT will simply consolidate our holdings in there and preempt any inroad by Putin's behemoth Gazprom. In this goal, I solidly agree with Bush. Can you try imagining for a minute what Putin can do if he gets hold of Nigeria's gas fields?! Unthinkable! He will have achieved his dream of forming a Gas Cartel bossed by Russia in much same way Saudi Arabia bosses OPEC. Can you imagine that happening ... at these times ... giving his antecedent oil-and-gas politics in Europe?!"

"Makes sense."

"Then, there are pockets of deposits out there that FLIGHT also looked into. It made prescriptions for Angola and Libya. Down in Angola, CHEVRON and a few others had set roots, established a beachhead, and secured a twelve billion barrel reserve locked in there."

"Libya?! Angola?!"

"Yes."

"No wonder our political relationship with the Libyans had been picking up of recent. We forget the Lockerbie thing and we get down to business with the black gold."

"How else do you access Gaddafi without soft-pedaling on Lockerbie and the tough talk?

"Political expediency!" flung Jennifer.

"Damn Right!"

"Don't swear at me, Alfred!"

"Look! Your reasoning; the way you talk! You are not exactly prepared for the role of a First Lady!"

"What's that mean?" growled Jennifer, turning to face Alfred Reeds on the huge bed as if prepared for fisticuffs.

"You are not exactly a spring chicken in this town ..."

"Meaning?"

"You ought to know by now that in politics, truth and apparent truth are not the same. I expect you to have better reasoning on issues than I'm picking up tonight. International politics is a whole lot more complex than morals, Jennifer!"

"Are you insulting me?"

"No! Just stating the obvious. You cannot say ... you cannot express these opinions out loud outside of this room! Good governance involves one form of political chicanery or the other."

"Didn't I just say that? Whose side are you anyway? Yours or Bush's?"

"Look, I am not against George's policy thrust in the Gulf or elsewhere in as far as our energy need is concern. No one in his right senses is going to stand by while a fourteen-trillion-dollar economy implodes because some dictator out in Africa or the Middle-East don't know which end is up! But I cannot stand by and be taken down by what I know nothing about. Period!"

"Clear enough! Can I ask you some questions?"

"Go ahead!"

"Let's look as the best scenario. Suppose we clinch the Oval Office, will you abort FLIGHT?"

"No! Americans need FLIGHT. I cannot abort it. Still, no President in his right mind will ever accept its existence."

"I see."

"But I cannot be identified with it now ... not

before I get into the Oval Office."

"Then the worst case scenario. Suppose the Democrats whip us!"

"The strong candidates in there are Hillary and Obama. My source says FLIGHT had been leaked to Hillary. Her stance is same with mine. We don't think Obama knows. If he did, he had not been letting on. But whichever way, if he clinches the White House, he will become aware of FLIGHT ..."

"Will he abort it?!"

"Never! Of that, I am dead certain! Phase Two is near conclusion anyway. All the incoming president has to do in Iraq is maintain some form of military presence. A huge military base tucked away out of sight is near completion. The base can be rapidly reinforced should there be the need. The cue is already there in Kuwait. The huge administrative staffing needed will be accommodated in an embassy setting, which is near completion. It's the sort we have in Kuwait and Nigeria. Oh no ... if Obama clinches the deal, he wont have much of a headache concluding FLIGHT's Phase Two. And Phase Three automatically spins off Phase Two. It is the self-propagating, final phase."

"All right. Clear enough. The thing now, Alfred is getting a proof of the existence of FLIGHT ready in case the bubble blows! Proof! If they did not see it fit to tell you as the country's NSA, it would be your words against theirs if the bubble blew! Just like the talks about town!"

"I've got the proof, Jennifer. You think I am stupid! I've laid my hands on a copy of FLIGHT ..."

"And the Presidential Approval Memo? There is always a PAM that ticks off the implementation of such top-secret projects!"

"Yes! I have that copy too!"

"Good! Is Lewis in on this?"

"What's that mean?"

"He's your buddy ... well, more like your political siamese twin. Nothing happens to you without him knowing and vise versa. Did he ... was he involved in FLIGHT?"

"No. But I told him! I had to. I may need his millions to pull this thing through, otherwise they'll bury me!"

"What thing? What thing are you pulling through?!"

"Jack is working on it!"

"Want to talk about it?"

"Not now! Let it take shape first!"

"You could do with my advice!"

"Not with this! Too dangerous."

"Are you sure you don't want to discuss this with me?"

"Not yet, Jennifer. Not yet."

It would have been a rude shock for Jennifer if she knew the fine details.

25

A few streets away, Kim and Neil were having their troubles as well.

They were the last set to leave the Christmas Party at the White House.

Behind locked doors at the CIA Washington headquarters, Kim said, "How is Terry Valentine coming?"

"I'm billed to see him soon. Contacts had been made and rendezvous set."

"Anything new about that thug Pablo? Is he working for anyone?"

"Not to the best of my knowledge. I've dug around; nothing! Not a whisper! Nevertheless, I'm keeping all options open. And like I said, so far we get the DVD-R off the market and eliminate all previous contacts, it does not matter whether or not Pablo works for anyone."

"Are you certain of this, Neil?"

"Certain!"

"It better be so, Neil!"

"Why? Anything on your mind?"

"Yes! Frankly, I believe something fishy is going on. I do not particularly like the way Reeds looked at me back at the party today. Like he knew what I didn't know ..."

"Reeds! Alfred Reeds?"

"Yes. Very cocky! I've been thinking since this thing with DRAINPIPE began. I mean ... why is Reeds not leaving the bloody cabinet yet? So sure of himself. I would have thought he needed all the time he could muster for his campaigns. So why hadn't he resigned to flag off his campaign? Why, Neil? What's he got that makes him so self-confident?"

"Well ..."

"Maybe he wants to bury me first!" Kim said before Neil could articulate a conjecture.

Neil laughed it off, saw the deadpan look on Kim's face, and wiped the expression off immediately.

"Jesus, Kim! You are dead serious about this?"

"Damn right! Ever thought of the possibility that Reeds may be after this same DVD? Hasn't it even crossed your mind?"

"Jesus Christ, Kim!" said an alarmed Neil.

"Uh huh! Try to imagine the damage he can unleash. What about the lift his public image can get from the scandals that would result from the disclosures of DRAINPIPE."

"What ... what would ...?"

"Just think about it for a moment. Using us as a ladder into the Oval Office! He will cut through with a beautiful picture. Good old ambitious Reeds heading for the White House at his pace ..."

"But Kim ..."

"Then he got into trouble for accepting to help his country under Bush. He then became enmeshed unfortunately by Bush's perceived political blunders. Now he is championing the annihilation of a monster called *Iraq Occupation* born by Bush ...

and DRAINPIPE born by Bush's boys."

"Yes," said Neil lamely.

"You can imagine the effect!"

"Yes."

"All these carefully set forth before the goddamn blue blood, dumb politicians populating the fucking Capitol Hill! That is against the backdrop of Reeds' oratory. Do not forget, Neil; the sonofabitch has a PhD in Law from Harvard and has spent half his life up in the Hill! They are in his pockets!"

"Yes! Right! Put this way, Kim," Neil said starting to perspire at both armpits, "Reeds would be washed clean."

"That exactly is what I have been trying to tell you!"

Neil licked his lips nervously. Kim had a way of unsettling anyone if he set his mind to it. He was utterly paranoid.

"And FLIGHT," continued Kim. "What if he knows about it?"

"Jesus! How? He was kept out! Strictly!"

"Still. He is chummy with that lily-livered Lewis these days. I wished I could have their offices bugged or something!"

"But Lewis is also not privy to FLIGHT," cried Neil in desperation.

"Awh come on, Neil! What remains secret around Washington forever? We all have ways of surviving. You think they know? Seriously?"

"No reason to think they do!" cried Neil. He was almost soaked in his sweat. "If Reeds did know," continued Neil, sounding really desperate, "wouldn't he have resigned … or at least told George about the possibility? And if he told George, George would tell you! That's what I think!"

"Aaah! Don't know, Neil! Really, I don't know!"

"I don't think he does!" emphasized Neil mopping a sweaty face.

"Good. So keep an eye on things every inch of the way, Neil. I want that goddamn DVD. Then you can go ahead and wipe off everyone ever connected with it ... every goddamn one!"

"Yes, Kim."

"Don't let that no-good Reeds come a mile of that DVD, Neil; I'm counting on you!"

"Yes."

"If he comes between us and the disc, we will have no choice but to take him out too!"

Neil could not believe what he had just heard.

"Take who out?!"

"You heard me! Or he will take us out! That includes you, don't forget!" said Kim stabbing the air in Neil's direction vigorously with a stiff finger.

"Jesus Christ! He is the NSA, for God sake! We can't get away with it!"

"The big question, Neil is: will he get away with taking us down?! Not much different from taking us out! All he needs is a copy of FLIGHT; the PAM from the Oval Office that got it into implementation; and of course the DVD from Nigeria ... and we are fucking dead! Both of us!"

"Kim! We do not have evidence supporting this ... at least for now! It's all your conjecture! Kim ... Kim, you are letting your imagination run too wild! You gotta calm down!"

"Oh! I am calm, Neil! Please prove me wrong!" said Kim with a leer. "Just remember those possibilities. I don't want any more surprises! We've got a business to run!"

"Let's concentrate on retrieving the disc for now!

Shall we?"

"Agreed. So what do you think about Terry?"

"Terry will pull this through but it will cost us a bundle."

"Of course! Usual fee!"

"Maybe more!"

"Why?"

"Terry will know we are in a fix, especially now."

"How?"

"He will read the situation in Iraq right! He may even know about FLIGHT. Terry has connections in the Intelligence community! That is one of the ways he can keep alive in his sort of profession – with information. That's what makes him special, thorough, never failing. Terry will know that we are cornered, desperate."

"What's your point, Neil?"

"Like I said, he will probably hike his fee."

"Pay him whatever he wants! Just get me that damn disc, Neil and wipe off anyone ... anyone at all connected with it! Tell that sonofabitch just exactly that!"

THE WIDE ROAD

BY

ÒGÚN YĘMÍ

PART   II

A VOICE FOR AFRICA.

A HEADACHE FOR IKEH.

104 - 135

26

Christmas had come and gone.

Even the New Year was becoming old. Unlike Washington, L.A never had a break for the yuletide season.

It was for this reason Fúnmiláyò had quickly returned to the city from her short holiday in Nigeria in the first week of January to throw the doors of ADÙN open.

As usual, clients trooped in. The atmosphere hummed tantalizingly, alive with West Africans and gastronomically adventurous non-West Africans of all races and castes trying to sample West Africa's rich delicacies.

ADÙN found a space between Grande Casino Plaza and Vermont Restaurant & Bar on Vermont Avenue right there at the other side of Barnsdall Park.

Emeka had walked all the way from his workplace on West Sunset Boulevard, around Kaiser Foundation Hospital, across Barnsdall Park just to get Dúró from his workplace on North Edgemont to ADÙN.

Hell of a guy! Always full of brimming optimism.

ADÙN served Nigeria cuisines under the able

management of Fúnmiláyò, an ebony beauty revered not only for her culinary talents but also her cheerfulness. Today, her hair was done in wrap-around braids which thinned upwards to end in Shùkú.

Presently, Dúró and Emeka were struggling to get a table.

"Come, my dear," said Fúnmiláyò appearing from thin air and exposing those snow-white teeth that set off her complexion with an alluring shine. "You are lucky today. There is a table for two just to the corner."

"*Nbo*? (Where?)," said Dúró in Yorùbá language.

"Just after Big Òjó," she said pointing at the hulk called Big Òjó where he sat hunched over his plate of Àmàlà and Gbègìrì, completely oblivious of his surrounding.

Dúró winced involuntarily. Fúnmiláyò noticed and said reassuringly, "Don't worry; he wont make a scene today. I gave him an extra plate of his favorite ... free. He's always griping about saving money."

Of course. Dúró had heard an earful from the Los Angeles Yorùbá crowd about the story of Big Òjó. Mired in penury for decades in Ekiti State before escaping its vice grip to the comfort of the United States a decade and a half ago; Big Òjó was consigned to a perpetual struggle against poverty even when there no longer was one in his life to fight.

Story had it that he was worth nearly a million dollars but would never part with a dime except it was decidedly lifesaving. While he stuffed his bank, Big Òjó went around L.A with mass transport. He did not think any of the automobiles was worth the retail prizes. Big Òjó was always cantankerous and forever irritable. The news was; poverty had taken Big Òjó's mind. He was poverty-scared.

Emeka was already rushing over to the empty table allotted them by Fúnmiláyò before other diners could beat him to it.

Dúró looked Big Òjó over thoroughly and whispered to Fúnmiláyò, "*Kí lo fi n se onje nbi?* (How do you get these delicacies to be this tasteful)? At this rate, Big Òjó is going to eat his fingers with his Àmàlà."

"*Ọlá yin ni, Dúró,*" said Fúnmiláyò with evident pride, "*Pèlú ọlá Ọlórun!* (It is by the grace of God, Dúró and those of our clients). Now hurry along. Yẹmí will come to take the orders."

"*Ẹ se;* (Thanks)," said Dúró joining Emeka who had somehow found Yẹmí and was already placing his order.

Dúró carefully tapped Big Òjó on his back and said, "*Ẹ kàá sán, Ègbón;* (Good afternoon, sir)."

Big Òjó looked up, grinned knowingly, and said, "*Aaah, Duro! Báwo?* (How are you, Duro?)."

"*Mo wà, Ègbón;* (Fine, sir)," said Dúró in carefully selected words.

"*Báwo n' sé?* (How are you doing at work?)."

"*Fine, Ègbón;* (I am just fine, sir)."

They exchanged light pleasantries in Yorùbá until it was Dúró's turn to order his meal.

Dúró went for Pounded Yam and Ègúsí. Emeka preferred Fùfú and Edikaekong. Each ordered a liter of fresh Palm Wine to wash down the heavy meals.

The atmosphere hummed with hushed conversations on a background of Orlando Owoh's soft philosophical music.

———

Halfway into their meals, Big Òjó was done, gave a loud belch, said goodbye, and lumbered off. Dúró heaved a sigh of relieve. No scene today.

Big Òjó stood at no less than six feet four, lugging around two-forty pounds. Which made his scenes scary.

Emeka said, "You did not even bother to ask me about my trip to South Carolina. Aren't you happy to see your buddy back ... in whole?!"

Emeka went visiting his friend who lived in Florence, South Carolina over the weekend and only returned on Monday evening. Dúró had deliberately kept off a discussion of Emeka's trip; he knew where it would lead. Dúró was not comfortable with the subject. Now, Emeka could not keep mum anymore on whatever it was he came off South Carolina with. Cautiously, Dúró said, "Of course, I am. How was your trip?!"

"Soul refreshing."

Here it comes, thought Dúró, who busied himself with his Pounded Yam.

"I said soul refreshing," repeated Emeka.

"Yeah! I heard you."

"Is that all?"

"What else? Well, except, how were Chukwudi and his family?"

"Great. They are doing well."

"Good."

"You should visit one of these days."

"Sure."

"Maybe then you'll see Chika's point in his *Capitalist Nigger*."

"There we go again. Always stirring the hornet's net! Don't start this, Emeka. Not now! Can we have a peaceful lunch, please?"

"It's the truth, Dúró. Really. I know you've read the book twice but one more time may do the trick."

"I've got all I need from that book. I'm done with it."

"Didn't you tell me never to scoff at anything?"

"Yeah, yeah, yeah!" said Dúró around a mouthful of Pounded Yam and Ègúsí. "Get the point; I am not scoffing at the book. I don't dispute Chika's observations. But I don't see the sense in writing about what is so obvious; especially when he had to keep repeating himself so often. The minute we got in here we could see the wide Black-White disparity. You could readily discern these things after a few weeks of walking the streets. Do I need someone to tell me about it in a book? No, Mr.! No."

"Still, it was a bold venture to put pen on paper and say it out loud … at least to promote public discourse on these rather sticky issues."

"Partly true! But his approach was wrong; completely wrong. It was so parochial it not only belittled the Black Race but also the magnitude of what happened to the Race. His approach and style reduced his entire effort to hardly anything more than a loathsome ploy to sell a book."

"He was dead right on a lot of issues, Dúró!"

"So you keep saying! And I agree. But a person running a sole diagnostic lens on an entire race can hardly expect to get anything right. This is a race with a combined population of a billion; scattered in at least three continents. All the viewpoints articulated in that book are his! Not only that, he kept stating over and over again that he did not care if his views were acceptable or not. Does that make sense? I would say that was as dictatorial as any of

the African leaders he berated with his tirades. No
one man can provide answers to the ills besieging a
race. Chika was not asking questions of the Black
Race. No! He was not piquing the curiosity of
members of the Race. No! He simply made a
barrage of observations and went on to say what he
believed was the root cause – *STUPIDITY*. You
don't promote public engagement by such rabid
attack. Four-fifth of the book was devoted to just
that, proving a case for Black Race's *STUPIDITY*. I
would have expected a more in-depth and objective
analysis of the causal factors. You expect a
newspaper man to be more objective. Interviews;
interviews and more interviews ... just to get at a
few of the root causes."

"Dúró. I was just in South Carolina. You were
not there. Chukwudi took me through the infamous
Corridor of Shame. It is appalling. Some slums in
there are worse than what we see in Mushin or
Oshòdì."

"No doubt. Everyone knows these ills. They are
everywhere you see us! What I am saying, Emeka is
that all of those observations could have easily gone
into a chapter in the book. Then Chika could have
devoted more energy to initiating and sustaining
public discourse on the possible root causes of those
ills by throwing up barrages of questions that would
have piqued anyone's interest – from the homeless
to the wealthy; from the stark illiterates to the
Professors. You cannot achieve that by devoting
four-fifth of a book to proving that the Black Race is
inherently *stupid*. It ought to be the Black public
digging for answers through various forums,
conferences, and symposia. His questions, if asked
just the right way, would have been the topic on the

lips of every Black Man out on the streets. His questions would have been bedtime discussions in each home. Chika would have started the greatest discussion of all times. Chika was aptly placed at the time he wrote *Capitalist Nigger* to give the world a robust, holistic exposé on the entire Black Race … in continental Africa and the Diaspora … but he blew it squarely. In actual fact, being a newspaper man with a newspaper that was affordable, the *Capitalist Nigger* was unnecessary. Chika could have serialized his observations in his newspaper through a column. But *Capitalist Nigger* had to be for what it had to be – make money for the Author by cloaking the Black Race in the worst attire he could come up with. Actually, that was clever. He set out by writing for the Caucasian population – by denigrating the Black Race. Made a beautiful business sense … now that I think of it."

"I don't agree."

"But he said and believed that Blacks generally do not leisurely read. In a racist society, all you need write is something like the *Capitalist Nigger* and you have a potential bestseller."

"No, no! I don't agree."

"It's your right to dissent. And I may be wrong. But that is the impression I came away with after reading the book twice. If the book had come from a Caucasian, it would have commanded less attention amidst Caucasians; it would have been an old and dying rhetoric. But coming from a well traveled, knowledgeable Black Man whose experience spans continental Africans and Blacks in Diaspora, it was news … a new kind of … news."

"Look, Dúró …"

"I'll tell you my reasons with two obvious

examples ..."

"Yeah! All right!"

"It would have been pardonable if anyone but an Igbo man had gushed so enthusiastically about the adroitness of Chika's East Indians in business and commerce. For a reason. The doctrine he raved about in his book is the economic watchword of the Igbo tribe from which Chika comes. What's more; other tribes in Nigeria admire – even envy – the Igbos for this. It is why the Igbos command such economic clouts in Nigeria. Every little baby in every household in Nigeria – possibly the entire West Africa – knows! Why would Chika choose to be silent about this? You tell me!"

"Aaah! Don't be melodramatic ..."

"Melodramatic?! One of Chika's grouse was that the Black Man typically lays around, whining about Slave Trade, Colonialism, Segregation, and Discrimination."

"Damn right."

"Well; he is wrong! Again, let's look at Chika's own backyard as a case study – the Igbos."

"What about the Igbos? What do you have against us?" barked Emeka, feigning anger as he chewed on Edikaekong.

"Oh quit this flippancy; you're getting on my nerves! The fact is, the Igbos did not sit around and whine about the future of the Igbo tribe in the contraption called Nigeria! Did they?"

"Oh! Nigeria! The Britons!" spat Emeka.

"Personally, I do not blame the Britons for slapping us all together under the threat of the gun. They did what suited their social, political, and economic interests at the time. It was what they had always done; destroying nearly half the number of communities the world over. But the thing here is; the Igbos did not sit around whining when their misfortunes began soon after our so called independence. They stood up promptly when they needed to and said, enough. They were leaving Nigeria. They were taking their fate in their own hands. It gave rise to the Biafra war in which millions lost their precious lives. Unfortunately, the nation was stillborn ..."

Now, Emeka brightened.

"It would have been unarguably the richest nation in Africa."

"No doubt Emeka," said Dúró. "Many of us from other tribes in Nigeria really hurt that Biafra failed. It was such a promising nation."

"Oh yeah," said Emeka, pushing a ball of Fùfú and Edikaekong down with Palm Wine. "We had our eyes on the oil and gas in the Niger Delta as well as the use of the coast. We were planning on being a Singapore, a Taiwan, a Malaysia and a Norway rolled into one."

"Aaah! There you go! Most Nigerians knew this thinking, Emeka! How can Chika not acknowledge this? A so called official of Biafra. All he could say of these efforts of his people is that they are part of a STUPID race? It was a ploy to create a bestseller."

"You are getting emotional about this. Don't take yourself so serious."

"Okay, my second example!"

"Which is?"

"The time scales involved here!"

"What about the time scales?!"

"Chika was also silent on that ... as important as it is to the issues he touched."

"He never claimed to know everything."

"Well, when you arrogate the power to assess the progress of an entire race to yourself, you have to get your facts right. Slave Trade began in the sixteenth century. It was followed by Colonization in continental Africa. Colonization is a whole lot more than physical occupation of Africa, you know."

"Agreed."

"The colonizers packed and left Africa past the middle of the twentieth century."

"Yes."

"Amidst Africans traded as mere commodities around the world, Slave Labour metamorphosed to Social Segregation."

"Correct."

"Good! When did the Social Segregation and the Lynching come to a grudging end in the US?"

"The sixties. About four decades ago."

"Aaah! Just as the colonizers were packing up and leaving Africa. That was only an eye-blink ago. Just around the corner."

"Agreed."

"For African-Americans for example, this did not mean four decades of easy ride. It only meant four decades of no-state-supported-lynching and no-state-supported-social-segregation."

"Something like that."

"Britain colonized mainland America. Yes?"

"Yes."

"America gained its independence somewhere in 1776..."

"Correct again."

"Ah hah! See? That was nearly a hundred years of nationhood, unity, and progress before America's Civil War, when a portion of America decided it was breaking off. That was America's equivalent of Nigeria's Biafra."

"What's the point here?"

"A hundred years, Emeka; not a hundred months or a hundred days; a hundred ... years! Nigeria began breaking apart only seven years after its independence. Seven! Doesn't that tell you how the various components just love to really stay together and build a nation?!"

"Yeah. Sort of."

"How does that bode for development in a state that was supposed to be a Federal Republic ... not a Confederate? As at the time Chika wrote his book, Nigeria was less than three decades post-civil-war; and less than four decades into self-rule and nationhood."

"Yeah."

"In contrast, the US was over one hundred and thirty years post-civil-war and over two hundred years into self-rule and nationhood. Two hundred! The Republic of South Africa was a paltry half decade into post-Apartheid self-rule and self-determination. Now, where is the sense in using the same yardstick to measure the progress of these races and nations and from that standpoint label the Black Race *stupid*?"

"Look ..."

"It took mammoth Russia nearly three decades to begin to rise from the abyss into which its economy was engineered in this same contest for supremacy ... this same resolute inclination to dominate. That was Russia; one of their own; a former ally that, in fact, aided America's independence. Russia even had the vantage of a world power. Americans never took Russians as

Slaves to work in plantations in the US for a couple of centuries! Did they? Americans did not go over to Russia to occupy their lands for four hundred years and wipe their identities clean! Did they? And still, it took Russia three decades to begin to rise again. Three decades! And someone out there thinks that we must have been a Race of *stupid* people for being unable to send probes to outer space four decades post-independent; four decades after five hundred years of broken life. Where is the sense in that?"

"Is he bothering you with one of his tiresome lectures?" boomed a voice.

Dúró looked up from his table and saw Big Òjó standing over the table, glaring at him. Dúró's heart skipped beats. He swallowed the food in his mouth and pushed it down with a nervous gulp of Palm Wine.

Big Òjó bent a little, scooped a bunch of keys from the table he had just vacated, and pocketed it. Obviously, he had forgotten it while he left earlier. Now, he was back to retrieve it. To Dúró, the timing was wrong. Now, Big Òjó was in a foul mood. His thick lips were in an angry pout.

Turning his gaze on Emeka, he demanded brusquely, "I said, is he bothering you?"

"Eh!" stammered Emeka. "No, sir! He is not. We are just ... just chatting."

"He keeps bothering people about Africa and this Black thing," rumbled Big Òjó.

"*Ègbón*! (Bro!)," said a nervous Dúró trying to placate the fifty years old hulk. "We are just ..."

"Been there all my life and could not feed myself despite a PhD in Physics," Big Òjó rumbled ominously, rudely interrupting Dúró. "Now I'm out here and doing well. And the likes of you won't let us rest with dreamy bullshit!"

"I …"

"Africa this, Africa that. Black here, Black there, Diaspora this, Diaspora that. Africa renaissance. Patriotism, Colonization, Apartheid, Blah, blah, blah!" Then pointing a fat threatening finger at the general direction of Dúró's nose, he warned, "You keep going around opening your mouth anyhow and they'll stop giving us jobs. So stop bothering people, and get a life!"

Then the big man lumbered off.

"Phew!" said Emeka. "What was that about?"

"Must be pissed at something."

"He is always pissed at something."

"Can't blame him. You heard him. PhD in Physics. And could not feed himself back in Nigeria."

"Fact!"

"But he needs to realize the roots of his problems. Maybe then, he will stop being mad at everything."

"Go tell him to his face!" challenged Emeka.

"Awh come on! He'll tear me limb-to-limb!"

"Discussions on race are always sensitive, so latch onto something else."

"Very well. Consider this. Chika arrived in the US in the late sixties and wrote the *Capitalist Nigger* in the late nineties. Thirty years or so in the US. That was a period of stupendous economic boom in the US. The US leapt in huge bounds in all fronts. Prosperity was everywhere. With economic prosperity came a loud voice. They told everyone what to do. They shoved their values down the throat of those who resisted. Free market, globalization, and democracy were the new songs

from the US ... and everyone must chorus. Chika
landed and lived for thirty years in the midst of this.
In same period, the Black Race in that country was
just emerging from a tumultuous struggle to prove
... just to prove that they are Human Beings ... with
all the accompanying psychosocial attributes you
would expect of a savaged Race. Chika saw these
sharply contrasting worlds. He simply blew his top.
The result was the raving in the Capitalist Nigger.
He thinks we are inferior and that we are stupid."

"Prove him wrong," challenged Emeka chewing
on goat meat.

"No! No, we are not; never was."

"Proof! I need proof!"

"Courtesy of science, we now know that the
modern man evolved and dispersed from Africa."

"Yes. Thanks to whom?! Yorùbá scientists?! No!
Caucasian scientists ... ranging from geneticists,
paleontologists to archeologists," said Emeka
cryptically, cutting a ball of Fùfú and scooping
Edikaekong with it.

"Aaah! What's the point?!"

"Make your point and I will mine! It's a debate!"

"All right! Let's assume Wells and the other guys
were right. The modern man dispersed from
Africa."

"Uh-huh!"

"Over the intervening millennia, each group
evolved to suit his surrounding and meet his needs
for survival in an untamable planet."

"Makes sense."

"Then we met again. And trouble began. The
thing is; why couldn't we have peacefully
coexisted?"

"They did not come for social visits, young man!

They wanted Slaves, Dúró. They needed machine-like guys to work farms over in the New World. They saw this is abundance in us. They saw a business opportunity and took it. I would say that was a very smart choice in survival strategy."

"You could be right. You could also be wrong. Now, I ask! Could it have been that the people who came to us are not so much capable of peaceful coexistence with others but their own? An operating concept of 'I before others'; 'I, myself, and me'. Is there that possibility, no matter how remote? It may provide some answers to a lot of questions. I'm not talking in terms of who is good or who is bad here! It's not about inferiority or superiority of cultures and peoples. We are trying here to know who we individually are in the light of emerging facts from science ... their science ... and how we affect each other."

"Fair enough."

"If you care, a pattern seems to shine through in the way the Caucasians colonized distant lands all the way from back then to now. Hitler epitomized the extreme form of this racial intolerance. International political plays of today are replete with this also. These guys simply go out there to search for whatever their race needs to thrive. And when they do find these, they promptly begin arrogating it all to themselves at the expense of others ... even when everyone could have peacefully shared ... even when the host cultures had no needs for these resources in their peculiar living styles."

"What do you suggest? Sit on the gold, the diamonds, the copper, the platinum, and the oil and let them go to waste?"

"Who says the best way to relate to diamonds and gold is to hang them around your person? And what makes you think crude oil would ever have featured in the kind of life our culture would have evolved had we not been colonized!"

"You believe your utopian dreams? It is impracticable."

"You may well be right! But capitalism, which lies at the other end of the spectrum, removes every shred of nurturance in humans. It reduces us to nothing more than puny, shallow-minded entities whose essence could not rise above things as petty as power and money. Anyway, my point is; was it possible that evolution over the intervening millennia had changed us all so radically that we are no more same? Or, at least, don't share same virtues anymore? Cats are cats; but a Lion is never going to be a Tiger. Still, they may have shared a common ancestral origin. Snakes are snakes but a Python is never going to be a Mamba. Still, they may also have shared a common ancestral origin. Is that why we have such profoundly negative effects on each other?"

"You've got to be kidding."

"A few decades ago, I would have said the same. Not so anymore. Science ... their science ... is making astounding discovery now, blasting off old beliefs, and implanting new ways of thinking. They say we share a third of our genome with plants."

"So we read these days. Kind of scary!"

"Well, do you see one-third similarity between you and the edikaekong in your plate, Emeka? After all, it's a variety of plant."

"Are you insane?"

"See your revulsion?! The fact remains that

plants and us are brothers."

"Are you crazy?! Edikaekong and I? Brothers?!"

"Your revulsion demonstrates how off the mark humanity had been thus far with his ways. There are new facts supporting this. *If we peel away the sentiments and get down to pure Chemistry, Humans are different from plants only in complexity. Both are agglomerates of atoms'. The simplest life form is an agglomerate of atoms as is the most complex life form. By implication therefore, if arranged on a Table of Atomic Complexity, all matters on earth will occupy a single straight line; for they are essentially same but with increasing complexity.* Still, we are all witness to the profoundly deleterious effects we have on the flora around us. A few hundred years down the line, we would have wiped off everything from the face of the planet with our warped ways; this so called civilization. Now my point is; could similar trends have applied to why the varying races can hardly coexist without recourse to disdain and decimation? All you could see in the other race is exploitation and annihilation?!"

"You're kidding, right?"

"Ask Wells."

"I sure will. Book him to see me in my office."

"I'm dead serious! I hate flippancy at times like these!"

"Relax or you'll have a heart attack or something!"

"Aaah! Anyway, the point is made!"

"What point?!"

"That we may never have been same species ..."

"Debatable! Highly debatable! Anyway, they are trying to decode the human genome. Few decades down the line, we'll know if you are lying to me ...

as usual."

"Don't hold your breath."

"I'm not."

"But suppose I was right. We were never same. Then they came to us, kidnapped us in millions, decimating us. In itself, that was not much of a problem. It was hardly anything more than the same scenario you get in wars. Except that here ... they began hundreds of years of destroying everything that was us ..."

"Of course. It's quite simple! How could you colonize a people and still allowed it its identity and the use of its mind? Would that make sense? You would lose control of the colonized if you allowed that. How could you make Slaves out of a people if you failed to destroy its identity? Everything that made it a people had to go – the languages; the traditions; the cultures; the beliefs; self-image; governance systems; healthcare; innate concepts of procreations; concepts of life; what living meant; what ageing meant; and what death meant. You would have to destroy the people's ways of commerce, communal relations ... everything?! Everything had to go! By whatever means! Only then would the people's subjugation and Colonization be complete."

"Good! Did anyone out there ever consider the effects of this on our psyche ... from generation to generation? Facelessness! No identity! Stranded in a dark tunnel! Marooned in a featureless sea, wondering about aimlessly trying to search for landmarks! Did anyone ever consider the implications of these on the day-to-day thriving of the Black People?! In this featureless sea, the only landmarks available as reference points are those of the people who colonized us. From this point forward, we began evolving in a different path – the path of those who colonized us."

"Look, Dúró. I ..."

"Hold on a moment!"

"Okay ... I'm listening!"

"The manner in which we evolved in continental Africa differs from that of Africans abducted away. Continental Africans were slaves in their lands, yes ... but they still had shreds of their roots; a little solid ground to stand on. Africans abducted away had nothing! Nothing! Absolutely clean! Blank! Again, Slave Trade and Colonization were not so much of a problem to the peoples of Southern Africa. In their cases down there, Apartheid was. Now, you tell me, what's Apartheid got to do with those ferreted away across the Atlantic to work the plantations? The effects of these cataclysmic elements differ on us. The journeys of these varying groups of Blacks and their generations ... generations ... therefore differ – socially, politically, psychologically, and intellectually."

"Agreed."

"What we have all been doing ever since shunted down the evolutionary road of the colonizers is learning the strange ways of the colonizers."

"What else is there to learn when we have been wiped clean ... as you put it?!"

"Well, in the process, we came off with a bad mixture of our innate self and the cultures shoved down our throat. By the time we had independence in continental Africa, we were saddled with a self-destructive socio-cultural trend called primogenitocracy."

"Primogeniture and democracy lumped in one?"

"Yep! Back then, some of them actually warned the colonial governing class about this horrible eventuality. One was Sir Gordon Guggisberg! He was a British colonial officer back then. Rare breed! Honest! He saw the goodness of primogeniture in the people of the then Gold Coast (now Ghana) and felt that the people needed to develop along this beautiful path that was unique to them; not the British – western – way."

"Oh yeah?"

"Oh yeah! Guggisberg told them pointedly what could happen to the thriving people of Gold Coast – and the Black People as a whole – if it were forced into western ways. His point was that, nature had molded the Black Race to relate to the world around it and make good livings off it in completely different ways from those of Caucasians. What Guggisberg did not realize when making those analyses was that he was not in the Gold Coast to better the lots of the Gold Coast people but to pillage the land for the development of Britain and Britons. On a psyche-brutality scale of one to ten, primogenitocracy is ten ..."

"In theory maybe!"

"Oh come on! It's so obvious! The brutalities; the murders; and the social segregations of Colonization, Slave Trade, and Apartheid were gross. Yes! But the real problem does not lie in the abuses! You could see the abuses a million miles away. That made them easier to fight. Not so the effects on the mind! You don't see those! Still, they are the factors that will unequivocally shape the victims entire life and those of the generations that follow. This is where primogenitocracy features."

"How?"

"It derived its hideousness from its insidious and pernicious nature! You never knew it was there."

"I don't think it is there! I simply think you are dreaming up excuses for a failed race. And that does not make me wrong!"

"Yes! Indeed! You just hit the nail straight on the head. Like schizophrenics, primogenitocrats are the last to realize the illness they harbor. You are probably one. God helps any community you govern."

"Don't insult me."

"I'm not. But where is the logic when a person remains Heads of Governments of his country for decades?! Decades! Where is the sanity?! This is with the facts that his people wastes away on the streets while he carts away the common wealth to communities thousands of miles away! Post-independent African democratic office holders treat their offices as those of Chiefs, Kings, Emirs, Baálès, or Sultans. They never want to let go until they grow old and senile! They handle their offices and countries like personal holdings."

"Isn't that exactly Chika's point!"

"But the good ones who had risen above primogenitocracy are out there also by the thousands!"

"Out of the combined Black population of about a billion?"

"Only a handful leads in any community; others simply follow. Only a handful led the Caucasians to the promise land of the sort of wealth and good living which meet their aspirations. And as you have been witnessing, only a handful is leading them downhill as well."

"Granted but ..."

"All we need are leaders who can locate the right landmarks ... the landmarks we lost when we began evolving down the wrong road."

"What? You want to go back to that sort of life?! Black magic and all?! Come on!"

"A famous scientist once said that *any sufficiently advance science is not distinguishable from magic.*"

"Get to the point."

"Far-reaching statement! He was right on the point. He could have as well been talking about the Black Race and what was once their ways. I am a Yorùbá and I can tell you lots from my culture labeled Black Magic but which seem to me like very advance forms of living. And if every Black Man out there can look far back and deep down into the little left of the core practices of his Tribe, possibilities are very high that he will make the same discoveries I did. All you need do is look beyond the stereotypes! Dig below the surface!"

"Come on! Let's take those Yorùbá practices for example ... those evil things! Who do you think is going to go back to them?"

"Emeka, the interesting thing these days is that, more and more, as the days go by, branches of science like Quantum Physics, Theoretical Physics, Neuroscience, Parapsychology tend to vindicate that these Yorùbá practices you call evil may in actual fact have been advance science ... but of another state of existence."

"Hah!"

"Really!

"Oh, come on!"

"Let's take one very important living style involved in today's hot issue of global warming for example – Spatial Travel. Our so-called modern methods of spatial travel."

"Don't tell me you prefer your ridiculous Egbé! This ... this thing of yours which works like Star Trek's Transponder ... but without the gadgets. Kind of comical. How shall I explain it? Yeah, you ... you tend to will yourself ..." chuckled Emeka derogatorily, chomping on goat meat. "You just will yourself into neighborhoods you want to visit irrespective of how far apart on earth points of departure and destination are. The disappear-here-appear-there type of ... faster-than-light flight ... jump ... journey or something. Like you see in kiddies' cartoon. You just bounce around the planet like a faster-than-light ping-pong ball! A concept of *'everywhere is literally a step away from everywhere else!'* Huh?! Come on! If you want a reasonable discussion with me, you'll be talking about machines as impressive as the F-22 Raptor, moving cities like the Aircraft Carriers, marvels like the Chunnel, the Millau Bridge, the Burj Al Arab Hotel, the Hubble telescope ... not Black Magic! Not ridiculous stuffs you yak about of your tribe's Egbé, Àpèpa, òkigbé, ayẹta, Kánàkò, Sàgbàdèwe, Àféèrí, Mágùn, and the hell rest of those evil practices."

"The principles of Egbé and those that guide the F-22 Raptor for example are probably same since they employ attributes of the planet ... the universe. Only, it is so advance in the instance of Egbé that Physics – as it stands today, without radical overhaul of its basic fundamental assumptions – cannot prove or stumble onto it. Just listen to a mind like Michio Kaku discuss spatial travel as it affects time. And you'll realize that he needs be told that there exists a race that had practiced something like Egbé and Kánàkò in spatial travel. That may be a break he had been hunting for. The question now is, is there any similarity between the theorized Wormholes and Egbé? Was the practice of Egbé and Kánàkò bending space to achieve such fit? What were these travel methods of the Yorùbá people? What were they?"

"What?! Kaku will have a fit listening to you. You wanna kill the old man, go talk to him about … about those stuffs. Ludicrous! Everyone being beamed about town like Captain Spock? Where then are we going to get the heavenly pleasure of driving such God-sent machines as the Italia Ferrari, the German Porsche, the Japanese Lexus, or the British Jaguar? Besides, nothing good comes cheap, Dúró. The earth is just a piece of rock floating around in space and trying its best not to collide with other rocks. As for it dying, they are trying revival strategies. You heard Al Gore the other day …"

"Of course. Nice guy. Commendable effort. But I'm still waiting to hear how the West will unhook two billion determined Asians – Indians and Chinese – from the mindset that equates civilization as well as good living with driving luxury, gas-guzzlers. And this happening at a time when for once in almost a century these Asians are on the prosperity road. Now, they have so much self-determination that they don't give a rat ass about what the West thinks or does not think. And while at it you may as well let me know what Europe is doing to stop sending the wrecks they sell at exorbitant prices to eight hundred million Africans as second hand cars?"

"Oh come on! Stop the griping! Back in Lagos, you had one of those cars you are now calling wrecks, man! As for the dying planet, they'll fix it.

Trust them! But if they cannot reverse the planet's death and the thing dies after all, they are going to evacuate us to another planet somewhere, you can bet your ass! They are already searching! There are billions of them out there! So get real, bro! I need a peaceful lunch!"

"Peaceful lunch my foot! Let's stick with your US Navy. Take their *smart bomb* you so much like to gush about for example."

"The BGM-109 Tomahawk Cruise Missile?! Hell of a weapon," enthused Emeka proudly, munching edikaekong. "Deftly plucked Saddam straight out of that hole in which he was hiding! Picked him up the way you picked fleas off that scrawny dog of yours back in Lagos and delivered him on his kneels smack dab in Bush's living room in the White House! Did you know that?!"

"Your headache! But I tell you this, compared to my tribe's Àpèpa; the Tomahawk is crude, undeservedly more expensive, and totally earth-unfriendly. That is not mentioning the Tomahawk's collateral damages, which the Generals on the battlefield have to explain all the time. From a remote corner in my village, Àpèpa can choose to kill just one person in any of the world's overcrowded cities! Just one soul … amidst millions! And what do we use in achieving this? Features as basic to the planet as gravity! Hundred percent earth-friendly!"

"Yeah! With unparallel targeting! Right?" said Emeka bursting into a guffaw.

In more serene environments, Emeka would have stood out and be stared down. But in the delectable cacophony, which characterized ADÙN, re-creating typical Ìsàlè-Èkó sceneries; Emeka's guffaw was one amidst scores of others.

"Unparallel targeting!" repeated Emeka as he calmed, his eyes streaming tears.

"Yes! Really! I'm not kidding! The Tomahawk Cruise Missile cannot do that! Too crude for that sophisticated level of targeting. It even overshoots targets as big as buildings. Other than these differences, both achieve same goal – remote killing!"

"You want me to take you serious?"

"You don't have to! These are verifiable facts! I've heard you talk with gusto about the stealth of the F-22 Raptor ..."

"One hell of a machine, Dúró!" beamed Emeka. "It's one hell of an impressive machine! Creeps on targets soundlessly! Ingenious!"

"Aaah! There! Still ... a mere whisper of Àféèrí in the remotest privacy of my room brings derision ... even from my fellow Yorùbás! Wonder why!"

"Àféèrí! The invisible man thing? Go stand in Times Square and tell the people about Àféèrí and see where it gets you! The shrink house!"

"For sure! I know that! That's why we are having this discussion! As we speak, scientists are sweating day and night finding ways to control hurricanes! Even how to seed clouds with chemicals in order to induct rain!"

"And they'll get there. They always!"

"Very well. But I don't see anyone labeling them magicians ..."

"Magicians?! Magicians?! Are you insane?! These are scientists practicing cutting edge science!"

"Aaah! Still, what do they think of Sàngó, an ancestral Yorùbá who commanded mind-boggling mastery of lightning? This is the same lightning which scientists now said is pure electricity; each discharge in excess of a billion volts. This is the same lightning which scientists of today know next to nothing about. Hundreds of years back, Sàngó and his people had control of stuffs like that?! And a Black man out there still thinks this person's descendants are *stupid, dependent people*?!"

"Truth stings yunno! Quit bickering!"

"And what do they think of Ògún, a Yorùbá ancestor with sheer mastery of metals? What do they think of our Rainmakers?! They say they are evil. Black Magic!"

"And they are right! These are incomparable things, Dúró! Take it from me. You don't compare these primitive arts with cutting edge science."

"Aaah, there! No wonder our politicians steal our money to buy bulletproof vests and cars ..."

"How the hell do you move around without one? Would you have preferred your ... what was it you called it? Aaah ... yeah, ayẹta. Or òkigbé or something. Huh? Traditional Yorùbá bulletproof, you said. You want that? I'll try getting you one from those old goats in your village ... if they've not all died off. It's a dime-a-dozen."

"So sad," said Dúró, shaking his head and swallowing balls of Pounded Yam and Ègúsí. "Black Magic they call these! Huh?"

"And I agree."

"We as a Race will have reclaimed our lost identity the moment the vibrant youths start seeing through the vein of this mental colonization and stop judging itself with the yardstick of another race. Only then will we be able to stop this perpetual prey on Africa and Africans. Only then will we be able to rise above primogenitocracy and self-destructiveness. Only then will we – ourselves – be able to stop the sort of predatory political plays we see in Sudan and the DRC."

"Don't gripe around. The United Nations is on these cases! We all know what's going on in Darfur for example. It's all about oil. The Chinese are playing the usual card of *divide-and-rule*. They know and are using the age-long animosities between the Arab Sudanese governing class and Black African Sudanese. The Chinese simply set them against each other just so they could get at the oil which is abundant in Sudan. But don't fret; we have the US and the UK around to checkmate the Chinese. And eventually, they'll get the Chinese puppet, Al-Bashir ..."

"Don't be naïve. China knows that the UK and the US play the same game. It knows that the UK and the US are even more brutal in this sort of game. What's the war in Iraq all about? The interest of Iraqis or democracy? Nonsense! It's all about the political survivals of the US and the UK! Period! Africa and the Middle East are simply pawns in the political chess. No one will stop this but ourselves. And we cannot do that without having a strong voice. We cannot have a strong voice except we discover ourselves and become proud of what we discover."

"Wonder what is left after the pillaging!"

"Of course, we have to start recovering the stuffs they stole from us. Egypt had started hers from Britain. Why shouldn't we start recovering ours? Here and there, Hitler's Holocaust victims are already getting compensations. Why shouldn't the Black Race be entitled to reparations for centuries of decimation? M.K.O. Abíólá died trying; his death should not be in vain."

"I agree with you on that," said Emeka. "I mean, take a look at those delicate royal necks in Europe. They are beautifully adorned by stones stolen from our land."

"The Cullinan Diamond is a typical example. It belongs in Africa. It was a supposed gift by the then Apartheid South Africa government to some Royal guy in England. Now, it had been cut up to adorn the royal crown, we heard. The news making the round is that the stones are now worth almost U.S. $650million! Combined!"

"Yeah! And they say we need their aids!"

"And we believe!" said Dúró, swallowing Pounded Yam with a heap of Ègúsí. "To me that is the problem. What they tell us is not the problem; the problem lies in what we believe as grounded truth. That's one of the reasons we need a reconnect with that point at which we were shunted down the wrong evolutionary road. If we pick up from that point, we can regain our identity and self-confidence and save Africans from guaranteed extinction."

"Wonder who is going to pioneer that?" said Emeka.

"I can give you a dozen impeccable names from each country in Africa, Emeka ... ranging from our Ambassador Ségun Olúsọlá, Professor Wọlé Shoyinka, to The Second Jesus ..."

"Who? Second what?"

"The Second Jesus."

Emeka's eyes glazed over. Dúró's jaw dropped.

"You don't know who The Second Jesus is?"

"Look ..."protested Emeka. "I ... I ..."

"My God! But you can write an encyclopedia on

Bonaparte Napoleon, William Shakespeare, Abraham Lincoln, and hundreds more!"

"Look man ..."

"Shameful! Shameful indeed!"

"What's your problem?!" cried Emeka at Dúró's condescension. "Do I have to know everything?!"

"No! No, you don't have to! But it is not only unforgivable but pathetic that there exists a learned Black African of the twenty-first century who does not know that Nelson Mandela is The Second Jesus," said Dúró, hurriedly washing his hands.

"Oh come on! Don't be melodramatic! It slipped my mind; what with all these struggle to make dollars and all."

Dúró wiped his hands with the napkin and stood up.

"Are you done eating?! Don't tell me you're going to waste half a plate of Pounded Yam!"

"Lost my appetite."

"What?! Because I could not remember who The Second Jesus was?! Oh come on, man!"

Emeka's telephone rang. He extracted the phone from its waist pocket, looked at the screen, and whistled in alarm before answering it. "Yes sir?"

"Lunch time was over a quarter-hour ago! I'll take it off your pay, young man, make no mistake about it!" screamed his boss at the other end of the line.

"I'll be there at once, sir," said Emeka in subdued voice. Turning to Dúró and shooting him with killer looks, he said, "See what you have done?"

"You started it; I was minding my Pounded Yam when you began this stuff about Chukwudi in Florence. It's your fault, not mine."

"Aaah; what's the point. Talk, talk, talk! Yak,

yak, yak! Shall we go please?"

Both Emeka and Dúró hurried out of the restaurant.

Two tables away, Ikeh sighed and stared glumly into his third gourd of Palm Wine. He had listened unnoticed to every word said at Dúró's table over a period of an hour. He knew it was an understatement to say Dúró was a big problem. The guy was a ticking bomb! What sort of person had Emeka brought into his life?

How Ikeh wished that Big Òjó would simply squash Dúró during one of his paranoid rages.

Ikeh knew virtually nothing about Dúró except through Emeka.

Ikeh and Emeka had grown up together in Orlu. They knew each other well enough to know that they thought alike and could agree on most issues. But this Dúró fellow? Trouble! A euphoric dreamer with his head in the goddamn cloud! What would Ikeh do?

How was Ikeh going to get a person this grounded in Afro-philia bullshit to deal in diamonds stolen from West Africa in exchange for a blackmailing DVD-R stolen also from West Africa?

Ikeh knew he was in serious trouble. As if his headache from Pablo was not enough, now he had to deal with a ticking time bomb right under his own roof! He needed help. He needed new tactics to deal with this predicament. But first, he needed to be dead drunk! Lifting his Palm Wine to his lips, he gulped half of the gourd-fill. He was suddenly very thirsty.

From the east coast, more trouble was heading Ikeh's way. His assassination was being contracted out to a killer. It was the second time in just a year this was happening. What made it particularly bad for Ikeh was; this was coming from a group separate from the first.

THE WIDE ROAD

BY

ÒGÚN YẸMÍ

PART III

GRANDE FINALE

138 - 313

27

2006 was dead.

Washington was beginning to shake off the post-yuletide hangovers. Neil walked briskly into The Tower Building in downtown Washington.

He headed straight for DC Coast Restaurant. In there would be Terry, he knew. In fact, Terry had ordered and devoured a meal of Oysters and was half way through an excellent bottle of wine when Neil arrived.

Neil took a seat facing Terry in the high-backed booth and said, "Hi, Terry."

Terry was clean-shaven. His head shone. His penetrating eyes had a deadpan look. He was done in a nice tailor-made ash suit, which did his ebony complexion a world of good. Terry sipped his wine as he surveyed Neil; then grinning knowingly, he said, "You look hassled, Neil. Relax. I got this isolated booth so you can feel secure."

"This place does not worry me," said Neil ordering his drink.

"What does?"

"I'm not worried!"

"Who're you kidding, Neil? Must be damn hot for Kim to send you out in this freezing weather."

"Yes, I won't mince words," agreed Neil.

A waiter brought his drink. Neil sipped and color seemed to return to his cheeks.

"Are you okay?"

"Yeah. Just working too much."

"Thinning hair, balding too fast, sallow skin, hollow eyes, a pouching middle. You ought to see a doctor."

"Look Terry! Are you some kind of a doctor now or what?"

"Just concerned, that's all!"

"Thanks," said Neil gulping his drink. "This assignment is delicate, Terry."

"How delicate?"

"Very."

"Figures!"

"What?"

"Your look. You're stressed."

"Didn't I just tell you I'm overworked?"

"Now you dump the problem into my laps."

"Sort of."

"So what do we have?"

"There is a DVD-R of information involved. A Nigerian based here in the United States is the peddler."

"Who's buying?"

"Pablo. Pablo owns half of L.A.'s underworld."

"Yeah, I know him. Mexican-American. Kills cops and has a way of getting away with it."

"That's the sonofabitch!"

"When is the exchange?"

"I don't know."

"Where are they to rendezvous?"

"I don't know."

"Where do you guys suppose the DVD-R is being kept?

"I don't know."

"You don't know much then, do you, Neil?"

"Look, that's where you come in! That's where your professionalism counts, Terry."

"What is the time frame?"

"I have no idea."

"So ... as a matter of fact the exchange could be slated for tomorrow for all you know?"

"You've got the general idea. But I do know this; this guy is taking his time. He got the DVD-R months back but simply went into the cooler. He only began looking for buyers a few weeks back."

"Any idea why?"

"Why what?"

"Why he laid low for this long ... months you said."

"No, I have no idea."

"How come you did not go after him back then?"

"I never knew he had the disc until a few weeks back when he started looking for buyers, Terry."

"Now that you do know, why not send your guys after him?"

"This has to be done incognito; no connection at all to the CIA, Terry. This is of utmost importance."

"To whom?"

"Me."

"And who? Washington power shots, Neil? Talk to me!"

"That's all you need to know, Terry. That's how you and I deal."

"Fair enough. Any other things I need to know?"

"Yes. Everyone who had come or seemed to have come in contact with that disc should be wiped out."

"Fair enough."

"Then we have to verify the authenticity of the contents of the DVD-R when you retrieve it."

"Yes. Naturally."

"When you have it, open it, and send the entire content to me via the usual designated internet site."

"Any passwords?"

"None that we are aware! But if there is any; hack through it the best way you can without loss of information from the DVD-R."

"And then?"

"The two of us will set a rendezvous so you can hand over the disc."

"Sounds good to me."

"Here," Neil said handing a Flash Drive to Terry. "It contains the files on all concerned; the little I have. The initiative is all yours from here on. Payment will be as usual."

"No, Neil! This one will cost the Agency 1.5 million dollars, U.S."

Predictable, Neil said to himself. Usual fee had always been five hundred grand or thereabout. Aloud he said: "Our agreed fee, Terry had always been five hundred grand."

"I know Neil, but not this assignment."

"Why?"

"You know why, Neil. I do not have to lecture you. And don't keep pretending. You make a bad job of it."

"I'm not pretending! I see no difference between this and previous assignments."

"Too bad then! The deal is off," Terry said emotionlessly and stood up to leave the booth. "Find someone else."

If Terry walked, Neil knew that Kim would have

him shot by evening. He said, "Sit down, Terry. Surely, this can be discussed. No reason we cannot come to an understanding."

"The only understanding we are coming to is 1.5 million U.S. dollars," Terry said gazing steadily at Neil as he slowly took his seat. "And please don't waste my time. You of all people should know how important my time is to me!"

"Seven fifty thousand, Terry, tops."

"One and a quarter million, Neil. You guys want the DVD-R fast, all contacts to be wiped out! That is an open-ended contract! Coming at this time, one cannot but notice that I will be saving you a lot of distractions stemming from Americans' uninformed reactions to these things in Iraq ..."

"What's that mean?" Neil growled.

Terry held Neil's gaze and said slowly, enunciating his words with care, "FLIGHT! Ever heard of that? Neil?"

"What are you talking about?"

Terry grinned. It was shilling. His eyes shone like a miniature sun. He sipped his wine and set the glass carefully on the table, perhaps with too much care.

"I know everything, Neil; I know all there is to know about FLIGHT."

Neil said nothing.

"Kim invented FLIGHT to address the country's economic exigencies; fine. It's only patriotic. I therefore don't expect him and his boss, Bush, to simply stand by and allow religious fanatics to derail a project as lofty as that under the pretext of Jihads or something. So Kim invented Abu Ghraib and Guantanamo. Okay! Now this guy crawled out of Africa with fresh sets of problems; you don't need the distractions. Fine. Logical. I agree with you. So you dump the load on me. No problems. But you're gonna pay for my services, Neil! Make no mistake about that!"

"Terry!"

"Seems Bush is discovering that it is almighty more difficult colonizing the Arabs today than his forefathers did Africans a couple of centuries ago. Maybe the Arabs did learn one or two things from the way Africa and Africans were destroyed over their natural blessings."

"Terry!" snapped Neil, "Can we leave the bloody politics to the politicians?!"

"Maybe! The politics is none of my business! Yes! But it's why you are here now, Neil, talking to me. So somehow, it becomes my business! So sit up and pay!"

Neil's baited breath came out of him slowly, an icy chill enveloping him like a shroud. Terry knew about FLIGHT. Who else did? Neil summoned courage, looked Terry straight on, and said: "I do not have the authority to pay more than a million, Terry. That's the truth."

"Fair enough. Half now, half on verification."

"Accepted. I will arrange for payments."

"You know to where."

"Yes."

"Then one other thing."

"Yes, Terry?"

"I hope this is not one of Kim's assignments within an assignment. I don't want any agency boys going anywhere I go, taking a pee anywhere I do."

"Nothing like that, Terry, I assure you."

"Good. Then I don't have to worry about any body-count."

"What's that mean?"

"If I see anyone dogging my tail, I'll put a bullet in him, knowing well I'm not ticking off your boys. Right?"

"Uh … well, yes."

"I don't like the ring of your voice, Neil. Is it a yes?"

"Yes, for God's sake, Terry!"

"Good. You know where to deposit my money."

"Yeah, I think so," Neil said, tossed off the rest of his drink and stood up. He could not get away from Terry fast enough.

"Good luck," Terry said after the departing Neil.

'Sadistic psychopath!' thought Neil, rapidly exiting.

28

The last two weeks of January had been very busy for Terry.

He had a virtual deadline. He did not know where Ikeh was keeping the DVD-R or when Pablo was going to conduct an exchange. But it was immediately obvious that Ikeh was the person dictating the pace of event. Terry's option then was to warm his ways into Ikeh's heart.

In the interim, Terry had found out that Ikeh wanted the DVD-R exchanged in an elaborate set-up at 3567 North Rexford Drive, one of Pablo's properties in Hollywood.

Why there? It did not fit.

An exchange of the type Terry envisaged could as well have taken place at the backroom of any of Pablo's casinos or Pubs or something. Even in a car over a few minutes. But a house like that? Bang in the choicest part of Hollywood?

Something was wrong.

Then payment style? Most unusual!

Pablo was to pay Ikeh in diamonds, uncut, untraceable, and of course smuggled in from one of Pablo's sources in war torn Liberia.

So much for the cry of South Africa about Blood Diamonds; Diamonds Trafficking; and the Kimberly

Process Certification Scheme.

Terry had built on the files handed to him on Ikeh and his roommates. Ikeh presented a fascinating picture.

He was an experienced police informant. Police informants generally had a common weakness. They were always ready to listen to you; perhaps in doing so they picked one or two things to peddle to their police contacts. Terry would use that to his advantage.

Again, Terry being an African-American meant it should not be too difficult getting into Ikeh's camp, taking up an identity that could be cheaply crafted and easily defended on Ikeh's scrutiny.

After a while, Terry decided on dual nationality. Nigerian-American. Profession? A lawyer who had stepped into the jewelry business but taking up diamond smuggling from the West African coast on the side. And wealthy in the process.

Vague but definitive. It would be in line. Gemstone smugglers were always presenting that sort of indeterminate profile.

He shopped around for a name and finally went with Godwin. He found out it was a very common name in the Igbo tribe in Eastern Nigeria where Ikeh belonged. Within days, Terry was complete with all the facts he could lay his hands on from websites on Nigeria tribes. Then he started visiting Ikeh's most frequented outposts.

That was when he realized that there was someone else on the Ikeh case beside him.

_____

By the third day, Terry had the tail on Ikeh laid out.

He was Thompson Orion, a white American in

the hitman business. Very efficient. Low profile. Operated mainly in Europe. Occasionally, he did some jobs in Africa as well.

A few more calls told Terry where Thompson had been in the last couple of months. Quite interesting. Thompson had been all over Nigeria, doing things for the CIA there.

Aaah! Fingers were pointing again to the same people! Neil Simon and Kim Holland.

Thompson was not tailing him, Terry. No, that was obvious. He was on Ikeh.

Conclusion? Neil and Kim had contracted a job to two! Neil had lied! Too bad. Terry was not splitting one million with anyone. Neil was going to get his first body count.

First, Terry was going to use Thompson as the ladder to ascend into Ikeh's heart. His plot was simple really.

29

Ikeh occupied a table for two at a corner in Temple Bar, his usual joint in Santa Monica.

There were no tables for one; otherwise, the romantic spirit that Temple Bar tried to encourage would come to naught.

He had been drinking for a while and was generally mellow. Now he took a long swig from his beer, eyes closed, while savoring once more the delectable taste. As he was settling the glass down, he opened his eyes. There was a stranger sitting in the only chair in front of his table.

"Can I help you?" growled Ikeh, lifting his beer again.

"I think we can help each other," said the stranger.

"Look, man," Ikeh said irritated. "I am in no mood to buy any insurance policy or whatever it is you have to sell."

"I think you will very much want to buy what I need to sell."

"I beg your pardon!"

"I may just have saved your life."

Ikeh's beer hand, which was heading for his lips, came back. Carefully, he set the glass of beer on the table.

"What did you just say?"

"The CIA put a tail on you all the way from Nigeria."

Ikeh took a long drag from his beer. His throat was suddenly as parched as the back of a pig.

"Who are you?" Ikeh managed.

"A friend who cares."

"You have to do better than that!"

Terry did.

He took Ikeh through Thompson's assignments in Nigeria.

"You see," Terry concluded, "It's all about the DVD-R."

"Who are you?"

"First. Do you believe me?"

"Let's say, some of the things you mentioned might be true."

"I'm Godwin Ofor."

"Godwin what? Ofor? A Nigerian? You are an Igbo man? Come on!"

Terry gave Ikeh the background he had cooked just for this.

"I don't believe this! How the hell did you get into this?"

"Same way Pablo did! My boss was also interested in acquiring the DVD-R."

"Who is that?"

"But you should know I would not tell."

Makes sense, thought Ikeh, saying nothing aloud.

"I made some inquiries and found out who was buying from you. I told my boss and he backed off. Pablo is dangerous. No one wants to mess with him."

You can say that again, thought Ikeh; staring intently at the stranger in front of him; and trying to size him up.

"But then I picked up this tail of yours and decided to give you a helping hand."

"Where is he?"

"Resting calmly in a van at the end of this street. You wanna meet him?"

"Is he ... did you kill him?" whispered Ikeh fiercely.

"Nah! Needs you and him to have a chat the way he sang to me."

"Sonofabitch!"

"Shall we go?"

"What's in it for you?" asked Ikeh suspiciously.

"Should be obvious. A slice of Pablo's diamonds from West Africa. A million and a half, I was reliably informed."

Ikeh felt dizzy. The stage was becoming crowded. He had decided to cut Emeka and Dúró in on the deal. Now this Godwin fellow.

"What makes you think I wanna play?"

"I helped you cheat death, Ikeh. Obviously, that's worth something!"

"Let's have a chat with that bastard first."

———

They were walking away from the van. After the chat.

"I met him at Bíódún's funeral back in Lagos some months back," said a shaken Ikeh. "Called himself Mark Foster. And something about being the SPO to the U.S. Ambassador there. So he killed Bíódún?"

"You were next!"

"Well, we'll see about that."

"So? Where do we go from here?"

"I need a day or two to think things through.

You obviously know how to get me."

30

Spago Restaurant in Beverly Hills was in a class of its own.

Conveniently tucked away on North Canon Drive off Wilshire Boulevard, it was where Hollywood stars with class dined.

Terry had chosen the five star restaurant in line with the wealthy image he had been portraying to Ikeh so far. A meeting was booked for today.

Since the first meeting, both had each other's numbers. And regularly conferred.

A few things had happened.

One.

No one had mentioned Thompson again. Terry had gotten rid of him. Ikeh was glad not to discuss him.

Two.

They both had brainstormed and solved the problem created by Ikeh's two roommates.

The two were to be involved in the exchange but believing a completely different plot. It was for a purpose. The plot would convince the two roommates to vacate the country with Ikeh. This way, Ikeh could vanish from the USA and be rest assured that Pablo would never find him. It was the only way Ikeh could feel safe from Pablo after the

152

transaction.

But Ikeh still had one little problem in trying to turn the table against Pablo. It was why he had called on Godwin (Terry) for this meeting.

Ikeh wanted Godwin (Terry) on his side during the exchange. It would give him the confidence he had so far lacked dealing with the very dangerous Pablo and his crop of gun-totting crooks.

In the last few minutes, drinks served, the two have been discussing that interesting point.

Terry was saying, "Did you ask to be paid in diamonds?"

"Hell no, but I like it."

"He probably knew you would! He did his research on you well enough, I guess."

"Maybe! What's the point?"

"He gave you an offer you could not refuse, Ikeh. Diamonds."

"So?"

"He could easily get the diamonds back," said Godwin (Terry), fanning Ikeh's fear to a fiery level. "The chances of Pablo getting them back were far better than if he was paying you cash."

"What are you saying?"

"Maybe he was not giving you the diamonds for keeps."

Exactly Ikeh's predicament.

"I suspected as well. Would you be willing to watch my back for a fee?" offered Ikeh.

"Depends."

"On what?"

"How much are we talking about?"

"Fifty thousand dollars worth of stones."

"Deal."

31

2007 had brought an atmosphere of tension into the minds of Emeka and Dúró.

They had been in the United States for about a year and now had a good grip on what obtained locally.

Right at the onset almost a year back, it was clear that they were only employable as menial workers despite having University Degrees. Dúró had a Bachelor of Art Degree in Philosophy; Emeka had a Bachelor of Science in Electronic Engineering. But in the U.S., they were shocked to realize that over and over again, from one job application to the other, they were not employable on those bases.

The corollary was shocking. How were they going to be the sort of financial successes they had dreamt of for years by engaging in menial chores in the US? Emeka worked as a Garage Attendant in West Sunset Boulevard. Dúró was a mere Front-desk Attendant at a bookstore on North Edgemont.

Yes, they ate well and were quickly able to reverse the markers of adult starvation they had had for years. Yes, they wore good clothes and sent a few dollars home now and again. But then, the sort of success Dúró and Emeka wanted exceeded these puny milestones.

On other fronts, there were more to worry about.

Gasoline was climbing to all-time highs from an agglomerate of factors playing around on the world energy stage. Predictions were no succors. Retail prices were steadily escalating. The credit crunch within the U.S. economy was becoming very worrisome. The mortgage crisis was visible now.

The results were predictable. Small and medium scale businesses in the U.S. were either downsizing or folding up.

Typical of the lower socioeconomic workers of the U.S. economy, Emeka and Dúró's funds were coming in depressing trickles. And there seemed to be no end in sight. Dúró and Emeka began panicking.

Were they going to be around here in the next two decades or so, and still on these chores! Very possible at this rate.

They needed to build houses in their villages. Buy cars for their parents. Set up businesses, which their brothers and sisters would run.

They needed to drive those posh cars, visit those exclusive restaurants, go on cruise holidays, and lazy around on the beaches every once in a while.

That was why they had left the familiar comfort of their home to the strange harshness of a place like the United States. They were not hoping to labor for life, living a subsistent life, and stranded within the welfarist confines of the United States, eventually living on government social hand out.

Again, Ikeh.

How had he been able to live this big – not only in Nigeria but also in the U.S.?

By all standards, Ikeh was a millionaire. Well ... in Naira. But a millionaire all the same. He had

estate properties in Ìkẹjà and his village; all bought
or built cash down.

In Nigeria, he drove a posh Mercedes Benz
bought outright; and that was not the only car. Here
in the U.S., he drove a Dodge sedan and lived all by
himself in a bungalow bang in Los Angeles at the
fringes of almighty Hollywood.

Aaah, something was not right. Now was the
time to find out. A heart-to-heart talk with Ikeh was
overdue.

32

The talk happened on a Sunday evening.

They were all cherry after the characteristic buoyancy which BILL COSBY SHOW gave. Now THE OPRAH WINFREY SHOW was starting.

Dúró felt that if Ikeh was allowed to get into Oprah mood, the chance for detailed discussion today could be lost. Ikeh was addicted to Oprah.

Dúró said, "We could still be at this daily routine for the next generation, Ikeh and we wouldn't be anywhere."

"What?" Ikeh said snapping out of an attention riveted on the TV.

"These chores aren't working for us, Ikeh," Emeka buttressed. "This toiling everyday at work is just not working."

"Oh! Why not? The pay is good. All you guys have to do is learn how to work hard and save, curtailing your expenditures. Learn from Big Òjó. Your chances will come ... eventually."

"Come on, Ikeh," Dúró picked up, "you know it's not going to work out. Big Òjó is an aberration. The truth is; savings are hard to make here in the United States doing the type of chores available to us ..."

Good, thought Ikeh. Now, Dúró was coming down to earth; not stranded in some afro-phillia nonsense. Reality was dawning. Good for Ikeh's mission.

"Look Ikeh, we are friends," picked up Emeka. "We are here at your instance. I mean, what could we have done without that guy you connected us with at the U.S. embassy back in Nigeria for example ..."

"What?" Ikeh asked his heart leaping. He forgot Oprah in an instant. If anything, now his roommates had his attention. "Johnson?"

"Yes," Dúró came in. "His fee was outrageous but he got us our visas and here we are. Now we are eternally grateful to you."

"I'm really glad you guys moved fast," said Ikeh as if the words were burning his tongue. "His enemies from the village killed him." The popular belief in Orlu about Johnson's sudden death was that his enemies got him through the services of the village witches. "It is a pity," continued Ikeh, "It is such a common occurrence. Those wicked village witches! They ate him in his sleep!"

"Yes," grunted Dúró.

"Well ... about this business, Ikeh?" said Emeka almost impatiently.

"Yeah, Emeka. See, you need to make a choice ..."

"Between what and what?"

"A choice between what you have termed chores and that of bracing up to go into business in this country. Bear in mind that leaving the safety of your regular jobs is a big risk in itself. Going into business of any type is even more of a risk. It may or may not work out. You have to keep that at the back of your minds. Sometimes you go into it and get a big break but a lot more times you end up worse than when you had a regular paying job ... you know all the deals."

Both nodded.

"Good. That's settled. Now I need to let you know some facts about my line of business. You may have been wondering ..."

There were nervous exchanges of tensed grins between Dúró and Emeka, each tending to say 'yes, we have been wondering.'

"Well, I tell you this. I do not touch drugs. That applies to deals having anything to do with totting guns."

"So what is it that you touch?" Emeka asked pointedly.

"Gemstones."

"Holy God!" Dúró exclaimed. He realized that it all made perfect sense.

Emeka was so surprised he was speechless for a while.

"Pretty smart, eh?" Ikeh said, laughing boisterously.

"Yes," Emeka said laughing too, "pretty smart, Ikeh."

"I will talk to you somewhere next week. You may have stumbled across a golden opportunity."

"What opportunity?" said Emeka.

"Let's say ... something in the gemstone business. Quite straightforward. Pays good. But not without its risks, guys."

"Nothing good comes cheap, Ikeh," said Emeka. "So ... what exactly is it?"

"We'll talk next week. Take a few days to think these things through. Business or regular works?

The decision is yours. We'll talk next week. Then I'll lay all the cards on the table ... that's if you are going with me on it."

"So be it." Emeka promptly said.

"My mind is made right now." Dúró asserted. Deep down, a warning signal came alive.

"Next week then?"

"Yes," both chorused.

Ikeh's head snapped back in position. In a few seconds, the hypnosis was back via cable TV; Oprah was still playing.

33

This time, Terry had chosen the fabulous Spark Woodfire Grill Restaurant on West Pico Boulevard in West Los Angeles to meet with Ikeh.

Ikeh was to update Godwin (Terry) about his two housemates. Their drinks were served.

At a table nearby sat Enrique Belucshi, Hollywood's current rave. He was the lead actor of the blockbuster movie *Bride of Summer*, just released barely a month earlier.

With Enrique was Elizabeth Adams. Of course. She was the famous host of the L.A.T.V. talk show, LIZZY'S. Not that Elizabeth was Enrique's type. Which she knew only too well. But being Los Angeles' number one talk show host, it made a good business sense for him to warm up to her a little.

Second in rating in the U.S. only to THE OPRAH WINFREY SHOW, LIZZY'S has nearly five million Americans eating from her palm once a fortnight. Whatever she said about *Bride of Summer* would count in the gate takings.

The third person at the table was Bradley Rithe, one of the hottest movie Directors in Hollywood. Ikeh gazed at these superstars, exhilarated at sharing a room with them.

"How's it coming?" Godwin (Terry) enquired.

Ikeh's head snapped around as he peeled his gaze off.

"Good so far," Ikeh answered, tasting his drink. "They are both exactly where I need them to be."

"Good. Can we go over the plot again?"

"Aaah! Yeah," said Ikeh taking another sip of cognac. "It goes like this. You are the big guy from a West Africa diamond smuggling outfit with tentacles in the U.S. Pablo's house in Beverly Hills belongs to one of your members'…"

"A woman, don't forget."

"Yeah a woman. A greedy one. Had been skimming consignments of diamonds from your bosses back in West Africa for years. Now, the big bosses found out. You were sent up to straighten things out with her. You got in her pants, found out she was salting some of the diamonds in a Safe at her home and decided to help yourself."

"Good going."

"Now to pull this through, you need my help to crack the Safe in the house. Then we need two more hands; one to crack the house electronic security and a third to handle the car. After the deal, all players will have to clear out of the U.S. If my two roommates are up to the task, they can fill up the two positions. The pay is good, unbeatable."

"Good. How are their mindsets?"

"Right where I want them! They are hungry for a break. Even Dúró the dreamer."

"Good. How's Pablo's contact coming?"

"I had convinced Clarke about the timing of the exchange so it gives Dúró and Emeka the impression that we are robbing a Safe."

"Did Clarke agree to deactivate the door alarm as soon as we start up the driveway?"

"Yeah. Took me all my wit. Clarke is more paranoid than a lab rat."

"What would you expect of Pablo's men?"

"Anyway, he finally agreed."

"Let's drink to a successful exchange."

They both did.

Ikeh left happy.

Far into the early morning, encased in the privacy of his room in Beverly Wilshire Hotel, Terry was still awake.

This African-American believed by Ikeh to be Godwin Ofor, a Nigerian-American in the gemstones-smuggling business, was busy studying the outlay of Ikeh's bungalow in minute details.

In half an hour, Terry had gone through all of the details except the design of the Korea-type heating system.

From the history available in the archive, Terry found that a Korean had originally owned the house, which he built to his personal specifications.

The heating system was custom-built to reflect the tradition back in Korea. This comprised an intricate network of subterranean tunnels all linked to a central heating unit located in the kitchen.

A separate service tunnel opened to these networks of tunnels with an exit near the wall fence that surrounded the garden at the backyard. Through this same tunnel, heat could be let off occasionally, thus serving as a sort of temperature regulatory system.

Called Ondol, it had been adjudged one of the most efficient floor heating systems that had ever existed.

Eventually the Korean had moved on, selling the

house. In the last ten years however, consequent owners of the house had abandoned the Ondol after it broke down. Ikeh was the last owner and he too had not bothered to reactivate it. Apparently, it was easier maintaining conventional oil heating systems.

One never knew, Terry thought. He was a man who took his assignments seriously. He overlooked no detail at all. Now, he began a careful study of the neglected Ondol.

34

Now time flew.

The pair of Dúró and Emeka were no longer bogged down by the usual dread premonition or the fear of the unexpected. The excitement of an upcoming new life, a new beginning, kept their mood at an all time high.

Two weeks had gone. Ikeh had had several sessions with them just to lay the cards on the table as he had promised.

They both had gone along. Then Ikeh had gone further to explain what parts they were to play in the upcoming business deal.

Now, as the D-Day neared, they began rehearsing their roles to perfection. Occasionally Godwin, the big guy from West Africa, came along in the rehearsals. Adrenaline was pumping. They were set to take on the Beverly Hill woman.

In the midst of this excitement however were flashes of depression.

Presently, Emeka stared a hole on the screen of the big TV in the living room, absorbed in self reflection. It was mid-morning on a Sunday. His aim was to summon enough inner energy for a good day in the city; but this had eluded him so far today. Even with his favorite programs lined up on cable

TV, he could hardly cheer.

"If only we can be as patriotic to ourselves as these western countries," mumbled Emeka sullenly, "I will not be in this mess."

"We cannot!" said Dúró promptly. "There had to be a commonness of purpose first. And there cannot be a commonness of purpose except we are psychologically independent of our mental Colonization, Emeka."

"Look! Look, man!" snapped Emeka. "Don't start this! I really am not in the mood for one of your speeches. I want to try and enjoy my Sunday, Dúró."

"Can you enjoy it? Really! Are you happy about all these?"

"I will try to make the best of it if you don't spoil my day."

"Your sadness has nothing to do with me but your running away from your country at the prime of your life ... as you once put it."

"What a preacher," said Emeka. "As if you are not in same shoes with me. Now, we realize we cannot have the sort of financial breakthrough we had thought when we stepped on that cursed plane from Lagos. Maybe the witches from our villages are at work. Maybe they cursed our journey."

"Come on!"

"Could be! Didn't you tell me to scoff at nothing?"

"Yeah but this is different ..."

"But ... look ... everything points to the machination of the witches ..."

"Calm down, man! Here, we know precisely why we are where we are. We can only be employed as menial workers. That's why!"

"That's what I'm saying! It's the witches! That's why these guys around here don't give a rat ass about our degrees! Those wicked witches cursed our degrees!"

"No! And you've got to calm down, Emeka. This is none of our faults! This has nothing to do with our intelligence or competence; it is a political issue. Don't blame yourself!"

"To make matters worse, this place is starting to fall apart ... just as we got in. Can you believe that?! I think we are jinxed!"

"The economic downturn around here has nothing to do with us for God sake!"

"Why not?!"

"Are you kidding?!"

"No I'm not! You look at the scenario. Why us? Why our time?! This place was ticking just fine until we stepped in! Now you hear of all sorts of *financial bubbles*' ... just as we got in here. Suspicious if you asked me!"

"My God! Listen to yourself! Why would an entire country be made to go down the drain because of you ... us?"

"Why not? Look what happened to Sodom and Gomorrah?!"

"You believe that stuff?!"

"Why shouldn't I?! It's in the Bible."

"Will you calm down, Emeka. We know why we are exactly where we are. And like I said, it is political; we are not cursed."

"Oh well! Wished I knew that answer a few years back."

"Come on! No matter what anyone told us back then, we would still have come. It was not so much as where we were going but where we were running from."

"Yeah!"

"The decay back home had blinded us to the realities out here."

"Yeah."

"You cannot come out here and have it easy! You have to realize that these guys out here had not designed their economies to be bled by immigrants under any guise at all, legal or not. Foreigners settling in the country, working and earning some pay and remitting this back to their home countries are doing just that – bleeding the economy. They know we are here, working, making money, and remitting some home. They know we are bleeding the economy..."

"Aaah! Don't make a mountain of an anthill. It's only negligible. What do we earn around here anyway? Peanuts! They don't mind."

"Negligible? Are you kidding me?"

"No! Despite the constrains, I'll say these guys still look after us really. We do the lowly jobs which their citizens won't. They appreciate the gesture and let us go away with some money ..."

"Look ..."

"Yeah, yeah, yeah! I know they cap what you can remit ... that's only logical. The bottom line is, these guys look after us really. Now, you send nice stuffs to your fiancée, Tóbi. And members of your family. Shoes, clothes, and stuffs that would have been beyond them had you not been out here. "

"Come on! It's beyond that. All you need do is follow World Bank statistics on funds remitted by Africans who had migrated out of Africa into Europe, Asia, Australia and the Americas. Believe me; it is in billions of dollars annually."

"Come on!"

"I'm not kidding. It conveniently doubles the combined sum of all Foreign Direct Investments and Official Development Assistance to Africa."

"For real?"

"Yeah. Check out the statistics when you have the time; just log onto the World Bank website. We are bleeding the economy. And they know! They juggle that with the benefits accrued from using us as cheap labour. Which is actually what we are – cheap labour sources."

"Really?!"

"Yeah! And if at any point they come to the conclusion that what Africans benefit from the deal outweighs what they benefit from us, they will promptly repatriate us home … under some concocted laws. Period. That's Big Òjó's fear. It's why he'll never be able to relax."

"My God! We work out here so hard and those corrupts politicians back home steal our common wealth and bring it back out here! Unbelievable!"

"It's the bitter truth! From Nigeria alone, in the last forty-seven years, starting with indigenous governance at independence in 1960, about £200billion had been stolen by our so called leaders … people who are nothing but psychotics. I mean … how else would you explain the mindset of these guys? You could steal your people's wealth and invest the loot in your country; your community! That may make some sort of odd sense! I may not have problems with that! After all capitalism itself isn't about being honest and nice! But to steal such enormous amounts; run to Europe and America across oceans and seas to hide the money; and then come back to the squalor in Nigeria and watch your people wallow in abject penury? As always?! That needs a certain amount of madness! That required a warped mind of some sort, completely detached from reality!"

"Yes! Depressing! £200billion stolen! Scary!"

"Really. At the rate Britain, for example, gave aids to Africa generally, it would take centuries for it to give as much in aids. Meaning in effect that previous financial aids from Britain to the entire continent of Africa were pointless. All Britain would have done to help Africa – if there was sincerity of purpose – was simply to return the loots from African leaders in its banks to Africa."

"If wishes were horses, Dúró ..."

"Aaah, there you go! The fact was simple really: the West served only the interest of the West, nothing more. It was only patriotic! You go out there and try recovering those monies. That's when you really begin to encounter the diehard patriotism of a Caucasian regarding anything Caucasian. You would be lucky to get a fraction of the loot. And by the time you got it repatriated, it had lost so much value that the exercise was pointless. See?"

"Yeah!"

"There is the answer to your question on patriotism."

There was silence for a while and then Emeka said, "I'm worried!"

"It's only normal, considering our situation."

"That's not what I mean!"

"How?"

"I'm concerned about you."

"About me? In what sense?"

"Your attitude!"

"What attitude?"

"Towards ... towards issues! The way you look at things!"

"What things?"

"Everything! This West, Colonization, and Africa thing! West this, West that! Caucasian this, Caucasian that! We are out here man! We need them. We've got to keep our mouth shut."

"I don't believe this! Like Big Òjó! Those are strictly my political viewpoints! I'm just sharing!"

"It shows in your attitude; your body language. And that breeds trouble!"

"How?"

"Take Godwin for example. He is not exactly like your typical Nigerian. He is a Nigerian only as far as his name goes; he is in all practicality an American ..."

"That much is obvious."

"He cannot even pronounce his name the right way! Nigerian father, American mother! Born in the U.S., bred in the U.S.! Was in Nigeria only once in his lifetime ... once in his lifetime ... to attend the burial of a grandpa he never met. That guy is not a Nigerian in the real sense of it; he's not an African, Dúró!"

"What's your point, Emeka?"

"That guy has no clue about all these stuffs you talk about and he does not care."

"He is lost!"

"And he does not give a rat ass! So leave him be! It's none of your business! He is another Big Òjó ... only he has been more civil in his approach to your hassling ... so far!"

"We need to open his eyes, his mind! Free him!"

"Look! We cannot all be you! If you two get into a clash of personality, the coming operation is doomed!"

"Oh! That? I see what worries you!"

"Thank God you do!"

"Don't worry. I understand Godwin enough."

"Do you?"

"Yes."

"Could you please simply leave him out of this lecture thing all day?"

"Yes, why not? No lecture when he comes in for practices. Satisfied?"

"Yes. Good. Thanks!"

"This is very important to you Emeka, isn't it?"

"Isn't it to you? It's our only ticket out of this cancer of poverty. I don't want to keep dangling at the bottom of the food chain all my life ... just getting by. We need to put in all we can to make this operation a success. This woman and her web of smugglers stole our diamonds; we are taking some of them back. I don't see that as stealing! We need to clear our heads, focus well, and concentrate, Dúró."

"You can count on me, Emeka. I mean it."

"Thanks. I just want to go back home. Back to Nigeria. Home is home no matter how bad. But first, the diamonds," said Emeka, his voice breaking.

"It's going to be all right, Emeka. You'll see. Just hold on. Okay?" said Dúró soothingly. Emeka rarely showed such deep emotions. It got to Dúró. "Are you okay?"

"Yes. God, I hate this."

"Just hold on, buddy."

35

It was late Friday in February.

In downtown L.A., Clarke sat on a familiar sofa in the all-too-familiar waiting room. He had an appointment with Pablo up in his penthouse.

Today was the day the boss was handling over the diamonds for the exchange, which was slated to take place in just about twelve hours.

He felt trapped in-between the crazy demands of Ikeh who was selling the DVD-R and the crazier instructions from Pablo who was bending over backwards to ensure he got the DVD-R.

Why Pablo was so obsessed with the DVD-R Clarke had no idea; just that he wanted it at all cost. Finally, an exchange was slated for dawn tomorrow at Pablo's newly acquired North Rexford Drive property. The house had been handed over to Clarke weeks ago just after the interior décor was completed.

It was to ensure that he and Denise got used to it in order to affect a hitch-free exchange; then Pablo would move in. The house was the love of his life – at least until he found the next.

Clarke looked up to see the imposing hulk of Mo, Pablo's personal bodyguard. His gaze was, as usual, penetrating and unnerving.

"Hi, Mo."

"Yeah," snorted Mo. "He'll see you now."

Both headed for the penthouse elevator that serviced only Pablo's office. A moment later, Clarke was ushered into the presence of Pablo who was sandwiched between two scantily clad damsels on a big waterbed. Pablo snapped his fingers and the girls disappeared, leaving Pablo bobbing comically up and down on the bed. Mo closed the door.

"Sit down, Clarke." Clarke did. "How is it coming?"

"Like clockwork, Boss. Everything is in order. The exchange is at dawn tomorrow."

"Good, I should expect the DVD-R at breakfast then?"

"I give you my words, Sir."

"Good. You have never failed me, Clarke. Besides, I did not wanna spook that clown; otherwise, I would have sealed that house off like it was Fort Knox. You assured me everything is under control."

"Yes, Sir, in perfect order."

"And no catfight, Clarke! That house is the dream of my life! In there, I'm gonna grow old and play with my grandchildren and great-grandchildren and the hell rest of them! So keep it neat!"

"Yes sir!" Clarke said while Mo, on his part, chuckled throatily.

"You think not?!" Pablo snapped in the direction of Mo, his accent showing through and reminding Clarke once again of Robert De Niro.

"No, Boss!"

"So what the hell is funny?"

"Nothing, Boss. But you don't like children."

"Aaah! I'll get over it! And you Clarke!"

"Yes, Boss?"

"Don't mess up my house by shooting it up full of holes. It cost me a bundle ..."

"Yes sir!"

"That's my boy after my heart. And tell Denise to keep her goddamn hands off your fucking prick for now, you hear!" Pablo said busting into a guffaw. "You need a clear head to be focused for this exchange."

"Yes boss."

"Mo, give him the diamonds," Pablo ordered.

Mo lumbered to a wall safe, spun the combination lock a few times, opened the steel door, and brought out a pouch with drawstring mouth. Mo tossed it at Clarke.

"One and a half million dollars worth ... check it."

"Hey ease on him, Mo! He doesn't have to! Now do you, Clarke?"

"No, Boss. Your words are enough."

"Good. Anyway, Clarke, it's a set of stones worth one and a half million bucks. Check it! You go with the stones and bring back the bloody disc."

"Yes, boss."

"One more thing, Clarke. I decided to give you Ron and Kelly to help you keep an eye on things," said Pablo.

Typical, thought Clarke. Pablo could never trust anyone besides himself. Clarke was sure that if Pablo were to come back in a next life, he would be reincarnated as a Black Mamba or something along that nasty, paranoid line.

Aloud Clarke said: "I appreciate the gesture, sir; makes things almighty easy for me and Denise."

"Good," said Pablo, his face contorted into that grimace which often served for his bizarre way of laughing. "Pick them up downstairs on your way out."

"Yes boss."

36

Terry checked out of Beverly Wilshire Hotel late Friday evening.

His first stop was Budget Car Rental in Santa Monica. There, he rented a Ferrari. His second stop was the elegant Shutters On The Beach, an out of the way, sea-front hotel in Santa Monica with a quick access to the Santa Monica freeway.

Terry felt he should make a quick access to the freeway part of his standby provisions; he might need it. So he got a room.

As night set in, Terry left Shutters On The Beach and drove the Ferrari to an all-night car-care park. He checked the Ferrari in. He had brought a change of clothing. In the men's room serving the car park, he changed into it.

Afterwards, he took a taxi to Midway Car Rental in Beverly Hills where he rented a Land Cruiser for a day.

He hid his Laptop and a loaded pistol adapted with a silencer in the vehicle. He then delivered the 4WD to a convenient, easy-to-reach spot opposite Pablo's Beverly Hills house.

Done, he took a taxi to Ikeh's house in Hollywood Boulevard. His other gun was carried on him, professionally concealed. The agreement between him and Ikeh was to carry a weapon each. This was Terry's.

What were not prearranged were the Land Cruiser, the gun adeptly hidden in it, the laptop, and the Ferrari. They were Terry's little secret, to further the course of his present assignment from Neil.

37

Dúró welcomed Terry into the house as Godwin.

A chameleon that he was, Terry too was now Godwin in all respects.

He was in a light gray suit over a sky-blue cashmere turtleneck. It was the only possession on him, which Dúró could see.

Godwin looked sleek and handsome. His dressing took care of the weather while allowing for agility. Considered in the light of what was in the offing at North Rexford, Godwin could not have been better dressed.

Godwin's arrival in this manner got to Dúró. For the first time, the stark reality of his decision was sinking into him. The operation was for the following day. From there on, they were all heading straight for Mexico where they would board the next flight out of the America continent. Never to return.

An uneasy calm descended on Dúró.

This was in addition to the games which his mind was playing on him in the last few days, acting out his morbid dread of what was coming – something he was going to do for the very first time.

Robbery.

About a quarter hour later, they went to bed to have a sound rest before 4am.

38

Clarke, Denise, Ron and Kelly arrived at North Rexford early night.

The four quickly settled in and began putting things in shape for the upcoming exchange.

"What do you think, Clarke?" inquired Denise.

"Ikeh is no trouble. His two hangers-on are no problems too. It is the big bodyguard we have to keep an eye on. I don't trust him, and I don't like his demeanor ..."

"Yeah ... too cocky, too sure of himself. Besides, we've checked around, delved into police records, and checked with contacts in the diamond smuggling business; no one seemed to know him. He is too vague, Denise. He is the bloke we gotta keep an eye on. We've been in this diamond business for far too long. Except he's new, we ought to have gotten a whiff of him somehow somewhere. Anyway, we have no choice. Ikeh wanted him keeping eyes on things before he can go ahead with the exchange; the boss is howling to get on with things and here I am, caught in between ..."

"We don't have to like any of them," cut in Ron, a scary rawboned Mexican-American who was part of Pablo's personal security. "We just get the fucking DVD like the boss wants and we hand over the diamonds."

"That pretty much summarizes it," supported Kelly, another mean-looking Mexican-American from Pablo's inner sanctum.

"Suits me," agreed Clarke. "The plan is still at go. Ron stays with us, sitting by that window," he continued, pointing at the window which overlooked the driveways. "Kelly stays behind the library door, ready. If they pull any trick, we get them all into a cross fire between us ..."

"I'll cut them off from the staircase," offered Kelly.

"Yep. If you see anything unusual, start shooting ..."

"We better screw the silencers on the guns then," suggested Ron with a mirthless grin. "You never can tell what may go down. We don't want LAPD crashing down the driveway just to get at us!"

"Sure," agreed Clarke. "You all do that."

"You think there will be trouble?" asked Denise.

"No, but I don't want to be taken unaware by some bunch of amateurs from the jungles of Africa looking for some diamonds."

"Beautiful summary, Clarke," said Ron as he screwed a silencer on a gun whose safety catch he had sawed off. "You'll live long enough with that principle of yours."

"Only if he pulls this deal through without messing it with American ego," snapped Kelly. "Otherwise, the boss will kill him."

"Aaah, he will pull it through! Wont ya, Clarke?" said Ron.

"Settle down, you guys," Denise said, nudging everyone to shape.

"All right everyone! Settle in," said Clarke.

"We've got a few hours of sleep."

Ron and Kelly left for other bedrooms in the house, leaving Clarke and Denise in the master bedroom.

"By the way," said Clarke, "the boss said to tell you to keep your fucking hands off my goddamn prick."

"He put it that way?"

"Precisely."

"Son of a bitch!" Denise said, turning around and wrapping her fingers around Clarke's testicles. She massaged them gently and Clarke moaned as he hardened. Then they started kissing, first slowly then with an urgency that had them both panting. In no time, they were into each other kissing and moaning as both worked their ways to a shattering climax.

39

On the other side of town, long after others had slept, Dúró laid on his back awake, worried. Tense.

All arrangements have been concluded. For everyone but Godwin, Ikeh had bought one-way flight tickets to Lagos via Mexico. Godwin preferred personal arrangements.

Ikeh had however insisted that he (Dúró) and Emeka not resign from work to avoid undue suspicions. Which made sense.

By now, they all know their roles inside out including the steps to take in case of the unexpected. They have confidence and are generally set to take on the greedy North Rexford woman.

Dúró's uneasiness had however persisted.

Maybe it was because of the act itself. It had been dressed in several layers of beautiful garbs. Dúró had only one name for it, Robbery.

In the United States of America, all the way from Nigeria and equipped with a Bachelor's degree in Philosophy from one of the best Universities in West Africa – he was simply a robber!

Dúró thought; maybe the tension within him was as a result of the defense mechanisms, which his subconscious was putting up against the stark reality of what he had accepted, and prepared to do.

So debasing. Was his subconscious taking a flight from reality? Finding it hard to believe that he was simply a common thief in Beverly Hills?

Suppose he was shot at? Suppose the cops were waiting? Suppose the woman was there in the house, waiting?

Suppose!

Dúró stopped himself. He was carrying on too far. All those possibilities had been considered by all of them in great details and solutions proffered.

Dúró tossed and turned. His mind was a jumbled whirlwind of frights.

"*Háà! Ó se!* (Damn!)," Dúró cursed deeply in his native language, punching his pillow.

What would his mentor, Prof Wọlé Soyinka, do if he realized that he, Dúró, one of his best products had resorted to robbing Safes of diamonds in Beverly Hills, thought Dúró? Poor Prof would roll over and die!

Dúró got off his bed, knelt down, and prayed. He begged God's forgiveness. Yes, the woman had stolen the stones. But taking them from her without her permission was doing the very same thing the woman did – stealing. He promised God that he would never participate in stunts like this again irrespective of the moral justifications.

He remembered his Tóbi as he often did when boxed into a corner. From under his pillow, Dúró produced a sterling silver locket.

He had bought a new one from a jewelry shop to replace the weather beaten original. It had been a gift from Tóbi when he was leaving Nigeria a year back.

Dúró pressed the knob and the shinning locket snapped open. There she was! His Tóbi. Captured with a unique brilliance in the miniature half-frame photograph.

The smile dominated the entire background. Dúró gazed at it for a while with intent as if seeking answers to his problems in the photograph.

He felt better. Maybe things would go smooth. Maybe in the next one or two weeks, he would be a frigging millionaire.

At 1:30am, Saturday, only a few hours to the North Rexford operation, Dúró fell asleep.

40

Dúró woke up at 3am.

Again, he prayed. Thereafter, he took a shower and started the meticulous process of dressing up to look his roles.

For the assignment ahead, Dúró had gotten himself a suit, which was a size bigger. It would give him the agility he desired behind the wheel of the Dodge as well as ample space to carry his essentials; and, of course, his share of the diamonds.

He put on a shirt. His silver locket, as usual, went into the left breast pocket. Putting it there, he patted it for luck. He knew that once again, Tóbi was close to his heart.

He picked his leather billfold and checked the contents. There was his Driving License and a total of U.S. $122. Satisfied, he slipped the billfold into his hip pocket.

He could not use his usual cologne; Ikeh had said it could leave a signature behind for LAPD to pick. He slipped into an unbranded rubber-soled pair of shoes and put on a silk tie. Thereafter, he wore the leather gloves, which Ikeh had insisted they all put on.

He ran a hairbrush over his crew cut, shook himself free of possible broken hair and then put on his suit jacket.

His International Passport went into the right inner pocket of the suit jacket. Parting his cheeks for reassurance, he felt he was set.

Overall, he looked about right for a Black striving to look acceptable in highbrow Beverly Hills or on his way from Southern California to Mexico for a weekend gig.

Well, except for the leather gloves. But then, it was winter.

He picked the ignition key to the Dodge and headed outside. He pressed a button on the key and the garage door whined open. Dúró went in, leaving the door open.

The previous day Emeka had taken the car to the service garage where he worked and had it thoroughly checked. All systems were in perfect working conditions.

Dúró opened the driver's door and settled in. Minutes later, the others joined. Ikeh occupied the front passenger seat, while Emeka and Godwin occupied the back compartment.

"All right, let's roll," Ikeh said tersely.

Dúró gunned the car to life and got underway.

From Hollywood Boulevard, Dúró weaved his ways through back streets rarely patrolled by cops. In time, he connected with Beverly Drive.

On the Dodge's leather seat, in-between Godwin and Emeka was the small pouch that housed Emeka's tools for his supposed job in North Rexford. Sticking out conspicuously was an ammeter.

The ammeter would assist Emeka in monitoring the current flowing through the house security circuitry. However, the ammeter would be necessary only at the end of the operation, when Emeka would be coupling back the wiring, not at the beginning. In this, Godwin saw an opportunity; perhaps this could work.

As Dúró weaved them through the ghostly business district of Beverly Hills, Godwin surreptitiously removed the ammeter from the tool kit and hid it.

As the group neared North Rexford Drive, they became jumpier. But at least, they had not encountered patrol cops. The scene encountered was that of absolute tranquility whose balance was only disturbed by the automotive hum of the Dodge. From rich areas, they moved to still richer sections. Everyone was silent.

Dúró needed no directions. As soon as he crossed Sunset Boulevard, he knew he was home. The houses were a kaleidoscope of architectural creativity. One competed with the other. The spaces were immense, all well set away from the street as if cringing from the likes of Dúró.

3567, North Rexford Drive was an all white two-story affair. The house was set at least seventy-five yards from the street, with two driveways. There were no vehicles in the driveways, which could mean one of two things. Either the woman was not in or the cars had been parked indoor.

Dúró pulled to the curb.

Ikeh got out first, gently closing the car door so it made no noise that could carry off into the early dawn.

Godwin waited, breath baited.

Then Emeka grabbed his tool kit and got out. Emeka did not realize he was missing the ammeter.

Good going. Godwin carefully dropped the ammeter on the floor of the vehicle where Emeka had sat. Then he got out.

"Good luck," Dúró said loud enough for the three to hear as they headed up the driveway.

41

"They are here, Clarke," Denise said peeping discreetly from an obscure corner of the bedroom window. "I can see three of them coming up the right driveway."

"Yeah," agreed Clarke also peeping. "The fourth is supposed to be in the car, the so-called look-out."

"Is the door alarm off?" asked Ron.

"Sure. The damn door will click open no matter which wires are crossed."

"Good," Kelly said. He left for his post at the library, which was the first door to the right of the staircase landing.

Denise left the window and began checking her gun.

Clarke said: "I'll wait at the landing."

He ran a quick check on his weapon as he moved towards the bedroom's door.

"Careful, Clarke," cautioned Denise. "What if the Emeka fellow comes up with them?"

"That wasn't part of the deal," snapped Ron. "He was to busy himself with the goddamn security panel at the main entrance playing James Bond. If he shows up here, then something is amiss. I'll take him out ... and any of those two who look even remotely suspicious ..."

"Not until we get the DVD-R please!" begged Clarke.

"Sure! I don't have a death wish ... Clarke."

"Good. Are we all set?"

"Let me check with Kelly," said Ron, talking to a small transceiver concealed in his left palm. Moments later he said: "everything is set Clarke."

"Careful please," pleaded Denise.

"I will," said Clarke as he left the room.

Denise and Ron took their positions in the huge bedroom.

42

Godwin watched with awe as Emeka deftly began rewiring the door security panel.

Even if the security hadn't been deactivated by Clarke, thought Godwin, this guy would still have expertly broken through. Few minutes elapsed and a green light came on. At that instance, the door clicked open. Godwin pushed through the door followed by Ikeh. Emeka stayed with the door security panel.

Still, Godwin observed, Emeka had not discovered that he was missing the ammeter.

At the staircase landing, Clarke was waiting.

Clarke was carrying a gun, Godwin knew. Though Godwin did not see the weapon, he knew it was there somewhere, concealed on his person. Clarke would be stupid if he did not, thought Godwin.

The three of them moved into the bedroom down the corridor. There, Denise waited. But there was another person.

"Who's that?" demanded Ikeh.

"Ron? Just one of us who decided to come along and have a look ... if you don't mind."

"I do! That was not part of the deal."

"I don't see any difference this makes, guys," said Ron. "Shall we get on with the exchange please;

dawn is fast coming."

———————

Dúró had been assigned to keep watch while the North Rexford operation was on.

He knew exactly what was required of him in order to be thorough. It would be unforgivable if LAPD crept on him while his gaze was fixed somewhere else. Ikeh and Godwin had tutored him in the act of *"keeping watch"*.

Dúró looked around, closely scrutinizing the properties on either sides of the house. The houses in the vicinity were so far off he knew 3567 was theirs without the fear of being seen.

Again, and gladly, visibility was poor, characteristic of most winter mornings in Beverly Hills. Moreover, the abundant flora also provided a much-needed cover.

Dúró turned the Dodge around and parked. As he switched off the engine, he heard the clink of metal against metal in the back passenger compartment. Using the rays of light from the street lamp, he searched the backseat.

"Oh boy!" exclaimed Dúró as he picked up Emeka's ammeter. It had dropped from his instrument pouch, thought Dúró. Should he run up the driveway to the house to hand it to Emeka?

Bad idea! That would be neglecting his duty post! And that might jeopardize the whole operation. Beside he knew that Emeka would only need the ammeter when winding things up at the end of the operation, not now.

Well then, not too bad. Dúró opened the crammed glove compartment and squeezed the ammeter in, then switched his mind back to his task.

If any of the overnight cops passed by, the

Dodge would not attract any attention since other vehicles were around scattered along the curb. Dúró could make out at least four. There was a BMW sedan, glittering with a million stars under the street lamp closest to Dúró.

Beyond it was the imposing grandeur of a Land Cruiser. In front of him was a convertible Mercedes Benz car and, further down the street, a sleek Cadillac SUV.

Dúró felt at ease. Fingering the metal locket in his breast pocket for luck Dúró began praying silently, eyes wide open, and surveying the street for signs of trouble.

———

The exchange had taken place in the house's master bedroom on the second floor.

Clarke and Denise had thought of all the angles, thought Godwin. The bedroom was spacious without furniture that could get on their ways should a fracas ensue.

Available was a laptop with which Denise could confirm the contents of the DVD-R before Clarke handed over the diamonds.

In minutes, the verification was complete. The diamonds were handed over. While Godwin stood guard, Ikeh began a crude authentication of each of the stones.

———

Despite the prayers, time stretched.

The waiting was interminable. Dúró kept glancing at the house occasionally but it seemed sleeping, devoid of activities.

On one hand, this worried him. It was as if everyone had evaporated. On the other hand, it reassured him. At least there were no bedlams of alarms set off. Meaning, things were working well.

Dúró kept a keen watch on the street, his ears wide open, listening, analyzing, and separating the natural noise of early morning from those of possible intrusion.

And he prayed.

Was the operation going as anticipated? It had to!

43

The authentication of the diamond took time but it was a necessary procedure, all five agreed.

Finally, Ikeh was through. Every one of the stones seemed genuine. While at it also, Ikeh had divided the diamonds in four. That would shorten his task downstairs.

It was time to leave.

The five shook hands. Ikeh exited first. Godwin followed carefully taking his time, his steps slow, the strides measured.

Ron was on his feet, looking alert.

Close behind Godwin was Clarke. From the corner of his eyes, Godwin saw that Clarke had brought out a gun, held casually, and pointing towards the floor. He knew Ron too would have done the same.

Denise had no visible weapon; she seemed busy with the DVD-R and the computer. The gap between Ikeh and Godwin had lengthened considerably now. Ikeh was halfway down the stairs in his hurry to get things over with.

Now was the time!

Godwin spun around as he drew his gun. He shot Ron over Clarke's right shoulder. The bullet made a precise entry in-between Ron's eyes.

Godwin had chosen to shoot in Clarke's direction but at Ron further away for two reasons. To distract Clarke. And to quickly eliminate the threat posed by Ron further away behind Clarke.

As it were, Clarke's maneuver at dodging a bullet that was not meant for him in the first place had distracted him and given Godwin the crucial split second he needed to outmaneuver Clarke. Godwin shot Clarke through the heart.

Both shots from Godwin had been so fast and close together, that Ron and Clarke began buckling at their knees at same time. Being muffled shots, Ikeh descending the stairs heard nothing. However, the sight of Clarke and Ron suddenly sinking onto their knees alarmed Denise. Her gun jumped into her hands so fast it surprised even Godwin. She squatted, lined up the gun and shot.

She missed. Only a popping sound from her silenced gun marked her effort at putting Godwin away. Godwin shot her through the heart.

Above the single muffled spit of his gun, Godwin heard a scrapping sound from behind. He knew what it had to be; a body getting through a doorway in one hell of a hurry.

Godwin knew the house inside out from the house plan he had studied in details. Besides, the unexpected presence of a meanly Ron had alerted Godwin into a state of supreme suspicion. His assumption was that there might be other surprises. This exactly was why Godwin had anticipated sneak attacks of the sort underway now.

Godwin wheeled around and went down at same time, facing up. There he was; Mexican features. Godwin shot him twice through the chest and once through the head. The Mexican went down noiselessly.

Godwin stayed down for a few seconds longer, all senses alert. Nothing! No more intrusions! He was done. He stood up and raced downstairs after Ikeh.

"Hey what's keeping you?" Ikeh demanded in hushed whispers as Godwin caught up.

"Making sure these fellas don't pull any tricks."

"Where are they?"

"Still fussing over their priced DVD-R, Ikeh," Godwin replied casually. "And Clarke said to shut the door on our way out. Yunno, it will automatically lock and the security will engage."

"He did?"

"Yeah."

Ikeh felt that, that was odd. A person as paranoid as Clarke would usually come to the head of the stairs if only to ensure that truly they were leaving the house and not planning some sort of double-cross.

Ikeh could not however begin arguing with Godwin. Emeka was close-by and he did believe they had simply robbed a safe full of diamond in an empty house.

Again, it was part of the agreement that Clarke and Denise would not come further than the head of the stairs when Ikeh and Godwin were leaving, otherwise, Emeka at the door would realize that something was not right. All together, the picture was still in tune.

Ikeh had brought four drawstring pouches. Now he was busy stuffing each person's share of diamonds into his designated pouch.

Ikeh would have loved to be out of North Rexford at that moment sharing the diamonds elsewhere but he did not trust Godwin that much. Therefore, he stuck to the original plan of sharing the diamond within the house. Through, he tossed Godwin's to him and Emeka's also to him. He pocketed his.

By now, Emeka had realized that he was missing his ammeter, had thought about where it could be, and had concluded it had to be in the Dodge. Not too bad. He would dash down to retrieve it.

"Look, Ikeh," Emeka said a little unsettled, "I'm missing the ammeter. I must have dropped it coming in. Without it, I cannot complete the assemblage of the security wiring."

My God, thought Ikeh! Anger took hold of him but he fought for control. This was not part of the script. He said calmly: "So what do you do?"

"Come, get hold of these two wires," Emeka said showing Ikeh the bare ends of two leads within the exposed security panel. "Make sure they do not touch the sides of the panel."

Ikeh did as he was told, then said: "Now what?"

"I'll get the ammeter ..."

"You may look in the car first," suggested Godwin. "If not there then we'll search the driveway."

"And if we can't find it?" asked Ikeh desperately looking for an alternate plan.

"I can complete the wiring but it may trigger the alarm."

"How long will that give us?" asked Godwin.

"Twenty-five seconds tops," answered Emeka.

"Hurry then; maybe you can locate the damn thing in the car," snapped Ikeh, barely able to contain his anger. "We gotta get out of here!"

"Sure."

"Here," concluded Ikeh, handing Dúró's pouch to Emeka. "Give it to Dúró. That will calm him down some."

"Yes," said Emeka disappearing into the early morning,

In actual fact, Godwin and Ikeh knew that the ammeter was unnecessary but they could not possibly tell Emeka. To do so would be giving away the carefully constructed ruse.

Ikeh turned to Godwin just to, jocularly, point this out but was confronted with a gun. Godwin shot Ikeh at point blank ranges.

Now, Godwin was back in Terry mode.

44

Dúró snapped to with a start.

It was Emeka, suddenly appearing from the graying dawn at the left back passenger window, trying to open the door. He seemed in a hurry.

Dúró was alarmed. Emeka saw the fear on Dúró's face and gave a muffled laughter.

"Relax," he whispered, reaching into the back passenger compartment where, earlier, he sat. Dúró knew that Emeka was searching for his ammeter and said, "You dropped the ammeter going in. I kept it in the glove compartment."

"Thanks."

"Is everything okay," Dúró enquired with mild trepidation as he opened the glove compartment and handed the ammeter to Emeka. In turn, Emeka tossed a pouch on Dúró's lap.

"Your share, Big Boy. From Ikeh with love."

"Is everything okay?" Dúró repeated, calming.

"Smooth, Dúró. Bread and butter stuff," Emeka said with a very bold grin.

Dúró knew now that things would be all right. He had not seen Emeka that genuinely happy in a very long time. Emeka walked briskly back up the drive to the house.

Dúró heaved a sign of relief.

His mouth was fairly dry, the throat parched. A little composed, he took hold of the pouch nestling cozily on his lap. His share, Emeka had said.

Carefully, as if there was a bird in there that could take flight, Dúró opened the pouch and peered inside.

There they were! Diamonds!

Even in the dark enclosure of the pouch, they glittered! He dipped his hand into the pouch and took two stones out of what could not have been less than a dozen.

On his palm, they caught the pale amber rays from the street lamp and instantly exploded into a kaleidoscope of brilliant colors. It was a sight to behold! Entrancing!

Dúró had never seen diamonds before, not this close-up. But the instant he saw them he knew they truly were diamonds. Pure! He put the two stones back with the rest and salted the pouch in a secure side pocket of his underpants. Then he resumed his guard while waiting for the operation to wind up.

Like others before him in 3567, North Rexford, Emeka walked into Terry's house of death and got a bullet in-between the eyes.

Then Terry raced . upstairs to the master bedroom. He undressed Clarke and Denise and lined them up in bed to portray the appearance of a couple sleeping. Thereafter, he scattered Clarke and Denise's cloths around the room.

He carried Ron and his gun over to the library and left him with the very dead Kelly. Then he came back to the master bedroom and extracted the DVD-R from the laptop before proceeding to smash it into bits. He retrieved Clarke and Denise's guns and headed downstairs.

There, he collected Emeka and Ikeh's diamonds, as well as Ikeh's gun. Then, with the utmost care, he carried both of them up the stairs, one at a time, to the living room past the library and past the master bedroom. There, he had them sitting upright on a sofa, side by side in a preferred posture.

As he had expected, they had both died suddenly and hadn't bled at all, their hearts having stopped beating long before each hit the floor. Thus, there was no evidence of them having died downstairs.

All these precautions Terry needed to cover his tracks and throw LAPD in the wrong direction should they come on the scene before Pablo. The final cap would be Dúró in the car at the curb.

Terry raced out of the house; taking the back door. In a moment, he was with his Land Cruiser. He dropped the DVD-R and the guns from Denise, Clarke, and Ikeh. Then he collected the gun he had hidden earlier in the Land Cruiser and went after Dúró who was just a street light away. From his position, Terry could see the vague outline of the Dodge at the curb.

Moments later, Dúró was distracted from his duty by a movement which caught his eyes.

It was to his left, just outside the window. His head jerked convulsively in the direction, especially given the unexpectedness of the situation. Blocking his view was the imposing physique of the man he knew as Godwin.

Just as Dúró was going to warm up to him, he saw what was held in the man's hands. A pitch-black pistol. A silencer was screwed on it and it was pointed at him.

Dúró's heart began pounding in his ears, choked with fear. As he gazed, dazed, at the weapon for what seemed to him like eternity, he saw Godwin's finger curled around the trigger. That movement, depicting an impending death, galvanized Dúró into action. He reached for the door handle but missed, realizing that he was pushing against a resisting door.

At that instant, Dúró heard an angry spit from the gun and felt a huge fist slam into his chest. The force threw him back into his seat, expelling the air within him. He felt himself washed over by a wave of thick blackness and total void.

Terry worked fast. He concealed the gun he used on those six in the house under Dúró's seat, and then went through Dúró's pockets to make sure his share of the diamonds was on him. Satisfied, Terry left. With him was the second gun, the one he had just shot Dúró with.

The message he was sending LAPD was simple – Dúró was the person who shot those six in North Rexford. Motive? Diamonds! The big question which LAPD would be scrambling to answer would be the person who shot Dúró. A double-cross would be entertained but entertainment it would remain. Terry had covered all tracks. Characteristic. That was simply how thorough Terry took his assignments. Leave nothing untied.

45

Dúró woke up with a start.

His chest was in flame. He looked around him and realized it was early dawn. Then he heard the angry protest of tires down the street.

A vehicle had just pulled off the curb.

Dúró looked in its direction. It was the Land Cruiser that had been parked there all along. It was on the move. The taillight disappeared down the street in a hurry leaving Dúró with his immediate problems.

Then it all came back to him in a cascade. He had been shot! By Godwin! Using a silenced weapon! A person he trusted so much and relied upon so completely. Unacceptable!

Now where was Emeka? What about Ikeh? What had happened? What was going on? In pure panic, Dúró fumbled for the door handle, jumped out, and ran for the house.

The front door was slightly ajar. Dúró pushed past it and found himself in a short hallway. A few steps further on, he saw to the left a broad, carpeted staircase spiraling upwards to the second floor. Ahead, slightly to his right was what he knew had to be the sitting room on the ground floor.

Dúró took the staircase three at a time. The

busted safe was supposed to be somewhere in the library which was the first door to the right of the landing.

The door was closed. About to open the library door, Dúró saw that the door further down was wide open. It was the master bedroom door.

A beam of light escaped through the door, making a pool on the floor of the corridor just beyond the threshold. Ignoring the library door momentarily, Dúró headed down the corridor towards the open doorway.

Carefully, he entered the room.

The room itself was immense, elegantly furnished, and uncluttered with thick sky blue carpeting. The ray of light that had shone through the doorway was coming from a shaded lamp. The lamp was next to a king-size bed located almost at the center of the room. On the bed, Dúró could make out two nude figures. Both were Caucasians. One was a woman and the other a man.

They were quite dead.

He looked carefully around the room. The only disturbances to its orderliness were the clothes scattered around, possibly in the frenzied act of getting undressed for sex. Then amidst the clothing, some other things came into focus. They were bits and pieces of a thoroughly smashed laptop.

His attention switched back to the dead couple. Dúró moved close to the bed.

Each of the two had been shot once through the heart, their faces frozen more in disbelief than fright. Carefully, Dúró made his way out of the bedroom. He had to muster all his will power to stop the wave of nausea coursing through him. He felt gagged, choked, stifled.

Under his suit jacket in the chilly dawn, Dúró felt like in a blast furnace. He reached for his tie and loosened the choking knot as well as the two top buttons of the shirt.

He was sweating profusely. Beads of perspiration coalesced, dribbled down his face and neck, and soaked his shirt.

He was now at the door of the library. He wondered how he was going to open that door without leaving his prints behind. Then it dawned on him that he was wearing a pair of leather gloves. He could touch whatever he wanted. He applied a light pressure to the door and it swung open.

The shaded ceiling light was on though dimmed by a gold-fitting light dimmer. He reached for the dimmer and turned the light a notch higher.

Dúró moved into the library, which, like the bedroom of death, was expensively but sparsely furnished. Everything was in neat order. The shelves of books were in rows extending nearly three quarters to the ceiling.

Dúró knew from Ikeh that the safe was somewhere on the other side of the shelves where the wall was thickest. He listened for sounds. There was none except the harsh note of his scared breathing. He started towards the far side of the bookshelves, and then stopped.

Scattered in front of him were two bodies. One had a red-petal rim of blood in-between the eyes. The other had a similar hole at the bridge of his nose and two through the general area of the left breast.

They were stone dead!

Dúró stumbled out of the library and flopped on the carpeted floor to the right of the door. The choking feeling was back. The floor, the ceiling, and the walls seemed to be closing-in on him.

Where were Ikeh and Emeka? He needed to find them! He had to check the other living-room here on the second floor before going down to the one on the ground floor.

For a moment, he lost his orientation, forgetting from the knowledge he had where exactly the living-room was supposed to be. Then he remembered. It was down this same corridor past the master bedroom.

Dúró lumbered to shaky feet; careening along, supporting himself upright using the walls. He got to and pushed through the swing doors. The chandelier hanging from the ceiling was burning brightly. He came to an abrupt stop. Sitting next to each other on a big sofa, their backs to him were the pair of Ikeh and Emeka.

They seemed engrossed in a conversation!

———

This instant, Terry was miles away.

He had opened the content of the DVD-R on his laptop; had found that there were no passwords; and had sent the contents to Neil.

By the time Terry got to the car rental, Neil's verifications were complete. He read the confirmation from Neil; shut off his laptop; relinquished the Land Cruiser; and hailed a taxi.

He was headed for the all night car-care where he parked the Ferrari. From there he would drive back to his hotel room at Shutters On The Beach. He needed a satisfying shower and a deep sleep. He needed the rest.

46

At first, Dúró thought that both Emeka and Ikeh were involved in a conversation, so he hissed a testy "Hey, guys!" and took a diagonal path towards their position.

He was angry, confused, and frightened at same time because of the incomprehensibility of it all. There they were sitting comfortably in seeming quite conversation. Meanwhile, two were dead in the master bedroom; two others were shot up full of holes in the library; and Godwin had just shot at him. None made sense to him.

What was going on?

Who were the four corpses? What were they doing in a house that was supposed to be empty?

Dúró was charged and fairly crackling with anger as he got to his two friends. Right there, he froze into momentary immobility.

Both Emeka and Ikeh were sitting upright all right but were dead, their faces frozen in cheer terror. His worst fears had been confirmed. His sixth sense started howling at him to get the hell out! And fast! In a daze, he headed for the outside.

He had no idea what he was going to do but he kept moving all the same. He was certain of one thing however; he was in a lot of trouble.

He got to the Dodge, got in, gunned the engine to life, and left the curb. He drove down the street and quickly crossed into Sunset Boulevard, hurrying. He needed to be home!

Home?! What home? There was no home anymore!

Dúró slammed on the brake and pulled to the curb, killing the engine. Now he was shaking uncontrollably. After a while, calm gradually returned. He checked the dashboard clock, 6:15am.

Dúró knew he was fast loosing control of himself. If he was to have any hope of surviving this terrible mess, he needed to be in absolute control. He needed to be calm, rational, and capable of keeping his emotions in perfect check. Otherwise, he was sure, he was going to end up dead too.

And pretty soon.

The first reality he had to come to terms with now was that there was no home anymore. All that had gone the moment they left Hollywood Boulevard at dawn. Again, there had been six murders, all traceable to him. At least, he was a part of it. The third reality was that he had to get out of California – in fact, out of the United States – as fast as possible.

At first, he had no idea where to start. Then out of his jumbled thought came Mexico. Yes, Mexico! That was their original plan had North Rexford worked out. He would get into Mexico and from there left for Lagos.

Now more composed and with a goal to achieve, Dúró gunned the Dodge to life. He headed for Highway 101 southbound. In no time, he was on Interstate 5 where he was able to make better speed and arrange his thoughts.

It all boiled down to the fast lane business and its attributes, shunning what he and Emeka had jointly termed the sun-up-to-sun-down chores.

That had produced the stranger called Godwin. And of course North Rexford.

He remembered the Land Cruiser, which had been parked at the curb. It had sped off after Godwin shot him! Was that Godwin taking off? Likely, in the light of present circumstances! Was this planned? Was the Land Cruiser part of Godwin's plots? Maybe!

Godwin had used them, somehow and had all along intended getting rid of Ikeh and Emeka thereafter. Dúró shook his head vigorously, disagreeing with himself, and searching his mental archive for more applicable explanations. Actually, Godwin had intended getting rid of them all not just Emeka and Ikeh.

Godwin's belief would be that they were all dead because he had shot all of them. How was Godwin to realize that after a shot through the heart, he (Dúró) was still alive and breathing?

Through the heart?!

Dúró's hands on the steering of the Dodge wavered and it swerved violently as a realization hit him. He had been shot at point-blank ranges, the huge impact knocking him back into the driver's seat, and rendering him unconscious for a moment.

And here was the tell tale. His entire chest hurt! Where was the bullet? It was not a blank, surely!

Controlling the wheel with his slightly numb left hand, he rummaged around under his suit jacket with the right. He found the bullet next to the metal locket in the left breast pocket of his shirt. He brought it to within his visual field as he drove and inspected the agent of death. It had been flattened by its impact on the metal locket.

The locket had saved him!

From the little he could see so far, Godwin seemed a one-bullet-professional. Every single one of the six victims – except one – had been settled with just a bullet ... appropriately placed. If not for the locket, he too would have been stone cold dead. The locket had saved his life! Tóbi's gift of love.

Tóbi's Pastor had warned him about cheating on her while in the U.S. Tóbi had taken him to her Pastor a few days before departure from Nigeria a year or so back.

After the customary prayers, the Pastor had said, *'a vow of love is a vow of God, Dúró. God is Love and Love is God. Irrespective of where a vow of love is made, it is binding before the Lord. You will be sorely tested while in the U.S. but love will see you through.'*

The Ifá god had said virtually the same through the Ifá Priest.

Dúró's mother had gone to the Ifá Priest at the village for guidance on ways to ensure success for him as he set out for the United States.

The Ifá Priest had said, *"You set forth in the foreign land amongst thorns and prickles; clouds and storms, but a man who remembers his roots will rise even if he falls. Remember your roots and never forsake your heart."*

Tóbi was his heart. Dúró had persevered, kept love alive in his mind through the physical presence of that locket amidst other things and had been protected through the valley of the shadow of deaths.

Dúró swallowed hard at the close encounter he had just had with death. He was practically shivering.

Other problems intruded into his mind. There was the white couple – or well, man and woman. Who were they? Why were they there? What about those two in the library?

They looked like bodyguards to the couple in the bedroom. Dúró's profuse sweating had returned though it was a chilly winter dawn. Trouble! Pure, unadulterated trouble!

Dúró threw the flattened bullet out of the car window, its impact muffled by the rushing of the wind as he sped towards the junction off to Santa Ana. He would detour into the town in order to change his route somewhat. Santa Ana would give him the desired access to Interstate 5 further along.

Dúró was back in deep thought.

What went wrong? The North Rexford house was supposed to be empty. The woman was supposed to be out of Los Angeles this weekend! Hadn't Godwin played his part?

"Oh he had! He really had," Dúró said aloud to himself as if by so doing the implications would sink into him more. The whole story as concocted by Godwin and told by Ikeh was a lie, a complete tale out of the moonlight.

A blind rage took hold of Dúró and he fought to control the wheel as dawn came in Southern California. He had been played for a complete fool, blinded by his greed. He had been led onto an altar of greed to be slain treacherously by his lack of foresight.

Dúró turned his face to the car window, hacked up a good measure of phlegm, which to him represented Godwin, and spat it into the rushing wind. Ironically, it came back showering his face. In this natural phenomenon, Dúró could see himself in great details as if examining himself in a mirror.

He had gotten what he deserved, he decided. He had wanted to be rich overnight and had not heeded his conscience; that inner voice that had repeatedly called him to order. The beckon of untold riches was simply too great. Dúró had ignored this and he was now paying the price. Reluctantly, he wiped the phlegm from his face and then reviewed the situation.

Was the story from Godwin really and completely a lie? What about the stones in his pocket, brought to him by a jubilant Emeka who had said it was his (Dúró) share?

At the thought of the diamonds, Dúró broke out in cold sweat. Had Godwin looked for, found, and dispossessed him of those precious stones while he was *dead*?

Frantically, he started looking for a lay-by on the freeway. He needed to stop the car and locate the pouch of diamonds, which he had kept in a pocket of his underpants. The freeway flew by; no lay-by. The lay-bys seemed to have vanished from the highway all of a sudden. Finally, he found one and pulled into it.

Dúró adjusted the seat of the Dodge backwards to give him adequate space to maneuver. He undid his fly and dipped his hand through, rummaging around for the pocket in the underpants where he kept the diamonds.

No dice! His hand was hitting nothing! He went into a blind panic. Godwin had dispossessed him of his rightful diamonds! They were his! He had worked to earn them. U.S$150,000 worth of uncut, unpolished diamonds. Dúró was choking from sheer fright and anger. What would he do now?

47

Dúró had been searching his underpants pocket with his buttock raised off the seat of the Dodge to give him ample space.

Now completely dejected, he sat down. Then he realized that there was a soft hardness underneath him. It was the pouch with the diamonds. His diamonds were intact. His mistake out of blind panic was that he had been searching the wrong pocket.

For the next few minutes, he simply sat back and composed himself. He needed to be self-possessed. Done, he got out of the Dodge into the chilly dawn. Using the window glass as a crude mirror, he touched up on his dressing. He needed to look well dressed and equanimous.

Soon, he would be encountering patrol cops. If an All Point Bulletin (APB) was already out on him, he wanted to be relaxed. He wanted to be able to convince any overzealous cop that he was on his way to Mexico for a weekend gig. Except of course the APB included photos. Then the game was up.

Back in the Dodge and about to get underway, Dúró realized that he still had those leather gloves on. Taking them off, he opened the glove compartment to salt them away. But it was crammed full.

He slammed the cover and opted for the underside of his seat. In the process of driving the gloves deep under his seat, his hand hit a cold, metallic object.

A strident alarm went off in his mind! The feel and the shape of the object were pointers to what it could be. He dragged it into the daylight within the Dodge and his worst fears were confirmed. It was a big handgun adapted with a silencer!

Dúró could have sworn it was the same weapon Godwin had shot him with except for the color. He was certain of the color of the gun Godwin shot him with – pitch black. This one was definitely different. Dull gray; there was no mistaking it.

Then it struck Dúró. Everything fell into place, all the pieces matching.

Godwin had killed those six with this gun, and then used the second weapon – the black gun – on him. While unconscious, thought dead, Godwin had hidden the murder weapon for those six under his seat.

Without any print at all on this gun, and with him found dead wearing leather gloves in front of 3567, North Rexford, the conclusion would have been pretty straightforward. The diamonds in his pocket would have served for his motive.

What mattered to Godwin was who would be nailed for the North Rexford killings. That would have been him – a very dead Dúró. Now Dúró knew that Godwin had carefully planned everything long before now.

Dúró needed a plan to outmaneuver Godwin. More than fear, he was now driven by anger. First was to search the Dodge for other possible incriminating trails that Godwin might have planted. Then he would get rid of the gun as well as the leather gloves.

Dúró started with the glove compartment and gradually worked his way backwards until the whole vehicle had been thoroughly combed. Nothing! Good going!

It was time to get rid of the gun and the gloves.

He dragged out the leather gloves from under the car seat and wrapped the gun in them. It made a tight bundle, the gun completely covered. He got out and went to the shoulder of the road, his figure a little obscured from the road by the bulk of the Dodge.

Mustering all his energy, he threw the bundle into the forested seventy-five meter drop off the shoulder of the road. It went so far away and so far down that Dúró could not pick up the noise it made going through the dense foliage. He prayed that no one found it, ever.

As Dúró turned around, he heard the wail of a siren, very eerie in the early morning.

Dúró jerked to a convulsive stop, eyes wide. His mouth went dry and instantly caught fire. A highway patrol officer pulled up and marched sternly to him, his right hand resting on his hip holster.

48

They had caught up, Dúró thought.

An overwhelming impulse to take flight and plunge into the bush behind seized him. From the forest, he would make his way to the vast Pacific Ocean. From there he would think of the next move. At least he would have bought himself some time, a few hours perhaps.

All the same, Dúró fought the impulse.

"Hi there, any problems?"

"No ... no officer," Dúró managed amidst a stammer.

"Are you okay?" the officer said looking the Dodge over, "Being in this lay-by and all! Kind of lonely and dangerous out here, man!"

"Oh! Thanks! Yes, officer, I am okay. I'm headed for Santa Ana. I just took a leak."

"Aaah!"

"Sure!" Dúró asserted. Confidence was starting to return.

"Well."

"I was about getting underway, officer," Dúró said feeling a bit better and somehow grateful that he had not taken flight.

"All right. Be careful on these lonely stretches."

"Thanks, officer," Dúró said moving shakily

towards the Dodge. The officer sauntered back to his huge BMW bike, gunned it to life, and zoomed off.

Dúró got into the Dodge and found that his hands were shaking. A minute crawled by, his composure coming back. Turning the key in the ignitron, he got going.

"The guilty are afraid," he mumbled.

His journey through Santa Ana was swift. He was back on the interstate. He picked speed. It was about 7am now with heavy morning overcast. He wound up the window against the chilly morning and stormed towards Oceanside. In deep thought.

What was North Rexford really all about? Who was Godwin? Dúró stormed past Oceanside and headed towards San Diego, taking care to keep within speed limit. He had only one goal; get into Mexico as soon as possible and get on a plane to Lagos.

The cops would soon want him desperately. For routine questioning, they would say. However, that would mark the start of his one-way journey to the gas chamber or the electric chair or whichever killing method caught the fancy of the presiding judge.

In San Diego, he would park the car in an obscure garage and cross by rush hour train into Mexico.

Dúró was in San Diego by ten in the morning.

As usual, it was a city bustling with mid-morning weekend activities. But everywhere Dúró looked, he thought people were unduly staring at him. Were they trying to picture his face? Had photographs of him been circulated this far out of

California?

Now that he thought of it, he did look a bit odd on a Saturday morning, in tie and suit. He decided to change all that. From a Shop, he bought a cheap turtleneck to go with the suit, discarding the shirt and the tie. He transferred his precious lifesaver – the dented silver locket – into the right pocket of his pant.

Looking at himself in the full-length mirror attached to the changing room, he looked more in tune with the general outlook in San Diego on a mid Saturday morning.

He drove off again in search of a garage where he would park the Dodge before vanishing. While searching, he thought. He felt tired and hungry. The situation was not much better half an hour later. But then other things began happening. Certain things began coming to him. Flashes of new thoughts. Now, various details of the whole saga he had never paid mind began coming to him, opening other possibilities.

In light of this and the fact that he was hungry, he abandoned the garage hunt. He decided to slow himself down, get rid of the adrenalin. He needed to be calmer, more self-possessed. He needed a clear head to align the set of facts newly assailing his mind. That required a full stomach. And therefore a restaurant.

Dúró began searching for an inconspicuous one by driving around back streets. He found The Diners up Fourth Avenue. It was sandwiched between The Princess and Tapas Picasso off Hillcrest Street. He parked in an alley off the south end of Fourth Avenue and came back into The Diners. At this time of a Saturday, there was, expectedly, only a scattering of clients. Just as well.

Dúró hunkered down at an obscure booth and ordered breakfast. Now was when he lunged for typical Yorùbá breakfast – Isu and Ikàn. A serving would push him twelve hours straight.

He ate slowly and in thought. Certain realities were dawning on him that made him very much afraid.

Dúró asked himself some important questions: could the U.S. government extradite him from Nigeria? The answer was a big Yes. Would they want to? Again, Yes. The government had all the reasons in the world – six murders in a highbrow district as wealthy as Beverly Hills, with diamonds stolen. Those were the reasons. Bush would make it a major assignment.

FBI and INTERPOL would invade Nigeria, combing every conceivable nooks and crannies just to get at him.

Dúró thought; if he ran, he had confirmed his guilt. If he stayed back in the U.S., things might be seen in a different light. This was especially so now that he had survived Godwin's murder attempt. If he had been found dead in the Dodge with the murder weapon and the motive, it would have been a different case entirely.

Again, he was sure that no one saw him leave North Rexford. Right now, there existed no concrete evidence that he had ever been in North Rexford or participated in the actual robbery. At least, nothing he could think of. Consequently, he could completely peel himself off the whole mess.

The only way to achieve this was to stay put in the U.S., in Ikeh's house. He would go to his usual place of work at the bookshop, pretending nothing had happened. This might work. It was the best option available to him at the moment.

As it stood, it was a Saturday, his day off, his weekend off. He would return to L.A. tomorrow evening … maybe into the waiting hands of the police. Maybe not. He decided to take that chance.

If the police caught him here in San Diego or in Mexico City, he would have a story ready. He would tell them that he had driven all the way to San Diego just for the excitement of it all, heading for a blissful weekend in Tijuana and Baja California, even Mexico city.

Why not in company of his friends, Emeka and Ikeh, the cops might ask. He would simply say that the two had left the house early that morning in the company of a third person.

His aims were twofold.

One was to keep the lies as simple as possible so he wouldn't trip on them in subsequent questioning by the police. The other was to establish in the minds of the cops of the existence of Godwin. To Dúró's plans, this was paramount. Now, he had a plan of action.

He finished his meal and left in search of a Safe Deposit Company. He wanted to hide the diamonds before driving across the border into Mexico.

49

Just as Dúró got to Tijuana, Terry woke up in his hotel room at Shutters On The Beach.

He drove out to buy brunch, which he ate in his room. Done he ran an on-line check of his bank account and was satisfied. The half million-dollar balance had been paid.

As he reached to shut off the laptop, Terry noticed a red beacon prompt, and he stared. It was a Windows page, the page from which he sent the content of the DVD-R to Neil. There was a comment for his attention about the folders and files in the DVD-R. He moved the computer's cursor to the beckon and clicked. The computer had something for him. It rolled this out in boldface fonts.

FOLDERS COPIED.
COPY DAY: SUNDAY; 19-11-2006.
START COPY: 06:01:12.
END COPY: 06:59:56.
COPIES MADE: 01.

Terry felt chilled. The DVD-R from North Rexford, had been copied. The time of copy was spelt out as well as the number of copies made.

A copy had been made of the DVD-R on Sunday November 19, 2006. The copying was done between the hours of six and seven in the morning.

That was months before the North Rexford exchange. The disc with him now was the original, but it had been copied. There was only one person who could have done that.

Ikeh! Now dead!

This would bring an unpleasant angle to the deal if Neil got this DVD-R because Neil would also know it had been copied. Terry decided to take a precautionary measure to protect his reputation with the CIA. He was going to make a copy off this original version again. Then he would give Neil the copy, not the original. That was Ikeh's mistake – out of inexperience. Ikeh had made a copy from the original and had traded in the original. He never knew that the original program had automatically documented that a copy was made off it.

If he had traded with the copy, Terry's computer – or any other computer for that matter – would have taken it for the original. It wouldn't have known that other copies existed. Terry decided that when he was through with Neil and Kim, he would locate, retrieve, and destroy the copy Ikeh made.

In half an hour, a copy was ready. Then Terry began comparing the two. He needed to be sure that both were identical, word for word, letter for letter, and punctuation for punctuation – otherwise Neil would know. He already had the content via the net.

In the space of the time needed for this arduous task however, Terry had gotten into the content of the DVD-R deeper than he wanted.

Normally, Terry would do his job, collected his fee, and disappeared until another unsolvable problem from the CIA cropped up needing to be dumped onto his laps. In all, he always took care never to get involved. It was the only way Terry knew he could keep the CIA his client and kept on living for as long as he chose.

Now that Terry had incidentally gotten into the disc's content, he was almighty curious. It was not at all what he had expected.

He was baffled.

The disc was a detailed chronicle of mining activities all over West Africa by a clique of power shots in Washington; all headed by Neil and Kim. These were activities, which if uncovered by governments in West Africa would be the beginning of a major confrontation with Washington. These were acts that could destroy the CIA, several top shots in President Bush's cabinet, and political heavy weights in the U.S. Congress.

Little wonder Neil was so stressed.

What Terry had always known was that West Africa, like most regions of Africa, was endowed with commercial deposits of varieties of precious stones.

But the sub-region had largely chosen to do nothing about the natural blessings. With the little he knew, affluent West Africans who could have come together in partnership deals to finance the capitally intensive mining operations needed to explore these precious stones had been content to tow a line of masterly inactivity.

Usually, they sat around and did nothing more than acted as fronts for *looters disguised as investors* who came with some dollars, practically stealing the deposits through deals heavily skewed against host countries. Then the local fronts hung around at the background collecting pittance as commissions.

This disc implied that Kim Holland had identified this untapped wealth while scouring the continent a decade back. He had perfected the business trend using the resources of State. He had fabricated DRAINPIPE.

The DVD-R listed all the participants in the program and how funds were disbursed to them from time to time in the last decade.

There was Todd Broadmann.

Terry knew Todd very well. Todd had been in the State Department forever. Unlike the politicians, Todd was a hardworking technocrat who had woven his way up the precarious ladder that was the U.S. State Department by sheer perseverance. Todd knew the State Department inside out.

Bush's second term had elevated Todd to the Under Secretary of State on Africa. You could therefore not pull any stint in Africa without him knowing. Which made him all the more important to Kim in keeping successive Secretaries of State completely uninformed.

Then Jerome Hughes!

Who wouldn't know old cat-with-nine-lives Jerome? Given his controversial role in Clinton's haunting Monicagate, it was inconceivable that George Bush – a Republican President taking over from a Democrat Clinton – would take Jerome in and right in his first term.

But most politicians are dumb. And so it was that Jerome warmed his way into Bush's camp. And promptly, he became enmeshed in more controversies. Interestingly, not only did Jerome survive the scandals unscathed however, he gained more political advantage and popularity with them.

As Bush's Senior Special Adviser on Africa,

Terry knew that DRAINPIPE would benefit immensely from Jerome who could keep it from prying eyes at the White House.

Then erudite Budd Haywood. The big prize.

Twenty years in the U.S. Congress. Now Chairman of the Foreign Relations Committee. He would have been the Secretary of State had irresistible Condoleezza Rice not existed.

Budd was Kim's personal buddy. A good business associate as well. How could Budd be in this shenanigan. Money? Inconceivable! But there he was with details of how funds were moved into accounts he ran in Switzerland and Venezuela. Obviously, Kim had been very convincing.

Terry scanned the details of the program's spread.

DRAINPIPE had operations scattered in West Africa. There were sapphire mines in Burkina Faso, topaz in Mali, and aquamarine in Guinea. The diamond business was especially booming in Sierra Leone and Cote d'Ivoire. In Nigeria, DRAINPIPE had chosen to concentrate mainly on its rich emerald deposits.

The operations were simple really.

Locals who were well disposed were identified and used as fronts to get mining permits from indigenous governments for the chosen precious stones. Precious stones that were targeted were those needing only crude methods to get at.

In most of the mining fields therefore, there was hardly any need more than shovels, excavators, tractors, earthmovers and a few dozen men with good knowledge of explosives. The entire workforce from the technicians in the mining fields to the clerks in the offices was by the locals and directly under the control of surrogate businessmen.

This way, mining activities were kept very rudimentary as would be expected of the locals. Otherwise governments of these countries might become suspicious and carry out investigations that could eventually lead on to the actual men behind the programs.

What made DRAINPIPE profitable was the share number of operations it had all over West Africa. There were hundreds of them. In Nigeria alone, there were seventy-five blue emerald mining operations, each very limited in size.

What was more; the simplicity of each of the mines made it possible to be operated not only at peacetimes but also at times of civil conflicts with barely any disruption of core mining.

From these mining activities, DRAINPIPE had made nearly five billion U.S. dollars in just a decade.

With this disc, Terry knew that Pablo could have these men by the balls. It was a political bomb waiting to explode. However, Terry knew that Pablo himself would not dare this. It was way over his head. Except he was buying to sell somewhere else.

Even at that, Terry was not satisfied yet. It did not fit. Something was missing. Whatever it was, was there hovering at the periphery of his consciousness, barely out of grasp.

Terry decided he needed to sleep over it. He needed to brood some more. He needed to read the contents of the disc more closely. Maybe then, he would be able to connect it all.

He shut down his laptop, packaged the disc, and left the hotel. First, he would drop the Ferrari with the car rental before heading for the rendezvous, preset, where Neil would collect the disc.

All together, Terry concluded, it had been a satisfying six-week outing.

50

Jack Nicholas had decided it was safest for all parties if Pablo met with him at a discreet hotel room in Las Vegas.

A hotel of Pablo's choosing.

Jack wanted Pablo relaxed and clear-headed. The more stressed Pablo was, the more he used some of the drugs he pushed. The more drugs he used the more careless and irrational he became. Lately, Pablo had been under a lot of stress.

As it stood, Pablo was a scared man.

Jack and his boss, Reeds, were threatening Pablo and Pablo was powerless to do anything, rich as he was. In fact, being wealthy had made Pablo all the more cripple. Now, he had a lot to lose.

Reeds practically owed him. Involved were past favors with the records supposedly buried. Apparently, records could be exhumed, dusted off, and brought back to life.

The incidence had been a long time ago, long before Pablo made his millions.

He had been an underdog in the East coast then. He ran some dirty errands for a New York bookmaker. He placed the bets, helped with debt collection, and invariably got involved with some violence.

One or two years of easy run had gone without any major incidence. And he was considering leaving for the west coast. Then there was that last assignment.

Debt recovery. From the wife of a powerful senator on the Hill.

She had been coming to New York City without the knowledge of her husband and had been having an affair with a Manhattan banker who gambled heavily.

Invariably, she also got into gambling and incurred debts. Debts, which the banker boyfriend was not ready to settle. She defaulted several times on payment and Pablo's boss ran out of patience.

Pablo got the assignment. It was just the usual method of debt collection. Pablo's boss wanted her shaken just a little bit. Throw some scare into her, Pablo was told.

That was all. All of a sudden however, things got out of hand and Pablo found a dead woman on his hands.

Faint with fear and half out of his mind, Pablo called his boss with the bad news. His boss reassured him that everything was under control and to stay put until help came. Then the unthinkable happened. His boss sold him out; he alerted the police.

Pablo would have been caught with all the facts but for a man who came out of nowhere to bail him out. He was the senator from the Hill, the woman's husband. He had trailed her to New York City, to that particular hotel. He had stumbled on Pablo's fresh scene of murder.

This Senator from the Capitol Hill had all the facts that could put Pablo away for life. However, he chose not. He let Pablo off, free. By doing this though, Pablo knew, the senator was avoiding a scandal, which could have effectively damaged his political career, possibly irreparably.

Letting Pablo off therefore had been mutually beneficial. Pablo escaped the cops by the whiskers. Pablo never saw or heard from the man again. Until now, fifteen years later.

Now, the man was the United States of America's National Security Advisor, a White House hopeful come 2008. A whole lot more powerful. And he was calling on the past favor.

He wanted a DVD-R of information, which he knew was in the market and which he believed Pablo was best placed to procure.

Easy meat. Or so it seamed.

Pablo had put his wealth as well as his network of resources into use. Four of his best. And a pile of diamonds. The team had tracked down the seller and spent weeks working towards a foolproof exchange. The more the day of exchange drew nearer the easier things became. Then poof, everything was gone! Like a mist! Everything that could go wrong did go wrong. Now, Jack wanted his balls for breakfast.

"Have you gotten the guy who did this?"

"Dúró?"

"Whatever!"

"I have my men all over the place looking. I will have him routed out one way or the other."

"Any idea why this happened?"

"Not for sure but I have a good something to start on."

"Which is?"

"See, Jack. This Dúró fellow is one of Ikeh's two

roommates. The two had come to the U.S. about a year back like a lot of their type all over the goddamn place running off Africa. They come in here wild and mean, searching for the shortest way to make money. Then they go back to their goddamn African jungle ..."

"Aahh! These stories!"

"It's the truth, I swear!"

"And?"

"Look, Jack! Ikeh cut the two in on the deal. So he came with the two to North Rexford. But one of them got greedy and did them all in. He double-crossed us all!"

"The Dúró fellow?"

"Certainly!"

"How can you be so sure?"

"Well, someone bloody well shot those six, Jack, and it wasn't a ghost! The goddamn diamonds are all gone! The disc had disappeared! Next thing I know ... Ikeh's Dodge was gone as well! And the Dúró person? Gone too! Almighty suspicious if you ask me!"

"So?"

"He is our man! I will hunt him down, Jack. Please gimme some time."

"These things ... killings ... they have no connections with us ..."

"Not even a shred of evidence remains at North Rexford, Jack! Besides, there is no way anyone can ever connect the deaths with you or the NSA! No way!"

"Good. Get the disc, Pablo. My boss is waiting! And Pablo?"

"Yes, Jack?"

"You wouldn't want Claire's record to get into

the hands of these ferocious cops!"

"Come on, Jack!"

"They hate you!"

"Yeah!"

"They'll be glad to pin you ..."

"Yeah!"

"Still remember her?"

"Aaah ... ye ... yes!" stammered Pablo.

"Her murder was never solved!"

"Right!"

"Still an open-ended case. Could be revisited!"

"Please! Look, tell the NSA I will deliver! I don't care about the fucking diamonds! I will get the disc, Jack!"

"I know you will," Jack said and let himself out. Despite the cold atmosphere, Pablo was sweating. Mo came in to inquire how he was doing and Pablo boomed: "find me that prick, Mo!"

"Yes sir," Mo answered quickly retreating.

51

The last twenty-four hours were the longest in Dúró's life.

He had checked into Glamoure Motel, a back street bed-only accommodation in Tijuana. It had the kind of reputation and façade that would suit his needs.

Dúró could hardly eat. If an APB had been issued on him, would his photographs be circulated as far out of L.A as San Diego? If so, could the patrol cop who saw him before Santa Ana connect his face to the photograph? Would the cops somehow discover the gun he threw away?

Suppose someone in San Diego had remembered his face? There were people in The Diners where he had his breakfast! There was the cloth shop where he had a change of clothing. There was the Safe Deposit Company! And there were law enforcement officers at the border with Mexico.

Was LAPD right now waiting at the border?

It was now an hour behind his schedule. Dúró braced himself, picked up the car key, and headed for the motel's car park.

Moments later, he was on his way to the US-Mexico border. In his mind, he was prepared for the possibility that he might be arrested anywhere between the border and home.

He resolved not to resist or be perceived to resist arrest. The cops were always looking for the slightest opportunity to waste any African seen contravening the laws of the land. His case was. He would be wanted for theft and multiple murders.

As he steadily got closer to the border, he rehearsed his story again and again.

52

Terry knew he had calls to make, contacts to heat up, and traveling to do.

Now having gone through the entire contents of the disc in minute details, Terry found himself getting emotionally involved.

Kim and the likes of him mined Africa's solid minerals and gemstones at give away prices. That was when they bothered to pay at all. Most times, they practically stole them.

What was worse, when they did make attempts at payment, they did so through arms and ammunitions. In so doing, they tactically fueled armed conflicts on the continent.

While warring factions were at each other's throat therefore, people like Kim crawled around in the existing darkness to steal the continent blind of its natural endowments.

On the international political scene, however they pretend to play the Good Samaritan role of *caring, civilized, democratic arbiters. This, in the conflicts they helped create in the first place.*

Terry remembered that one Ambassador Ségun Olúsọlá, a Nigerian political elder statesman, had rightly depicted this sort of Afro-American relationship in a series of stage plays in Kenya dubbed '*The Arbiter'*.

He wondered what the old man would feel deep within him if he got his hands on the DVD-R from the U.S. embassy in Nigeria.

Terry was quite surprised at the way he felt about this sensitive issue. Was it the African in him acting up? He wondered. Maybe he felt a kinship with the oppressed, impoverished, and exploited peoples of Africa. Why not, he was one of them. In there was his ancestral home. Somewhere! Maybe it was time he traced his roots. The genealogists could help these days.

Then Condoleezza Rice. She was taken off her academic tuft and thrown into the hot pot of Middle East's increasingly complex diplomacy. Could not possibly survive it all in spite of being the most powerful African-American woman in the history of the U.S. politics. Interestingly, Condoleezza had taken over a controversial State Department from Powell who was forced off political prominence.

Colin Powell happened to be one of the first high profile victims of the Iraq debacle. What was going on in the East Coast? Were power-shots in Washington deliberately roping promising African-Americans into these tarnishing imbroglios to derail their political futures?

It was a foregone conclusion that Powell was a White House candidate as far back as the Bill Clinton era.

Powell had gone under too conveniently.

If anything, it would maintain the status quo in America governance. As at then, Powell was unequivocally the most influential African-American in the U.S. political terrain.

Yes, most ordinary Americans had moved off the

racism road built by those old, long-gone, no-good, transatlantic adventurers. Even conservative Britons had shuffled ahead, perhaps grudgingly, from core racism, Paul Canoville would admit. But the facts remained that pockets still lurked in dark, dingy corners. Old beliefs died hard. Conservatives rarely changed; it was why they were called that – conservatives.

It seemed, as it were, that such caste had constituted themselves into groups of powerbrokers in Washington who were after all still not prepared for an African-American presiding over a fourteen trillion dollar economy. It seemed then that Obama's fate was sealed though his record, while not as lengthy as any of Rice and Powell, was nevertheless as impressive.

Terry sighed; taking a moment to reflect on the future of a race he belonged.

Obama coming into the race for the White House had introduced another dimension to the responsibilities which had been hitherto shouldered – perhaps tacitly – by the political leaders over in South Africa since the dawn of its democracy.

One after the other, African states had, predictably, gone into disastrous ruins soon after each had finally wrestled the remains of its battered soul from the savages of predaceous colonialism. Which left the Black Race with only one nation as its last foothold – South Africa; running one of the most sophisticated economies of the world's Emerging Markets.

By default therefore; South Africa shouldered the responsibilities of determining before a watching, skeptical West what direction the entire Black Race would be perceived to be heading – above or below

water. It was the only way the West knew; it was
the only way it could relate to Africa and Africans –
how were they going to perform in the strange road
they have been forced to walk?

If Ọbásanjó could pull off the coming democratic
election, Nigeria would have joined the West-
brewed democratic system whose waves were
sweeping through the entire world these days.
Having had about four decades to clean up its acts
after its devastating civil war, such a successful
democratic culture would be instrumental to the
desired political stability, which Nigerians needed
for economic prosperity. Only in this milieu could
the entrepreneurial skills of Nigerians yield
dividends for their economy. After all, prosperity of
the sort brewed by the Caucasian-dictated living
style in present civilization can only be propped up
by a prescribed critical combination of governance
and commerce on a backdrop of ongoing science.
The three factors must constitute a closely
interactive and mutually beneficial tripod.

Besides, Nigeria would be better placed to
prevent the sort of exploitative and destructive
politics that had devastated Sudan under Omar al-
Bashir.

On the back of abundant natural resources and a
vibrant, hardworking, and intelligent population
that accounted for nearly fifteen percent of the
entire continent, the stage could be set for a country
that could be to Africa what China had been to Asia.

Maybe then, Nigeria could have the political and
economic shoulder strong enough to share with
South Africa in the Herculean responsibilities of
charting a path for the down-trodden Black Race on
an alien terrain.

African-Americans would probably have shared in these responsibilities but for one thing. Though liberated – somewhat – like any other Black Race all over the world, they were still short of full participation in the race's complete self-determination within the United States' political system. Reason? They have no country to run. Yet! Which was where Obama came in.

If Obama could clinch the White House, it was reasonable to believe that the Union Building would have less of a headache carrying the Black Race on its shoulders. If he failed, the existing weight of responsibilities on the Union Building would simply increase in geometric folds. Simple. Except Nigeria could pull its acts together.

Terry switched his mind back to the issues of Pablo and the DVD-R, leaving Union Building's headache to Union Building, Aso Rock's rough road to Aso Rock, and Obama's problems to Obama.

The question now was how this DVD-R could have interested Pablo, a mere Casino owner who happened to have come across some crooked millions.

Again, Terry was assaulted by that frustrating feeling that the key to it all was somewhere close to his conscious awareness but somehow out of his reach. He however had a starting point, Pablo.

Terry needed to dig.

As dusk came in LA, Terry set about his assignment.

53

Dúró came into Ikeh's house late night.

Throughout the long drive from San Diego, Dúró had monitored several radio channels. Not a whisper about the North Rexford saga. During a meal break in Santa Ana, he had been on the lookout for television news that might allude to the murders or the robbery. Nothing.

Dúró was a bundle of contrasting emotions.

Happiness because he had driven all the way from Tijuana across the border without the police arresting him. Confusion and fear because he simply had no idea what was going on.

What had happened at North Rexford?! It was now more than thirty-six hours! Had no one found out about the robbery and those who were dead inside the house? Surely, someone was bound to notice something! Whatever! What about the woman who owned the house as well as the diamonds? Hadn't she found out? Hadn't she returned from out of town or something?

Back in the house, Dúró carefully went from one room to the other looking for any clue that LAPD had visited. Nothing. Six gruesome murders and diamond robbery in a highbrow Beverly Hills house, not a whisper. The silence was too deafening!

244

Dúró decided he was going to be taking one day at a time. He would not panic otherwise he might give himself away. Having taken such a stoic decision, he braced himself to face the fact that any moment now the police would show up mean and wild. He was prepared.

Twelve midnight had come and gone.

It was now early Monday. Dúró had not been able to sleep. Each time he heard distant sirens wailing, he decided the time had come. His mouth would go dry and his heart would start racing but nothing would happen.

Settling noises of the night originating from the house's superstructure would set his blood boiling. Maybe it was a group of police officers creeping up the corridor outside his bedroom to affect his arrest. He was all chewed up.

Despite the bone-weary tiredness of the long hours of driving, he was unable to sleep. His mind was whirling, alert, and full of jumbles of conflicting thoughts. He had turned on and turned off the TV a dozen times! He could not concentrate.

Headache came and went. He hadn't even the energy to go to the first aid cupboard at the bathroom for an aspirin or something. What was he waiting for? The worst he decided.

At 3 O'clock in the morning, Dúró got off his bed and decided to prowl through the flat. If anything, it would give him something to do beside self-immolation.

He started with Emeka's room.

He could not help but produce a sad grin as he turned on the light. The room was crowded but

orderly and cozy. It combined a sitting room with a
bedroom and a study. It was Emeka's little world;
complete in itself.

The big bed was to the left of the door, pushed
against the wall adjacent the only window in the
room. Emeka loved the arrangement. It gave him an
impressive view of the lush garden at the backyard.

The drape was thick, giving the room an artificial
coolness and privacy that Emeka had always loved.
Under the window was a bedside reading table, a
reading lamp, and stacks of books. At a discreet
corner of the big table were framed photographs.

One portrayed the tall beautiful frame of
Emeka's fiancée, Chiamaka. Another showed
Emeka. Others showed Emeka and Chiamaka
together in varying poses. Still, others revealed
Emeka's entire family of father, mother, four
younger ones and two elder brothers.

Dúró stared at the photographs for a while
wondering if he would ever see these lovely people
again.

He sighed.

Had the demise of Emeka anything to do with
the vows, which he took at the shrine with
Chiamaka in Nigeria and broke? He had caught
Emeka with a lady! And when Dúró pressed, Emeka
had finally admitted there had been several ladies.
Was that the cause? Was that a curse? Dúró just
couldn't tell. He figured however that the answer
ought to be 'yes' if he, Dúró, believed it was Tóbi's
love via the locket that had so far saved his life.

He closed the wardrobe, put off the light, and
exited, closing the door.

Ikeh's room was down the hall, the farthest, most
private, and the biggest. It was the bungalow's

master bedroom. Ikeh always kept the door locked.

Dúró produced its key from the bunch with him which he had retrieved from the Dodge's glove compartment and opened the door.

As usual, the immensity of the room awed him. Ikeh had class and taste, and the money to feed them. The room was like Emeka's in arrangement, only it was uncluttered and expensively furnished.

Here and there, there were collector's items, which Ikeh had picked up over the last few years from auctions, exhibitions, and garage sales.

There was an antique lamp stand, a reading table, and two footstools. A funny-looking bedside telephone box reminded Dúró of movies cast in nineteenth century Europe.

A stride from the big bed, towards the right was a hand-made, all-brass coat stand that could not have arisen from anytime later than the nineteenth century.

The curtain rails too belonged to the same era. Close to the French window were two sofa beds placed so Ikeh could catch both the early morning and the late evening sun.

Quite odd that Ikeh would readily consent to leave all these behind, Dúró thought fleetingly.

The wardrobe next to the door to the bathroom commanded his attention. It was a walk-in type with four doors. The lighting had been designed such that as soon as a door was thrown open the soft brilliant glows came on. It was like a small low-ceilinged room.

Ikeh opened the door and walked into a soft glow of neon lighting. The rows of clothes, shoes, and accessories were all neatly arranged like it was a departmental store. There were scores of them.

Dúró walked among them, feeling fabrics and leathers and taking in the distinct odor of factory sprays on most of the patent leather shoes. These were sure to cost a bundle. To think that Ikeh was leaving them all behind.

Dúró sighed. Ikeh was dead, murdered.

He turned to head for the exit from the wardrobe and caught a movement to his right. He jumped with a start hitting his head on the low ceiling.

The guilty were afraid, he thought. He had only walked in front of the wardrobe's floor-to-ceiling dressing mirror to his right and his reflection was the movement caught in the periphery of his vision.

He turned to the mirror staring at himself. Much as he had tried since leaving North Rexford early Saturday, the strain still showed.

The bloodshot eyes and the bags under his eyes meant he hadn't slept well. He leaned against the wall; head drooped and wept, overwhelmed by it all. He hadn't meant to. Nevertheless, he couldn't help it.

His crying was however cut short as he found his palm, which was against the wall going inwards, into the wall. Dúró jerked his hand off and stared at that section of the wall. A chunk was receding like a piston within a cylinder. It was a round chunk sinking noiselessly. Dúró stared, amazed.

54

As soon as the sinking section of the wall stopped moving inwards, the floor-to-ceiling mirror started sliding along a horizontal axis to the right.

A small closet was revealed.

The closet was divided into four sections. Each section housed an assortment of goods and weapons. On the first shelf were two pistols, some clips of ammunitions and gun silencers. There were also other gadgets that Dúró could not recognize.

The second shelf housed a laptop bag with the laptop locked in. Beside it was an executive type briefcase with combination lock.

The third shelf contained pouches of various types and sizes. Though much bigger, the pouches share similarities generally with the pouch that contained his diamonds from North Rexford.

Dúró ventured into the pouches and was shocked. They all housed one type of precious stone or the other. Dúró was not versed in these stones but they sure looked a sight.

They shimmered brilliantly within the pouches, seeming to possess their own inner light. These were bound to cost a fortune. They were Ikeh's trading commodities. How could he have chosen to leave all these behind?

Suddenly, Dúró was intrigued.

The fourth shelf contained electronic gadgets, which Dúró thought must be listening, or recording devices. Maybe even, radio transmitting devises. What was Ikeh doing with these sorts of things, including sophisticated guns?

Ikeh had said he never dealt in guns! Oh yes, Dúró answered his own probing, but he never said he did not have one ... or two. With silencers to match. And clips of ammunitions!

Now, Ikeh was really fascinated.

Dúró decided to lug out both the briefcase and the laptop and take a look at the contents.

The combination lock might be tough to break, Dúró decided, so he took the fastest and surest method available. If he began guessing randomly, he might still be at it until daybreak. Instead, he began from the very beginning.

There were three number slots on the lock. The combination possibilities would not exceed one thousand. He would start with the least: 000 then proceeded to 001, 002, 003 ... on and on and all the way to 999, which would be the last of all the possibilities. In between those one thousand possible combinations would be the one to the lock.

He felt that he could spin a combination number within five seconds, possibly a whole lot faster since each new number combination was simply a flick of the last digit to the right. He only had to flick two digits once in every ten and all three once in every hundred.

It was therefore a very liberal timing to have assumed five seconds as the average for each combination. Going at five seconds per combination therefore, Dúró felt he could spare five thousand seconds. That was eighty-five minutes or thereabout to open the briefcase. Liberally, two hours! Tops!

As it turned out, the combination was 624, which took about an hour.

Neatly stacked in the briefcase were four dossiers. One at a time Dúró went through the dossiers, all four. They were bombs!

The first three were on three people, one to a person. They were the three who ran a company called LAZULINE. There was a Chief Executive Officer and two assistants.

The fourth dossier was about the company itself, everything neatly catalogued.

Going through the dossiers, one would readily realize that this was the company for which Ikeh worked. Clearly, Ikeh had compiled all the data.

Dúró went through the files repeatedly, making sure to understand the implications.

It was shocking!

Ikeh had neatly chronicled everything, which a typical prosecuting attorney would need to sink the company. From the details provided, the company was more or less an elaborate smuggling outfit.

On the other hand, the dossiers could be very effective at blackmailing any or all of the subjects concerned.

Was Ikeh doing or hoping to do just that? One could never know now.

Nevertheless, one thing was bound to happen when this case busted open. Someone in LAPD would come searching this house and these compilations would be found. FBI would undoubtedly become involved, and INTERPOL would get into the picture. Dúró knew for certain that the ripple effect was bound to touch him somehow.

Already, he was tied in with the North Rexford murders and diamond robbery. Now this. It would be a media circus, all desecrating Ikeh's memory. No, he could not afford to rubbish Ikeh's name posthumously, not this way. There was only one option – destroy the files.

He thought about this for a while and decided it was just the panacea to his predicament. Before that however, the laptop.

55

In one of the inner pockets of the Laptop bag was an unlabelled DVD-RW.

Dúró put that aside and descended on the computer first.

An hour later, Dúró was still battling to get into the computer. It was password protected, expectedly.

Dúró felt he was invading Ikeh's property, his private life and he felt ashamed of his act. Especially now that Ikeh laid dead somewhere in Beverly Hills.

Nevertheless, something told him to continue with his intentions. Dúró succumbed to the second inner voice. It was about time he started heeding his inner commands, he thought firmly. Just then, he got through; he was in the computer.

Running through the folders, he realized that many of the files contained therein were again password protected. He was fed up. If getting into the mainframe could take this long, getting into each folder, each file would take even longer.

Besides, what was he looking for anyway? He turned his attention to the DVD-RW. He inserted it into the DVD-ROM drive and opened it in a Windows page. It opened right away. No passwords! It contained four gigabytes of data. Huge. A program called DRAINPIPE laid before him! Owned by American businessmen! Hidden within the America embassy in Lagos! Dúró spent hours reading through. Shocking! It was more or less a detailed version of the dossiers.

The big question now was; who really was Ikeh? What had Ikeh got to do with it all? What was he doing with these sophisticated gadgets? And guns? Who really was Ikeh?

Now Dúró debated with his conscience whether to destroy the disc along with the dossiers.

What these American businessmen had going in West Africa was not only illegal but against the well-being of the economies of the countries involved. Granted that the primogenitocratic governments of these countries were doing worse to their economies and peoples. Still it ceded no right to these American businessmen to milk the sub-region dry.

DRAINPIPE was better exposed. LAPD would blow the top off it when the disc was discovered. Dúró was not going to destroy it. In the very competitive milieu of the American society, the police department would crucify the people behind DRAINPIPE. In addition, Dúró knew that the America media, as well as the public, would in turn crucify the government. Especially with the ongoing Iraq imbroglio.

As dawn came in Hollywood Boulevard; West Los Angeles, Dúró destroyed all four dossiers and flushed the burnt remains down the W.C.

Now the briefcase.

There was a slight problem. Half of it was metal and would not burn down to ashes unlike the dossiers, which were mere papers. Again, he did not want to return it empty into the closet. It might be suspicious, more so that the cops might find his fingerprints all over it.

His predicament was soon solved when he remembered those pouches of precious stones in the closet. He loaded them into the briefcase. Then he meticulously wiped the briefcase free of his prints before returning it to the closet.

56

Terry had traversed the United States from the West coast to the East, searching and probing but discreetly.

Pablo was the starting point. Terry had taken the archive apart and pressured contacts with deep reaches here and there. The expedition had paid off. Now everything made a perfect sense.

Pablo was buying for Alfred Reeds, a political heavyweight in the Bush administration and a 2008 Republican presidential contender.

Now it all made sense why Pablo was in such a frenzy to get at the DVD-R. He was being blackmailed by Alfred Reeds to acquire the DVD-R.

A political chess was going on that was a direct fall-out of Bush's FLIGHT.

Yes! So!

A very ambitious program was concocted by a man with honed instincts at preserving the prosperity of his country – and by extension, race. Terry had no problems with that. It was only patriotic.

Whatever anyone said of Bush; irrespective of who deserted him while he pursued FLIGHT, the fact of it was simple really. Bush wanted every single drop of oil he could lay his hands on not only in the Middle East but in the Gulf of Guinea to keep America's economy ticking like never before. And he was getting it. In itself, this was not Terry's worry.

Problem was that this was making Terry's life a living hell. Which was where Terry drew the line.

The main players were in two camps. There was Kim Holland and his DRAINPIPE buddies in one camp while Alfred Reeds, Jack Nicholas, and Lewis Howitzer were in the other.

In the ongoing game, the political death of one group was the triumph of the other. No in-between. No compromise. Both camps were so deep in the dirt that they could not back down. Backing down would be tantamount to self-destruction.

The DVD-R on DRAINPIPE was the determinant factor that could dictate the fate of each group.

Who was right and who was wrong was a question of morality, which was never Terry's terrain. One thing he did not like though, he would not take kindly to anyone trying to sacrifice him on the altar of personal greed.

Kim Holland had.

Terry was angry with himself. He was getting too careless. He ought to have seen this long before going after Ikeh and that DVD-R. Nevertheless, not all was lost. He intended getting to the bottom of it all. The first step was the retrieval of the copy Ikeh had made.

He decided to start with the house in West L.A. If the DVD-R were not there, he would think of where else to look. There would be clues. There had to be. There always were. All he had to do was buckled up and did his jobs well.

Now that the politically embattled National

Security Advisor was in the picture and in Terry's grips, other possibilities crept into light. Terry felt that if he played this game just the right way, he stood to make more gains than he had previously envisaged.

The National Security Advisor had in his possession what could afford Terry vast wealth and influence. This could be unfettered access to data and information from the National Security Agency and its seemingly impregnable Fort Meade. Alfred Reeds went around with the key to this.

Now, more than ever, Terry devoted more attentions to the details.

57

Today was Wednesday.

It had been two days since Dúró destroyed those files from Ikeh's wardrobe. Still he could not halt his gradual slide into madness. Nothing made sense. His dead friends had disappeared into nothingness. He lived in constant fear of ending the same way. And still there was nothing he could do about it.

His nostalgia for Emeka was stifling. An inseparable pair, they argued most times, disagreeing in principle. Nevertheless, they got along beautifully.

Emeka was an open, welcoming extrovert. Dúró was generally calm, suave, and more of an introvert. They complemented each other, creating a sort of balance that wouldn't have been had they not been who they individually were.

Until now, Dúró did not really know how much he was fond of Emeka, how much they meant to each other. It was this harmony that was so missing.

He felt so alone, so isolated from everything that constituted sound living despite the fact that he worked and walked amidst a teeming population.

Home was worse! He scarcely ate. These days, home was a screaming silence that would eventually dispossess him of his sanity if things continued this way.

In the previous two days, he was at work. Though nothing had happened; closing times were a dread. The two previous nights were like a lifetime in hell. However, the sedatives from the first aid cupboard helped.

In this stifling loneliness, a thought came to Dúró. If he continued to await an unknown development, he might be found guilty of complicity by silence. He felt he had to make a preemptive move.

His resolve therefore was to call the police by the close of work today. He was going to report Emeka and Ikeh missing. And he was still going to stick to all his stories.

Hopefully, he would be asked to come down to the police headquarters to make a signed statement. What was more; it would be a long session of questions and answers. After this, he would think of something else to occupy his time.

"Hey there, D," a colleague shook him by his shoulder. "Time to go."

Dúró jerked around from his ruminations and looked up. The time was ten minutes overdue.

"Thanks, Fein," Dúró said dolefully.

"Yunno, man," Fein said, offering one of her beautiful smiles. "Maybe you need to see your doctor. You're really not looking good."

"Yes."

"In fact you look like shit. Anything I can do to help?"

"You've done it, Fein, showing that you care. Thanks."

"All right, man. See you tomorrow then."

"Yes! Tomorrow," Dúró said and headed home.

He never got home. He was expertly abducted from a sidewalk.

58

Dúró woke up to pitch darkness.

His chest ached. He reeked of chloroform, which was pressed against his nostrils to send him unconscious as he was abducted.

He was splayed out face down on a crucifix. His head was held in a big vice. He could hear voices around him, somewhere beyond his head. From the way the voices of his captors echoed, Dúró knew they were in a warehouse. Pretending to be unconscious, he tried to concentrate on each of the voices. There were at least four or five. One seemed to be the boss.

They were in a heated conversation. But Dúró could not make out the sentences clearly. Then suddenly there was a lull and someone pronounced: "He is awake, boss."

"Give me the gun," a commanding voice snapped. Dúró wetted his pants and began struggling against the restrains. It was useless.

He could barely move a muscle! These people were professionals in this sort of thing, Dúró realized. Again, it seemed they were going to torture him! The questions were: for what? Who were they?

Dúró wanted to shout, to talk, to beg, to cry, but

he could only make throaty goggling noises deep inside him.

These people could start cutting him in half and he would not be able to utter a sound. The shuffling of feet told Dúró they were coming towards him.

"Make the vice tight!"

"It's tight, boss!"

"Make it tighter!"

Someone shuffled near and a split second later, Dúró felt his head threatening to crack open as the tight vice was made even tighter.

"Make the goddamn vice tight, goddammit! He's not feeling the pains! Or is he dead?"

"No, boss, he just can't make a noise is the problem."

"Why's that?"

"His mouth is downwards, boss, against the vice. We have to place him face up; otherwise he can't fucking talk!"

"Then do it! And make it snappy! I've got things to do! And blindfold him!"

Few men rushed to Duro's side and in a minute had the crucifix turned the other way round. Again, his head was back in the vice and a blindfold in place.

"Please," Dúró mumbled, his throat dry, his voice quivering. "I will do whatever you want, just don't hurt me."

"Shut your mouth until you are asked to open it!" a voice snapped rabidly. "You shot four of my people! That was a big mistake! Now, I don't care a hoot what you did to your fellow African thieves but you left their corpses in my house, my sofa ... and you made away with my properties!" the voice said, shouting the last sentence.

Against the backdrop of the previously whispered, viciously hissed words, Dúró felt the shout like a thunderclap. He wetted his pant again.

"My hard-earned diamonds!" the vicious words continued. "My DVD-R ... and ... and you smashed ... you had the gut to smash a forty hundred dollars worth of computer hardware! Now you think you can walk the streets anywhere in the America continent?! Too bad; it's just too goddamn small for the two of us!" Then Dúró felt something crash down on his head. Once again, he lost consciousness.

———————

Dúró woke up sometimes later.

How long he had been unconscious, he did not know. Just that now, he hurt more. His head ached badly, threatening to split open.

The vice was tighter. He was completely wet from the icy water they had been throwing over him to make him come around. Plus his urine.

At least now, Dúró knew one thing. This was the misery of North Rexford all over again. These people had mistaken him for Godwin. All the same, he was still confused. Who were they?

"He's around boss!" someone howled.

Feet shuffled close.

"Where are they?" the boss snapped in Dúró's ears.

"What?" Dúró croaked, his voice cracking.

"Don't play games with me or I'll fucking crush your head right now and be done with it!"

"No boss!" a voice cautioned, alarmed. "We gotta know where to get the disc first!"

"And my bloody diamonds!" the boss boomed again. "One and a half million!"

Dúró was shivering. His bowel loosened.

"It … it was … it wasn't me … Godwin … he did it … killed everybody …"

"What's he talking about? I'm talking about …"

"It was Godwin, Sir. I swear to God it …"

"What's that smell, Mo?" the boss demanded, momentarily ignoring Dúró.

Someone sniffed around Dúró's frame then made a pronouncement. "He shit, boss! Can we go clean him?"

"Hell no!" the boss boomed. A split second later, the muzzle of his gun was jammed against Dúró's genitals. "I will count to five. If you don't tell me where my diamonds and my disc are, I will blow off your fucking prick." He began counting.

"One!"

"God! No! It wasn't me …"

"Two!"

"Godwin. It was …"

"Three!"

"Please!"

"Four!"

"I only have my share. Please. Oh God!"

"Five!"

"Noooh!" Dúró shouted, as he heard the loud crack of the gun. He lost consciousness again.

59

"Wake him up!" Dúró heard someone shouted.

Another was hitting him hard and repeatedly to inflict as much pain as possible.

"He's awake, boss."

"All right," the boss answered coming close. "You are a very lucky man."

Indeed. Dúró was lucky. The boss had forgotten to thumb off the safety catch of his gun while trying to shoot Dúró's genitals.

What Dúró had heard therefore was the sharp crack of the firing pin hitting the metallic guard between it and the single bullet in the chamber. Dúró had fainted out of fear.

"Your share, you said," the boss was saying, his voice now very calm, almost courteous. "Your share of my diamonds, you were saying."

"They gave it to me, Sir."

"Who?"

"Emeka. I was in the Dodge at the curb. I was the lookout. I didn't go in."

"So?"

"It was he!"

"He who?"

"Godwin ..."

"We don't know about any Godwin, mister, you

266

better start thinking fast."

"Please, Sir. Let me tell you the whole story."

"The summary. In two minutes."

Dúró poured out his guts. He sang about everything. This included the false closet in Ikeh's room, the computer, the disc in its drive, and what he felt of Ikeh.

Pablo did not believe Dúró's story though he listened to him attentively during the narrative. However, Pablo learnt some things and heard some reassuring words like: *'the disc in the laptop in the wardrobe'* and *'the diamonds in the pouch in a safe deposit box in San Diego'*.

Pablo was tingling all over with the anticipation of retrieving the elusive disc. How it could have gotten into Ikeh's laptop after Ikeh died, Pablo had no idea given Dúró's account. He wasn't ready for logics.

All he wanted was the disc. Then he would send a bunch of his men down to San Diego to retrieve the diamonds. After that, he would work on Dúró some more. Dúró had to know where the remaining diamonds would be.

First the disc. With that, he could get the NSA off his back.

The entire group of five was ready in half an hour.

In the interval, Dúró had been accorded the dignity of cleaning himself and a change of clothing.

About to leave, he was again blindfolded. Ankle and wrist cuffs were clamped on him. His ears were stuffed with wads of cotton wool.

In effect, some of his vital senses were taken away from him to achieve as much disorientation as possible without the recourse to drugging.

No one trusted Dúró really but the scent of the disc at Ikeh's house was too strong a beckon to ignore. Pablo had to check it out while Dúró was used as the insurance package that would guarantee delivery.

As the group drove towards Ikeh's home, Dúró had time to put his thoughts together.

———————

Now Dúró knew why nothing had been heard about the saga at North Rexford. These people under the leadership of the one called The Boss had obviously been behind it all. The boss – and not some claimed woman – owned the house, those four dead people, the smashed laptop, and the diamonds.

The summary brought everything out in its stark reality: *Ikeh was in North Rexford to exchange a data disc for the diamonds.*

Now the big question was: why had Ikeh involved him and Emeka in whatever deal he had going at that Beverly Hills house?

Dúró had no answers.

60

After what seemed forever, someone took off the blindfold across Dúró's eyes and removed his earplugs.

The sound of the humming engine was like the roar of a waterfall as he emerged from a previous graveyard silence. The journey continued while his eyes adjusted to the darkness within the back compartment of the SUV.

He could make out three figures with him. The man opposite him was white. He was about fifty with a hard cold look from a taut face. The man pushed his face close to Dúró's and said in a menacing tone: "You make any sound at all except you are asked; I will blow your head off. Make no mistake about that." Dúró shivered. "Here," the man continued, raising his gun for Dúró to see. "I'm not like him," he said, jerking his head to indicate the boss who was in the front passenger seat. "The safety catch of this piece is always off. I sawed it off myself. I pull the trigger, a bullet comes out. Got that?" Dúró nodded nervously. "Good," the man said, "for you, that is."

The rest of the journey was in silence, mostly through alleyways and back streets. The nearer they got to Ikeh's house, the more frightened Dúró became.

What would they do to him after retrieving the disc? What if he had mistakenly wiped out the content of the disc when he read it the other time? What if it was the wrong disc? Or even worse; what if the disc had been stolen? His mind was a whirlwind of frightening contemplations.

Eventually, they got to the street, parked at an obscure corner, and led Dúró to the house. It was getting to dawn by the streak of graying in the eastern sky.

One of the men produced the house keys taken off Dúró earlier and whispered fiercely: "I hope for your sake this key works with the lock as you said."

"Yes sir! I swear it works," Dúró whispered back. "The key has an electromagnetic chip within it primed to turn the house alarm off once it is inserted into the lock. If it is the wrong key, merely inserting the key will set the alarm off."

"Good," said the man as he inserted the key into the lock and turned it once, his head cocked, listening.

The bolts could be heard sliding off the locks. The man pressed the door handle, pushed the door open, and then quickly stepped to one side. This left Dúró framed in the doorway. If anyone had shot from the inside, Dúró would have stopped the bullets with his body. That was not Dúró's worry; he knew the house was safely theirs. What worried him was what lay in the wardrobe.

A powerful wave of nostalgia suddenly seized Dúró. He wanted to go home. He wanted to go back to Nigeria, to his fiancée, his parents, brothers, and sisters. Home was home.

"Get going pal!" snapped the man who had

opened the door to the house. Another shoved him roughly from behind jarring him awake from his self-pity. Duro preceded the party into the living room. All had guns drawn.

"Mo," Pablo said, "You and Ben, take a look around."

"Yes, boss," said Mo motioning to Ben.

They took the corridor off the dining area towards the study to begin a methodical search. Dúró realized that Mo was the mean-looking one. Ben looked a bit more agreeable.

"Duke?"

"Yes, boss!"

"Go round the house and keep your eyes open."

"Yes, boss," said Duke as he headed for the back door.

"You," Pablo motioned to Dúró, "let's go get the frigging laptop and the disc. And remember, you will be the first to go if anything happens."

Dúró nodded and shuffled towards Ikeh's room as fast as the ankle cuffs would allow. In the bedroom, Pablo released his handcuffs and stepped back.

"Keep the wardrobe doors open and take the clothes on your path off the hanger as you proceed to … to this mirror of yours. If anything obstructs my sight, 1 will immediately start shooting. Am I clear so far?"

Dúró nodded. "Yes, sir."

"Remember … this time the safety catch will not be mistakenly left on."

"Yes sir."

Pablo stepped back, his gun aimed. Dúró heard the soft click that said the safety catch had been thumped off. He was faint with fear. He threw open the two doors in front of him and the lights within the wardrobe came on glowing brilliantly in the early dawn.

He proceeded into the wardrobe, removing clothes from his path. He got to the mirror and pressed a palm on the false wall to its left until it started going inwards. He looked towards Pablo whose gun was still pointed at him and shivered. He diverted his attention to the task at hand.

The mirror slid to one side, revealing the closet.

Dúró's mouth went dry. The laptop was gone.

61

Dúró stared speechless at Pablo, not knowing what Pablo would do to him.

At that point, Dúró heard a rather urgent call from the corridor outside Ikeh's bedroom. Pablo heard it too. It sounded like Mo's voice.

"What the hell is it?" Pablo shouted with a hushed tone, his eyes still on Dúró.

Silence.

"Mo!"

Silence.

"Ben!"

Not a sound.

Pablo forgot about Dúró and turned towards the doorway. He took two steps in that direction and suddenly stopped as if he had collided with an invisible wall.

From Dúró's position, he saw a look of surprise come on Pablo a fraction of a second before he heard the familiar angry spit of a silenced gun.

Dúró did not wait to see exactly what was happening. He knew what it was! The signature was clear enough!

From the corner of his eyes, Dúró saw Pablo sink onto his knees still staring in the direction of the door, gun in hand.

Dúró hid himself in the farthest depth of the wardrobe as best he could. Then he heard the deep rumble of Godwin's (Terry) voice.

"You came in too late, pal. I got it first and I'm keeping it."

Then there was a slight shuffle and Godwin (Terry) came into the wardrobe. Bent over because of his height relative to that of the wardrobe, he looked around briefly then exited.

Dúró stayed in hiding. He counted up to two hundred before deciding it was safe enough to venture out of the wardrobe.

Pablo was on the floor, dead, a hole with a red petal rim in between his eyes. He was still clutching his gun. Dúró moved into the corridor. There, Mo lay. He too was dead, his gun still in hand.

The picture was all too familiar. He knew Ben would be dead somewhere in the house. Outside the house, Duke too would be as dead as a doornail.

In the sitting room, Dúró found Ben, but he wasn't dead. He was propped up on a sofa with a bleeding shoulder wound. Ben was right handed; the bullet had been through his gun hand. A tourniquet was applied to the shoulder wound; still he had bled profusely.

Ben saw Dúró and gasped: "Too late. It was the man; the one you mentioned ..."

"Yes ... Godwin. It was Godwin."

"Whatever. I told the boss back at the warehouse it couldn't have been you, but he wouldn't believe me. He just wanted someone to take the fall."

"Well ... uh ... I tried to warn you."

"Yeah, yeah! He didn't kill me because ... because he ... he needed to send a message to the guy after Pablo ..."

"Pablo!"

"Yeah, the boss. Someone is after him for that ... that goddamn disc."

"Godwin's got it and Ikeh's Laptop."

"I know. He told me as much. He came in here after killing Mo and the boss and woke me up. I guess I fainted when he shot me," chuckled Ben wincing with pains. "He then applied this tourniquet. Didn't want me bleeding to death, he said. He figured the cops would come in to rescue me after he was gone."

"What about ... the ... the guy with the SUV?"

"Paul? You think he will let Paul live. Not a chance. Don't leave me, will you?"

Dúró nodded; his mouth aflame.

This was a familiar scene. Death all around him. He had survived Godwin's frontal assault once again. He sure was a cat with nine lives.

Ben said not to leave him. Where would he go? What the hell, he chided himself. Nigeria of course. Sweet home! Home was always home! With things as they were, if he got Ikeh's Dodge and drove hard, he would be in San Diego by 10am. He would retrieve his diamonds, confirmed his ticket, and got on the plane this day.

As if Ben knew his thoughts, he said, "The cops will get you, man. Don't even think about running."

"How?" Dúró blurted out frantically, "How would they get me if you didn't tell on me?"

"Oh I wouldn't! Just that by running away you would have confirmed your complicity and guilt in all these. Look around you, man! Make no mistake about it; the U.S. government will extradite you! You saw what they did to the Saddam fellow. They even jailed Noriega, a president in his country.

Picked him right off his presidential palace ... all the
way here to the U.S.! And jailed him! Think, man!"

"Yes," said Dúró distantly. He was rapidly
calculating, considering his options. He had little
time. If he was to do anything, he had to do it fast.

Ben was still talking.

"If you stay and stick with your fancy little story,
you just may make it. If the Godwin fellow doesn't
know you are alive, he will not come after you. If
somewhere along the line the cops pick him up,
then you can help them nail him."

That could be true, thought Dúró. His mind was
racing, sieving mounds of jumbled options.

"Whichever one," continued Ben, his breath
labored from the exertion of merely talking.
"Whichever one, the Godwin fellow wouldn't be a
danger to you."

Makes sense.

"See! If you stayed, you were more likely to
make it through. And when things were settled, you
could retrieve your loot and scrammed."

"Why are you doing this?" stammered Dúró.

"Doing what?"

"Why are you telling me these?"

"Because we can help each other. Help me make
a call and we can be moved out of here before the
cops come."

"We?"

"You don't intend staying here, do you?"

"Well ... I ... I think I ..."

"You definitely can't stay here, man! Suppose he
comes back looking for something? Besides, the
cops will be around soon. You don't wanna be
found with all these, do you?"

Dúró knew Ben was right. He said: "Where will

we go?"

"That's the spirit," enthused a breathless Ben. "Jack will take care of us."

"Who's Jack?"

"Jack is the big shot after Pablo."

"Oh! Well, what makes you so sure he will help us?"

"He will. Oh, he will! If he doesn't … well … then I'll refuse to play ball. Right now he needs us as much as we need him."

"You're not exactly in a position to deal."

"Believe me, man, I am. Thanks to your Godwin."

"He is not my Godwin!" roared Dúró.

"Hey, calm down! I don't have any problem with that."

"What's next?"

"Make the call."

"What's the number?"

Ben told him.

As soon as Dúró hung up, he heard the wail of sirens.

"Time to go, man; goddamn Godwin had tipped the cops off."

"What about my ankle cuffs?"

"In Mo's left pocket."

"What?"

"The keys! In Mo's pocket."

Dúró scrambled to where Mo laid dead and fumbled around in his pocket, got the key, and with shaky hands released the ankle cuffs.

He ran back to the sofa where Ben lay propped up, oozing blood. He looked so white now. Dúró practically carried him out of the house through the backdoor to the discreetly parked SUV.

Paul in the SUV was stone dead.

"Drag him out! Quick!" Ben mumbled half-conscious.

"Onto the side walk?"

"Yeah, sure! You don't wanna keep carrying a corpse around town with the cops on our tails; do you?"

"No!"

"Then hurry with it!"

The siren was almost at the house now.

Dúró dragged Paul onto the sidewalk and then slotted Ben into the front passenger seat. Done, Dúró got behind the wheel of the SUV.

Ben said, "I gotta tell you something!"

"What?" said Dúró gunning the engine to life and leaving the curb.

"The man you know as Godwin is not who you think!"

"What's that mean?"

"Remember I said the man gave me a message to Jack?"

"Yes!"

"Well; what he said was: tell Jack that Terry Valentine wants to meet with him. That's what he said."

"Terry! His name is Terry Valentine?"

"Yes."

"He isn't a Nigerian?!"

"A Nigerian! Are you kidding?! Hell no! There is only one Terry Valentine, man! He is a CIA contract killer. I know him as One-Bullet-Val; OBV."

"My God!" exclaimed Dúró as some pieces fell into place. Indeed. One-Bullet-Val.

"Hell of a guy, OBV! I am honored to have met him," enthused a breathless Ben. "Only few know exactly what he looks like. All we know is that the guy is African-American and damned good; one of the CIA's best."

"He shot you for God's sake!"

"So what? I'm not dead; am I? Still glad I met him."

"Well I am not and never will! He killed my friends!"

"Bad about your friends, man. I am sorry."

The rest of the drive was in gasps of directives as an exhausted Ben steered Dúró to their destination.

62

The murders at Ikeh's house were heating up L.A.

In addition, the gory details had generated controversies not only in the United States but also most countries of the world.

For a number of reasons.

One. Nigerian legal immigrants with no previous police records were involved.

Two. The manner in which they were involved was intriguing – they had all simply vanished.

Three. The pattern readily evident at the murder scene was not typical of mindless gang shootouts. In effect, this was homicide with interesting components.

Four. Pablo, an infamous crime lord, was involved. With Pablo in the picture, the flourishing trade in stolen diamonds became a focus.

Diamond smuggling outfits run by Pablo from West Africa came under intense press searchlights.

In no time, the press had exhumed all the dirt that existed on Ikeh. With it came the relationship, which bound him to LAPD. Simply put, LAPD was culpable by accessory to the facts of Ikeh's smuggling of gemstones from West Africa.

Though LAPD strongly denied this, claiming it

baseless and without merit, popular opinion was to the contrary. The public and popular editorials chewed them out then descended on the politics of blood money and blood diamonds.

Things were not made better by Leavitt's recently released blockbuster movie *"Blood Diamond"* getting rave reviews in not only the US and Europe but also Latin America and Southern Africa.

In West Africa, no one needed the movie around. The people lived the sordid live everyday. It was all around them! All the same, *Blood Diamond* had taken a peep into Africa's agelong exploitation by the West.

Thus, sections in the press were devoted to mineral-producing countries of Africa – which virtually included all – and the devastating effects these had been having on old and evolving military conflicts in same countries.

Talk shows began a circus on blood money and diamonds in manners deeper than Leavitt's movie. The Kimberly Process Certification Scheme came under focus again.

All of a sudden, the discussion veered to civil wars in Africa and the roles of the West, western agencies, and recently China, in the notorious supply of arms in exchange for precious stones and minerals.

It was argued that arms sales to Africa should not be treated as simple commercial exchanges since each transaction actually meant far more than money in exchange for goods.

Each transaction in arms to a typical African state meant that hundreds of thousands of Africans – perhaps millions – stood a very good chance of being murdered, maimed, and rendered homeless by their leaders.

It meant hopes shattered! It meant dreams aborted, aspirations stillborn, growth stunted, development halted, and civilization stopped.

Examples ranged from Angola, the DRC, Rwanda, and Burundi to Somalia and Sudan. The genocidal campaign in Darfur gnaws at the world's conscience with its gory details.

Entered a very politically vociferous Kanye West. Another Mohammed Ali. Could not keep his mouth shut about such injustices even if his life depended on it.

The superstar rapper came onto the scene to fuel the conflagration. After all, it was Kanye who did the hit song 'Diamonds From Sierra Leone', which had been making waves for the last three years. Pablo's strongest diamond smuggling links were into Sierra Leone and Liberia.

Kanye's music howled from every musical box on the continent. It was the first play on every club and radio station in Lagos. The Molụẹ commercial bus and the Danfo commercial mini-bus slammed it all day.

In South Africa where issues to do with diamond smuggling were always big events, Kanye's music blared from every taxis. It was the first play in every club on Rivonia Boulevard in Johannesburg ranging from Teazers to Monaco. It blared from every musical box in the cities, townships, and squatter camps all the way from the Northern Province abutting Zimbabwe to Cape Town.

Tickets to cinemas featuring Leavitt's movie were sold out in instants. The DVDs were instant sellout.

On other fronts, LAPD was still very much baffled about the disappearance of Ikeh, Dúró, and Emeka without a trace. Their descriptions and photographs were with every police organization and news media in the west coast.

By the fifth day, with no headway, LAPD put huge ransoms on each of their heads.

Dúró followed these developments while in hiding.

He and Ben had become friends of some sort. Even Jack Nicholas, who he discovered was a Personal Aide to the country's National Security Advisor and a Republican presidential candidate.

By the end of the first week in the hideout, Ben was up. As Ben recovered and regained his strength, the rapport, which had started at the bungalow in Hollywood Boulevard, was consolidated.

From what Dúró had been picking up, he was starting to see how his life had intertwined with those of Emeka, Ikeh, and Terry; not only in the last four weeks, but from the moment he headed for the U.S. with Emeka.

The whole thing was a tragedy really. If Terry hadn't double-crossed them, maybe it would have worked out.

The corollary was sad indeed. Dúró realized that he and Emeka had signed and sealed their death warrants the moment they decided they were leaving Nigeria to Ikeh's house in California a year or so earlier.

Now he had survived. The thing was; would he survive to the very end? And when was that end?

63

In far away Washington, things were not very cool.

"Why all these publicities?" asked a very suspicious Kim.

"With Pablo it was unavoidable ..." began Neil, but Kim cut into him.

"You think it's got to do with the DVD-R?"

"I got hold of Terry and he said no. It's got nothing to do with us or the disc. We know for sure that Ikeh, Emeka, and Dúró are dead. Terry said he took them out. What most probably happened here was the obvious. Pablo blamed the North Rexford operation on Ikeh and his two dead buddies and descended on Ikeh's house ..."

"Then why the carnage? Who killed them all? Who took out Pablo and three of his boys?"

"An anonymous caller tipped LAPD about the deaths, remember?"

"How the hell will I forget?!"

"He also said that one of Pablo's men got away. To me the person who got away was the double-crossing factor."

"The big question then would be why they turned against each other? What were they doing with handcuffs! And ankle cuffs!"

"The only way to know is to wait until LAPD picks the runaway ..."

"Except he is halfway across Mexico."

Neil shrugged noncommittally. Kim continued: "You think other copies existed?"

"No. Remember we wrote the program in such a way that any copy made off it would be automatically documented. So if a copy was made, I would have known ..."

"Except a copy was made from the original and you are sitting with a copy, not the original."

"What!"

"Think about it!"

"Why would Terry do that? He never operated like that!"

"There is a first time for everything! You think Terry is trying to double-cross us?"

"Why would he? It was not in his character to! Kim, you do have a wild imagination!"

"It's why I'm ahead in this game, Neil. This disc is as important to us as it is to that sonofabitch Reeds! Anyway, anything from Nigeria?"

"Terence had a meeting with Yòmóyè in LZL. He let him know that we are aware they were pinching bits from our 90% share. The Ikeh saga had brought that out ..."

"Thieving bastards!"

"He asked Terence if we had anything to do with Ikeh's rumored death, which is all over the news in Africa. Terence said no, that it was Ikeh's shady deal with LAPD and LA underworld that caught up with him. He ran back to Ikeh's wife with the news. Seems the wife was threatening fire and brimstone."

"Compensations would shut her up and she could get another sucker to fill her lonely bed!" Kim snapped.

"Yes! Precisely what Terence had ordered ..."

"How much?"

"Two-Fifty thousand dollars."

"Goddamn!"

Similar worries were eating into the innards of Reeds and Jack.

"I'm not so comfortable with the wild publicity, Jack! What if Kim and his boys got suspicious of the whole thing?"

"I doubt that. There is nothing to tell Kim that we may be on to Pablo. Besides, it seems the publicity is deliberate by Terry. He tipped the cops to the murder scene deliberately ... going by Dúró and Ben's accounts."

"Why?"

"I can't pretend to say I know why. He must have his reasons. In my opinion though, by bringing in the cops, he had limited what Kim may want to do ... and what Pablo's remaining boys may want to start too. Right now, Pablo's men are in hiding and will remain so for a while. That will be good cover for Terry as he conducts an exchange with us. That's what I think."

"Maybe, Jack! Maybe!"

64

The meeting had been at a Royal Suite in Washington Hilton.

Both knew they had a lot at risk and were discreet.

Reeds waited in the living room of the suite. With him were the two bodyguards arranged for him by Jack. It would be political suicide to use men from the National Security Agency.

Terry walked in and wordlessly took a seat opposite Reeds.

Reeds waved away the bodyguards. Now they were alone.

"You want to see me in person, I understand," Reeds began.

"We both need to talk."

"Oh."

"I guess so. Seems your little pawn Pablo could not tie his shoelace without messing things up. That was how he got into your trap in the first place."

Reeds' heart skipped beats. He said: "What do you mean?"

"You had a hold on him because he was the one who murdered Claire fifteen years ago in that hotel in New York City. Pablo is dead; your hold on him is off. Now you deal with me. You need the disc. I have it."

Reeds' baited breath came out of him slowly. He had a consolation; nothing was ever beyond the reach of this psychopathic CIA killer. "What makes you think I want to deal with you?"

"Then one wonders why you are here ... complete with bodyguards! Besides, I've got all the aces. I have all the discs! You want them; you can only get them though me! Of that, I am certain!"

"Discs! There is more than a disc here then?"

"There are three. I have the original and a copy. Kim has the third, a copy, which he thinks is the original."

"I need to know why there are three discs."

Terry told him.

Reeds nodded his agreement and said: "How much?"

"A million U.S. dollars to be wired to a specified account. Full payment before I deliver."

"That's absurd. Where do you suppose I can source a million. A quarter million is affordable. Half tomorrow and the other half on delivery."

"You weren't listening, Reeds. The price is a million U.S. dollars to be paid fully into my account before I hand over the discs. Otherwise, no deal. I would have thought a million was a small price to pay for the White House."

"I cannot afford a million."

"You've got backers."

"I like to pay the piper. It's the only way I can dictate my tunes."

"It's up to you."

"I can pull half a million, Terry."

Terry was thoughtful.

"I really need that discs," said Reeds. "Half a

million."

"Fully paid before I hand over the discs."

"Agreed; payable before I get the discs."

"All right. Deal! Have it wired to HT 600290V North Oceanic Bank, New York City. I'll give you three days to pull it through. Then I'll set up a rendezvous."

65

The call came at 2:30 pm of the fourth day.

Reeds took it on a secure line in his limousine, heading towards Capitol Hill.

"Smart decision," Terry began.

"Now your end of the bargain."

"We meet in California on Friday."

"Where in California?"

"Bobby Hotel, Santa Monica, Room 52. Be there at 2pm."

"Okay. But I need to be able to verify the contents of the two discs, Terry."

"Naturally."

"I'll bring a laptop."

"Fine with me. I'll come with the discs."

"Deal."

Both hung up. Reeds was in thought. He did some rough calculations.

Bobby Hotel was on Wilshire Boulevard a few blocks away from Fairmont Miramar. Today was Tuesday. Friday was three days away. That was too much rope Terry seemed to be giving him. Why? A trap in the waiting?!

Reeds thought about what Terry could possibly be up to. But he could not put his fingers on anything. Was he being paranoid?

Anyway, concluded Reeds within him; the only way to put an end to this game was to take out Terry. It was the only guarantee that other discs would not crawl to life in future. His half million dollars and his career would amount to nothing if one of his political enemies came up with copies of the disc few weeks down the line. Terry had to go. That decision taken, Reeds called his Aide, Jack Nicholas.

"Yes, sir! Jack here."

"He's setting up a meeting at Bobby Hotel in Santa Monica in three days. I will be in the office in about an hour. Let's discuss the details."

"All right sir, I'll be waiting."

An hour later, Reeds was in a close deliberation with Jack.

"We need to seal that place off, Jack. When I get the discs and I'm satisfied, I'll give the signal. Then we take him out. No matter what happens; Terry must not leave Bobby hotel alive."

"Yes, Sir."

"Then the Dúró fellow."

"Yes, Sir?"

"Bring him along for the exchange. Get him into a cross fire and tell someone to take him out."

"Yes sir."

"With him gone, no one can connect us to the killings. We'll get the diamonds later."

"Yes, Sir."

"Then Ben! He is too streetwise. He will not trust us the way Dúró does. If you bring him along, he will be gone before you can say Jack. Right, Jack?"

"Right, Sir."

"So keep him back in that house. Tell him he still

needs some rest. Give him some more money to make him feel he had helped like Pablo would. Then when the exchange is over, let someone get rid of him. The cops will blame it on Pablo."

"Yes, Sir."

66

2pm Friday.

Reeds was sitting in Room 52; Bobby Hotel, Santa Monica. His laptop sat in front of him. He was ready.

Across the hallway was Room 51. Two men sat there expectantly, armed and ready. Jack's men dotted the hotel. The elevator boy had been replaced. Even the bellhop and the door attendant.

Bobby Hotel was equipped with a rooftop helipad. A helicopter had been rented and on standby with two sharp shooters. It could be airborne and atop Bobby in minutes.

Across the road was a shopping mall. Jack had sharp shooters at strategic positions overlooking the hotel front entrance.

Every exit out of Bobby was covered. Terry would be trapped within. And taken out. Reeds had no choice.

Dúró felt he ought to be one of those in strategic positions; he too armed and itching to shoot Terry to avenge the death of Emeka and Ikeh. Jack had however insisted otherwise; he had asked Dúró to keep his mouth shut as well as stay out of sight.

Parked at the curb close to the hotel's frontage was a rented Cadillac SUV with darkened windows.

It served as the command center. Jack sat at the helm of affairs. Two men were with him to coordinate audio reports from the men in the hotel. Jack was ready.

———

Precisely at 2pm, the telephone rang in Room 52. Reeds jumped. He picked the telephone; it was Terry.

"The exchange will take place at 9:30pm at Ikeh's bungalow in West L.A."

"That wasn't part of the deal."

"Why are you whining, Reeds? You've still got five hours," said Terry. Reeds' heart raced. Was Terry suspicious?

"It's not a question of time, Terry. We had a deal; and you are changing the playing field."

"You wanted the disc; you paid for the discs; and you would get the discs, Reeds."

"Why the change of rendezvous?"

"Call it nostalgia, Reeds. It all began in Ikeh's house; it could as well end there."

"9:30 then."

"Yes."

Reeds hurried out of the hotel room calling Jack as he walked. "He just changed rendezvous, Jack. He called!"

"Yes. We monitored everything."

"Why would he want Ikeh's house?"

"He is limiting our number. That place is a residential neighborhood. There is a limit to what we can deploy against him."

"Do you think he knows about our small army?"

"I think so. We would do well to assume he did!"

"Good. Are we set for him, Jack?"

"Yes."

"Let's move! And bring that Dúró fellow."

"Yes sir,' Jack answered knowing that as far as Dúró's fate was concerned now he had no say, no choice. If he did not produce Dúró at the Hollywood house, the NSA would know he was trying to play games. That would be bad news for him. In his mind, he said a hearty adieu to Dúró.

"Do you have infrared night vision there?"

"I got sixteen."

"Beautiful. Now move, Jack, move. We've got no time."

67

9:30pm, Reeds' men were in place.

Ikeh's house sat in darkness, completely unlit. The glow of LAPD's no-cross lines marked the frontage. As Reeds headed for the entrance to the house, his laptop in his left hand, the no-cross line was a surreal reminder of the carnage that took place here two weeks earlier. And unavoidably still, there had to be another this night. Reeds felt a bit edgy.

Back in the Cadillac SUV, Jack watched his boss cross the police lines. Besides him was Dúró. Turning to him, he asked, "You said there are just two exits."

"Yes, Sir; this front one and a rear exit adjacent the kitchen. But the windows at the back can also be used."

"Good, good."

Reeds got to the door and tentatively turned the doorknob.

The door opened. He knew that Terry was waiting.

Immediately he got into the short hallway towards the living room, a shaded ceiling light came on. Terry's imposing physique dwarfed him from across the room. He sauntered over.

"Sit down, Reeds."

Reeds sat; his laptop on his lap. He said: "The discs, please?"

Terry produced the two discs from the inner pockets of his suit. Reeds couldn't help notice something about Terry these two times they had met; he was a smashing dresser. Terry's suit was dark gray and soft. It was impeccably tailored.

Terry was relaxed, disarming, and so casual that his coolness was unnerving. Was it a natural proclivity or an adaptation that served to mask the stark ugliness that was Terry's core, Reeds wondered, shuddering involuntarily.

He diverted his attention to his laptop, which he switched on. In a quarter of a minute, it was ready.

"The discs, please?" Reeds repeated again. Terry gave him. Reeds noted that one was a DVD-RW and the other a DVD-R.

Reeds' observation did not escape Terry's sharp eyes. He said, "The DVD-R is the original from Nigeria. The DVD-RW is the copy Ikeh made."

Reeds inserted the original copy into the DVD-ROM drive. In an instant, the computer told him the status of the DVD-R: that a copy had been made off it, stating as well the time it was copied.

Whoever wrote the program for the CIA's West Africa operations was good; it was riddled with bobby traps.

Terry was looking over Reeds' shoulder at the screen of the laptop. He said: "Satisfied?"

"I have to see the folders first."

"Be my guest."

Reeds began; punching buttons, opening folders, scanning files, and going through some fascinating details.

Back in the control SUV outside, Jack was in touch with four other SUVs and men ready for action. He was jumpy. His system was full of adrenalin. His heart slammed away.

His boss had not been talking much so Terry would not suspect that he was wired.

Jack began raising men in each of the SUVs to put them in states of heightened alertness. Were field glasses working well? Were the guns checked and double-checked? Were the multi-channel transceivers all operational? Everything was set.

68

Back in the bungalow, Reeds had, in the meantime, gone through the original as well as the copy discs.

He felt satisfied. He switched off the laptop, pocketed the two discs, and stood up. He was confronted by Terry, a handgun adapted with a silencer pointed at his head.

Reeds froze.

Terry had his left index finger on his lips, telling Reeds to hush. Reeds did not utter a word. Then from his pocket, Terry produced a sheet of foolscap paper. On it was written a script of dialogue that was to be between Reeds and Terry. Terry pointed to it and gave it to Reeds.

The first line was an instruction for Reeds to 'drop the laptop'.

So that was the catch!

Reeds' Laptop!

That was why Terry had allowed so much time before the exchange. It was to enable him device this ingenious method to snatch his laptop. It was why Terry changed the rendezvous from Bobby Hotel.

Why hadn't Reeds realized this?

There were about a dozen of such laptops in the National Security Agency. They were specially designed for top-level officers with the highest levels of security clearance. Each unit was a mobile, wireless access to the huge archives of the National Security Agency from any part of the world.

Granted that access was only possible into a unit through the palm print of the attached officer; Terry might have a way around that. If Terry made away and broke into Reeds' computer, Reeds was finished. Now, more than ever, there was a case for eliminating Terry.

Reeds gently dropped his laptop on the sofa he had just vacated and backed off a step.

The second line in the dialogue said that Reeds was 'expected to read out aloud only his line on the sheet and make it look real'. 'You may be carrying bugs', the line said in emphasized italics.

Reeds read his first cue, "It's good doing business with you, Terry."

"Glad we can pull it off," Terry replied. He had memorized his lines, Reeds realized.

"This will go a long way in correcting a lot of ills in our government," Reeds read.

"It is none of my business, Reeds. I have delivered. Go on and be on your way with your little army. Remember, I see anyone I will shoot to kill. If I were you I would hurry out right now to call off the boys with the guns."

"No such thing, Terry, relax," Reeds' line said.

"Well, good to hear that. Now Mr. NSA, be on your way. And good luck at the Republican Convention."

End of the script.

Reeds pocketed the sheet and made for the door in carefully measured strides. His heart was beating so loudly he could hear it within his ears.

Predictably, the light went out. Reeds had hardly gotten to the door when this happened. He opened the door, expecting a bullet through his back but none came. He exhaled, closing the door behind him. Then he began talking rapidly for Jack in the SUV to act.

"He is still in the house and he's got my laptop. My last couple of sentences was a script he made me read aloud at gunpoint. He is armed and he knows you guys are around and ready. I have the discs. Go after him, Jack. Get men sealing all exits from the bungalow and the grounds. He is ready for us."

Reeds could see men scurrying around. Two ran towards him, whisked him off the ground, and practically carried him to the control SUV.

The SUV filled with crackles and static of radio waves being monitored by Jack's men. Reports coming in said five men were searching the house, combing it thoroughly. Men on the grounds said there were no signs of Terry outside yet.

"Where's he gone?" Reeds said worriedly.

"The ceiling?" Someone offered.

"He wouldn't," Jack said. "That would be a cul-de-sac. He would know that. No, he wouldn't. Nevertheless, send in two more men to check the ceilings. Let them go with night vision."

"Yes, Sir," the man said and got on the transceiver.

A minute crawled by. And two. Then three minutes. Yet, nothing.

"What's going on?!" Reeds cried. "He couldn't just turn into thin air and evaporated through the cracks in the windows. And with my fucking laptop?!"

All units were reporting nothing. The ceiling

search was clean. All wardrobes in the house had been ripped out. The one in Ikeh's room with the false closet was taken apart. Nothing.

Cupboards in the kitchen were ripped out. All the bedrooms were ransacked. All windows were opened, toilets searched. The garden was thoroughly searched. Still nothing. Terry had vanished!

"What are we missing here, Jack?"

"I don't know! Where could he have gone?"

"Any cellars?!" suggested Reeds.

"No!"

"Oh!" Dúró exclaimed, a distant look on his face. All eyes in the SUV turned on him expectantly.

"What?!" Jack cried.

"The Ondol!"

"What?!"

"The Ondol!"

69

"What the hell is that?!" cried Jack, eyes wide with worry and anxiety.

"It's a Korea-style floor heating system built originally with the bungalow. It is a series of tunnels built under the floor. Someone can crawl through slowly. If Terry can squeeze well enough, he may be able to pass through."

"Where is the entry?"

"The kitchen."

"Wallace, send men to the kitchen," ordered Jack.

"Yes, Sir," Wallace said getting on the radio.

"What about the exit?"

Dúró was already scrambling out of the SUV. Jack sent two men after him.

Dúró was running; so the two lagged behind. Dúró ran towards the house; veered to its right side and headed for the garden. Just before the high-wall fence that separated the garden from that of the neighbor behind was the service exit for the Ondol.

It was overgrown with shrubs. He parted the shrubs. Even with the darkened backyard, he could make out the marks. They were fresh. Also, the lid was not in place. A gas mask with a portable canister of oxygen lay nearby.

It made perfect sense! Terry had crawled through the tunnels to the outside, breathing through the portable oxygen tank.

70

As Dúró searched around, he heard that unnerving but familiar sound.

Terry's silenced gun. Two spits. Then one more. Dúró knew it meant three dead, two of who must be the ones running to keep up with him.

He did not know from what direction the shots were coming because no sound emanated from any of those people shot. Which made sense; they were usually dead the moment they were shot.

Terry preferred shooting between the eyes or straight through the heart. Either way, death was instantaneous, giving the victim no time at all to make a sound or even bleed. Neat, cute, mercifully professional.

Suddenly, two booms sounded, each from opposite directions. Flashes of gunfire momentarily split the darkness. Then those spits again. Dúró craned his neck searching the dark backyard.

There, he was. Dúró saw the huge bulk of Terry. He was standing over a body, gun in one hand, and a laptop in the other.

Voices were coming closer. Terry looked up ready, ducking slightly. His suit was dark. He rhymed with the background. He was so perfectly positioned that he could skulk around the dark backyard merging with the flora and the ethereal darkness, which he seemed made for, picking them off one after the other until they were all dead.

At that instant, a security light came on. It was on a lamppost next to the fence beyond the garden, just behind Dúró. Sometimes, Ikeh worked in the garden with it at night. Someone had found and thrown the switch from the kitchen. The light outlined Terry clearly.

Terry realized his precarious position and headed for the nearest cover. He was almost there when he saw Dúró amidst the shrubs, silhouetted against the dark shrubs and the glare of the light behind.

Dúró thought he must have looked like an apparition for the reaction his presence elicited in Terry. Terry came to a sudden stop as if he had collided with an invisible wall. His eyes went wide and were fixed unwaveringly on Dúró; eye-to-eye.

Dúró was so frightened he remained rooted to a spot, not even blinking. He just stared at Terry who in turn could only stare back. Both men were completely transfixed.

Terry had thought him dead two weeks back. It most certainly was what elicited this shock in an otherwise shockproof Terry. If Dúró was not paralyzed into immobility, he had ample chance to have shot Terry a thousand times. But he too was as transfixed as Terry though for completely different reasons – fear and shock.

At this instant, the noise of men coming from around the house intruded into the stillness of the moment. Terry snapped out of his trance, momentarily forgetting Dúró. He whirled around and shot the two men coming at him. The muted spit of his gun was however drowned by the sharp reports of automatic weapons from the men.

Dúró saw the two men go down like sacs. Terry had gotten them. But Terry too had been fatally shot. In spite of his injury, Terry's attention began refocusing on Dúró. Terry turned back ever so slowly towards Dúró who was still standing on one spot unable to move; not even lift an arm. Dúró had completely forgotten that in his hand was a gun.

Now, Terry was again face-to-face with Dúró. This made it possible for Dúró to see the full extent of Terry's injury. It was ghastly. The right side of Terry's face was a bloody pulp; the right eye gone with it. It was like a horror movie. Terry's mouth moved but no sound came. Then he began sinking on his knees like a slow motion picture. His remaining eye was still locked onto Dúró's.

Blood gushed down the right side of Terry's neck and Dúró knew that Terry was dying.

Now more men came, saw Terry's vulnerability, and began emptying their clips into him. Dúró watched as Terry's partially obliterated face, still fixed on him in shock disbelief, was blown off from behind. Then the almost headless body toppled over and lay still on the grass.

Terry was still clutching the laptop.

Men were running around now, none seeming to be aware that he, Dúró, was in the shrub and shivering.

Amidst the confusion, Jack appeared and pressed a package into Dúró's hand, wrenched the gun from his nervous grip, and whispered fiercely to him to run.

"When you get around some block, open that

parcel and read the instruction."

"What is ..." Dúró began to ask.

"Just move and avoid the cops, you'll see detail instructions in there. Now move!"

Dúró ran. And ran. From street to street.

Sirens wailed, coming from different directions all heading to the war zone. LAPD was in full gear.

Finally, Dúró felt far removed from the scene and safe enough to open the parcel from Jack Nicholas.

It housed five thousand U.S. dollars, an address in Santa Monica, and a telephone number to call immediately, stating who he was and from who.

———

Dúró located a telephone booth out of the way and placed a call-collect to the number. It was answered on the first ring.

"I am Dúró from Jack Nicholas."

"Where are you?" the voice said in urgent whispers. Dúró gave a detailed description of his location.

"Wait right there! I will be with you in a quarter-hour, tops. Are you shot?"

"No."

"Good. Are you okay?"

"Scared shitless!"

"That's okay! Hang in there."

"Thank you."

The line went dead.

71

"Hi Dúró. I'm Harper."

"Hi!"

"Relax. You're safe now," said Harper as he pulled the car off the curb.

"If you don't mind my asking, what's going on?"

"It seems someone wants you dead."

"LAPD for example?"

"Yeah but also Jack's boss."

"What?! Why?!" Dúró snapped.

"Well, I understand how you feel."

"No, you don't! Why would he want me dead?"

"Tie loose ends, man. Leave nothing to chance."

"God Almighty, why? I am no danger to him!"

"Sure until LAPD grabs you and you spill your guts about all those deaths, ranging from North Rexford to that bungalow you just scrammed from! Catch my drift?"

"But the cops already know these!"

"To a certain extent, yes. The fact is; none of the deaths can be connected to Jack or his boss. If LAPD grabs you, you can establish that connection. That's the real problem. Jack and his boss know that LAPD or the press will cut a deal with you ... or the devil himself ... just to get juicy scoops on political heavyweights in Washington as themselves!"

"But ..."

"See those guys totting guns all over the place shooting at everything and themselves ... they are pawns, Dúró. They are very expendable. Those are the ones people like Jack and Reeds use for dirty deals like these. All will be blamed on Pablo, Ikeh, and that CIA contract killer you know as Godwin. I heard he had taken you through hell!"

"Back and forth, surrounded by corpses with bullet holes. I never saw so many dead bodies in my life. He kills people like we kill chickens at Christmas back in Lagos."

"You are one lucky guy, Dúró; you know that!"

Dúró nodded unable to speak for a while. Then he said: "Why would Jack help me, risk his neck?"

"You gave him a big break, Dúró."

"How?"

"By not running out on Ben. Otherwise Ben might have died and Jack would have lost the discs. For Jack, that would've been bad news, very bad."

Five minutes of silence stretched between them, then Dúró said: "I have to retrieve a parcel down in San Diego."

"It's waiting for you in the house."

"What?"

"We've retrieved the diamonds, Dúró. At a conservative estimate, they are worth five hundred and seventy five thousand dollars, U.S."

"My God, I never knew they were worth that much. Thank you, Harper ..."

"Don't mention."

"So what's next?"

"Some experts are waiting at the house to make you into another face. The documents are set. I will fly with you this night to Miami, Florida. It is cooler on the east coast as it is. From Miami, I will put you on a flight to Jamaica. There, someone will put you on another flight enroute Lagos. Back home, you can peel off the make-up and be Dúró again. End of the show."

"How do I carry the diamonds, Harper?"

"You can't. You'll be caught. We are not taking any risks. The stones are hot ..."

"Meaning?!"

"We believe they are Blood Diamonds! Coming from Pablo, they could not have been anything else. He had a web of smuggling rings stretching all around the globe. West Africa was one of his richest sources. We really expect that somewhere in the disc that's in the middle of these bloodsheds Pablo may pop up. He was that connected to gemstones smuggling cartels in West Africa ... the sort we are trying to burst open."

"So?"

"We've bought the stones off you; we'll sell them later. You cannot carry the cash and we don't want to attract attention by wiring the cash to you. So a special courier will carry the cash. He will be flying with you each moment of the way. As soon as you are on home ground, he'll deliver the cash into your lucky little hands and find his way back to the U.S."

"Thanks, man. I will never forget you guys."

"Hell you could write a book about this some day. Something like: 'a cat with nine lives'."

Dúró grinned broadly. It was his first show of gaiety since a long time back.

72

One and a half years was enough for relatives of Africans seeking greener pastures to expect everything to have turned around.

But for most, it took far longer.

For long periods at a time, communications were cut off. Hopes were never lost. The dollars would eventually come. The second-hand goods would also come; some for use, others for sale.

Occasionally however, the traveler would return in a short while immensely wealthy. Others might come back dejected and wretched. A lot more might never come back. Hope was always alive.

The pattern had been predictably so for about twenty years.

Dúró's return to Nigeria was therefore not seen as anything out of the usual.

Alfred Reeds resigned from George Bush's Cabinet on February 2nd 2007; barely a week after he got the discs from Terry.

By mid-February, Reeds' presidential campaign took off full swing. Six months later, he was the only candidate left in the Republican's Presidential campaign strong enough to present a substantive counter to the huge momentum of the Democrats.

September 2007 saw Reeds taking a break from a successful campaign. He was back in his familiar tuft in the Capitol Hill appearing before a Congressional Oversight Committee. On the day of the first sitting, Dúró sent a postcard to Jack under the name Godwin and wished Jack the best in life.

By this time, Florence, the wife of Late Ikeh, had moved from their Ìkẹjà resident to a plushy house at Victoria Garden City, a Lagos suburb meant only for the exclusively rich.

From what Dúró learnt, the house was bought outright and worth several millions of Naira. Dúró wondered where all that money could have come from. He remembered having destroyed those dossiers on LZL.

The questions he now asked himself were:

'Were there other dossiers?'

'And with whom? Florence?'

But there was a good side to it. Dúró did not have to concern himself with the financial needs of Ikeh's family. Florence and the children were doing well. That halved his headache. Now, he would only have Emeka's family to carry along. Africans looked after their own because their subconscious was rooted in *umuntu ngumuntu ngabantu*; a core belief that *they existed and were real because of the existence and the realness of others.*

END

EPILOGUE

The advent of 2008 had varied gifts for different continents of the world. It had affected peoples in different ways.

Hunger, poverty, wars, and diseases were still ravaging Africa, yes! But the continent had won another battle in Europe. The Cullinan Diamond was coming back home where it belonged.

Agreed, it was now returning home having been majestically rent limb to limb for the royal needs of Her Highness. Still, the bits 'n pieces were coming home. Finally.

Alfred Reeds had scored three goals. He had left George Bush's Cabinet with his chin up; had emerged as the Republican's Presidential Candidate; and had done well in the Congressional Oversight Committee hearings.

The hearings had lasted six weeks. In the end, the lid had been blown off DRAINPIPE. Kim Holland and Neil Simon had resigned their positions. The FBI had invaded West Africa trying to piece together the bits and pieces of DRAINPIPE left as David Terence raced to dismantle the program.

As a result, diplomatic rows were breaking out with Washington by the day as governments of Cameroon, Nigeria, Ghana, Cote d'Ivoire, Mali and Sierra Leone laid their hands on leaked copies of DRAINPIPE and the infrastructures in individual countries that proved the disclosures right.

Scores of surrogate businessman in the sub-region had been arrested. But a few had fled before the bubble entirely blew. All the same, search warrants had been issued for their arrests.

Interestingly, there was not a single mention of FLIGHT throughout Reeds' Congressional Oversight Committee hearings. It seemed that the US presidential hopeful was already preparing for the likelihood of his clinching the White House by clandestinely walking his hidden thoughts and talks on FLIGHT. He was of the private opinion that FLIGHT was a program that was vital to the well-being of the US economy

***

Mid-2008 saw Barack Obama winning his party's presidential nomination ticket. His official nomination came later in the year and served as a beautiful runway from which his campaign roared off full throttle.

In the end, Obama's campaign had generated the most widespread interests in US politics from around the world and in manners never before experienced. This ranged from Japan where Obama shared a name with a town called Obama. Across Indonesia, where he once lived. Through Africa, his ultimate root. Over in Eurasia, where his approach to international relations was a welcome change. And Latin America where *Obamania* had almost assumed a cult status.

For the entire world, Obama was hope in a time of thundering hopelessness. Appreciation of the *Obama course* was not so much for the much-desired change, which he epitomized but more for the sharp contrast his path had against the egotistic, deeply predatory policies, which the Republicans had pursued through an egocentric president as he traveled – for eight consecutive years – down the meanest road that capitalism could construct.

For every member of the Black Race – dead and alive – however, *Obama* transcended the Obama person. In the twinkle of an eye, Obama had metamorphosed from the name of a mere mortal into a *course*. Obama had seized being a human face but a *rebirth*. Obama had become the *end to an era as well as the start of another*. Obama had turned into that all-so-enlivening *breath held for nearly five centuries*, and now being slowly exhaled. Obama was *dignity-returned; an entire Race redeemed* from the abyss.

For African-Americans like General Colin Powell (swallowed by Washington politics) and Condoleezza Rice (who was not expected to come off Bush unscathed), *Obama* was complete *resurrection*.

For Barack Hussein Obama himself, the journey up to the Fourth of November 2008 had made him as Catholic as the Pope. The race he would never be able run away from – no matter how hard he tried – started on same day. This would be: could Obama *eventually become more Catholic than the Pope*? Obama's assessors were not only going to be from the American public but from every continent of the world. It was why, in the first instance, his election into the White House commanded unprecedented world-wide interests.

For Africa and Africans specifically, the dice had been cast a long, long time ago. Obama was not likely to make any dramatic difference except in moments of individual introspection and as the ultimate reference in charting individual's philosophical path. Only on such springboards would Africans be able to launch a new era in Africa renaissance. Only in this milieu, besieged by regenerated ordinary African folks who would no longer settle for mediocrity, would the primogenitocrats have a change of heart. And turn away from the self-destructive path that decimated Africa and fellow Africans. Without this, Obama (and *Obama*) would remain to Africa only what the crowd at Chicago's Grant Park looked on the Fourth of November 2008 – a resplendent spectacle.

Even in our present seemingly downtrodden position, Africans say to the conservative forces over in the United States of America: *Obama must not end up as another John F Kennedy.*